A Pocket Full of Murder

Also by
R. J. Anderson

A Little Taste of Poison

A Pocket Full of Murder

R. J. Anderson

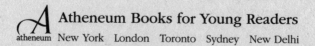

Atheneum Books for Young Readers

atheneum   New York   London   Toronto   Sydney   New Delhi

A
atheneum

ATHENEUM BOOKS FOR YOUNG READERS
An imprint of Simon & Schuster Children's Publishing Division
1230 Avenue of the Americas, New York, New York 10020

This book is a work of fiction. Any references to historical events, real people, or real places are used fictitiously. Other names, characters, places, and events are products of the author's imagination, and any resemblance to actual events or places or persons, living or dead, is entirely coincidental.

Text copyright © 2015 by R. J. Anderson
Cover illustration copyright © 2015 by Tom Lintern

ATHENEUM BOOKS FOR YOUNG READERS is a registered trademark of Simon & Schuster, Inc. Atheneum logo is a trademark of Simon & Schuster, Inc.

For information about special discounts for bulk purchases, please contact Simon & Schuster Special Sales at 1-866-506-1949 or business@simonandschuster.com.

The Simon & Schuster Speakers Bureau can bring authors to your live event. For more information or to book an event, contact the Simon & Schuster Speakers Bureau at 1-866-248-3049 or visit our website at www.simonspeakers.com.

Also available in an Atheneum Books for Young Readers hardcover edition
Book design by Sonia Chaghatzbanian
The text for this book was set in ITC Garamond Std, Akron Handscript, and Oneleigh Pro.
Manufactured in the United States of America
0916 OFF
First Atheneum Books for Young Readers paperback edition September 2016
10 9 8 7 6 5 4 3 2

The Library of Congress has cataloged the hardcover edition as follows:
Anderson, R. J. (Rebecca J.)
A pocket full of murder / R. J. Anderson. — First edition.
pages cm
Summary: In Tarreton, where the rich have all the magic they wish and the poor can barely afford a spell to heat their homes, twelve-year-old Isaveth's father is accused of murdering an influential citizen and Isaveth, aided by eccentric street-boy Quiz, tries to solve the magical murder mystery before her father is executed.
ISBN 978-1-4814-3771-4 (hc)
ISBN 978-1-4814-3772-1 (pbk)
ISBN 978-1-4814-3773-8 (eBook)
[1. Murder—Fiction. 2. Social classes—Fiction. 3. Magic—Fiction. 4. Fantasy.
5. Mystery and detective stories.] I. Title.
PZ7.A54885Poc 2015
[Fic]—dc23 2014040718

TO PAUL,
WHO WANTED DRAGONS
(SORRY ABOUT THAT)

A Pocket Full of Murder

Chapter One

PROPPED ON THE FLOUR-DUSTED stand, the Book of Common Magic looked as innocent as the ordinary cookbooks tucked behind it. Only the tremor in Isaveth's fingers as she turned the pages betrayed her apprehension. She'd never made spell-tablets all by herself before. Perhaps she should go to Aunt Sallume's and ask . . .

But then she'd have to pass the Kerchers' house again, and Isaveth didn't like that idea at all. Not that their cottage was much worse than any of the others on Cabbage Street: There was nothing unusual about soot-stained brick, peeling paint, and a porch cluttered with old beer crates, even if the hole in the upstairs window did look like a fat spider sitting in its web. She'd been bold enough earlier that morning, with Mimmi clinging to her hand and Lilet scowling at her heels;

she'd marched her sisters straight past the Kerchers' and around the corner to Aunt Sal's without a second thought.

Only, the porch had been empty then, and now it wasn't. Through the window she could see her schoolmate Loyal Kercher lounging on the front steps, with his elbows at the top and his legs stretched all the way to the bottom, smacking a mouthful of chew and waiting for his next victim to walk by. As soon as he spotted any girls or boys young enough to intimidate, he'd jump out in front of them, all sneering mouth and leering eyes, and he wouldn't move until they told him their business and begged him to let them pass.

The thought of submitting to such injustice made Isaveth hot all over. She'd rather die than give Loyal the satisfaction, no matter how big he'd grown this past year.

Anyway, it wouldn't be right to trouble Aunt Sal with her dithering, especially when she already had Lilet and Mimmi and her own two little ones to look after. Isaveth was almost thirteen now, not a child anymore. It was time she learned to make magic on her own.

Lighting the stove didn't worry her; she'd done that plenty of times when her sister Annagail was late coming home from the shirt factory. And though Isaveth might singe her fingers if she got careless, making spell-tablets wasn't really dangerous. Her biggest fear was wasting binding powder and their even more precious store of magewort, neither of which would be easy to replace with her mother gone. Worse still, what if the magic didn't take? Isaveth would have burned good coal, and turned an already too-warm house into a furnace, for nothing.

Yet if she didn't try it, nobody would, and the ingredients would go to waste anyway. Lilet and Mimmi were too young to make spells, let alone sell them. And though by rights the book belonged to Annagail, her older sister never touched it; she had no gift for spell-baking, and she'd been hesitant to do it even when Mama was alive to help.

But if Isaveth turned out to have even half her mother's talent, she'd be able to peddle those little squares of heat and light for five citizens each. A hundred cits to a merchant, five merches to a noble, two nobs to a regal, ten regs to an imperial . . . not that Isaveth had ever seen that much money, but she'd often dreamed about it. Even fifty cits—a mere ten tablets' worth—would be enough to buy a big loaf of crusty bread and a fresh egg for everyone in the family. How wonderful that would be! It had been so long since Papa had steady work, they'd been living mostly on beans and potatoes and the few scraggly onions they could coax out of their garden.

Even the cheapest meat was a luxury, and Isaveth could scarcely remember the last time she'd eaten a whole egg all by herself.

Mustering her courage, Isaveth prepared the baking pans, greasing them well with falsebutter so the tablets wouldn't stick. The recipe in the Book of Common Magic looked simple, but all around it were notations in a familiar, delicate hand: *Double magewort and halve binding powder in cold weather. Sift flour for neevils before mixing. Wash hands thoroughly!!!*

A familiar ache rose in Isaveth's throat. It had been half a year since Devra Breck died, but her presence still lingered in this kitchen, as though she had only stepped out and would be back at any moment. Softly Isaveth repeated the notes to herself, listening to the echo of her mother's voice in her memory. Then she dragged the big stoneware bowl out of the bottom cupboard and started assembling the ingredients.

An hour later Isaveth had flour all over her apron, a sifter full of wriggling neevils, and hair limp with sweat. But the tablets had come out from the first baking golden and firm to the touch, just as they ought to be. She sprinkled them with binding powder and cut them into squares with the silver knife—a sacred heirloom, and the only valuable thing her family still possessed. Once that was done, she slid one pan back into the oven and hurried to set the other in the brightest shaft of sunlight she could find. In a few minutes she'd know if her magic had worked.

It was hard to believe that even such simple spells had once been beyond the reach of ordinary folk like herself, the crystals and precious metals required too expensive for any but nobles and the wealthiest merchants to afford. The ways of magic were sacred, the early Sages claimed, and too sophisticated for uneducated people to understand.

Yet there'd been a few poor folk who defied the ban, working out cheaper ingredients through trial and error and passing on recipes by word of mouth. Little by little the craft had grown and spread—especially among Isaveth's Moshite ancestors, who had excelled at finding herbs and minerals with magical properties—until the nobles could no longer suppress it.

So they'd called it Common Magic, to distinguish it from their own more elegant and refined Sagery. And though at first most nobles deemed the use of such magic beneath them, they soon came to appreciate the economy and practicality of those spells, and adapted them for their own use as well. Now half of Tarreton ran on spell-power, and there were whole factories dedicated to turning out tablets much like the ones Isaveth was making. Stored heat, stored power, stored light . . .

Was it her imagination, or did the kitchen feel cooler? Cautiously Isaveth approached the oven. A glance through the peephole assured her the burner hadn't gone out, but when she held her hand close to the door, she felt no warmth. The tablets were soaking up all the heat. Her magic was working! Isaveth clapped her hands together with delight and dashed to the front of the house to see how her other pan was doing.

It was harder to judge this batch, since no spell could possibly capture *all* the light streaming through the window. The only sure test would be to take one into a darkened room and crumble it or drop it in a glass of water. Yet the flecks of magewort that dotted the tablets were glowing, and that was a good sign.

Isaveth let the pans sit a little longer, to be sure they'd soaked up all the light and heat they could hold. Then she dusted both batches with more binding powder, said a blessing over them—that wasn't in the recipe, but it couldn't hurt—and set them on racks to cool.

She'd done it! She'd made real magic all by herself. After all the filthy, miserable hours she'd spent collecting rags and scrap metal to help her family, Isaveth could only regret she hadn't worked up the nerve to try spell-baking sooner.

The town clock tolled the hour, and Isaveth looked up in surprise. Could it really be three bells already? Wiping her hands, she closed the Book of Common Magic and put it away. Then she crossed to the open window and leaned out across the sill. A pack of scrawny boys half her age were running about the street, calling to one another in shrill voices—"Gimme the ball, it's my turn!" "Hey, that's no fair!"—but Isaveth ignored them. If she concentrated hard enough, she might be able to hear . . .

The distant whistle of a peddler, his cart full of clinking bottles. The flap-snap of Missus Caverly's sheets drying on the line. But though Isaveth felt sure that someone in the neighborhood must be listening, she heard none of the music she yearned for—the triumphant opening theme of *Auradia Champion, Lady Justice of Listerbroke.*

It came on every Duesday afternoon, the most exciting talkie-play Isaveth had ever heard. It even got repeated on Fastday evenings for those who might have missed it. But Papa had sold their crystal set six months ago to help pay for her mother's memorial, so Isaveth had been reduced to eavesdropping on her neighbors ever since.

Sometimes she was lucky enough to overhear part of the story. But not today.

With a sigh Isaveth stepped back and let the curtain fall. It would be unfair to blame her father for selling the set, and there were a lot worse things to miss. But according to Morra Caverly, who'd heard last week's episode while she was working, Auradia had been captured by a handsome thief lord who tried to charm her into pardoning his men, and when she refused, he put a knife to her throat. Of course Auradia would thwart him and escape, but Isaveth was itching to know *how*.

There was no help for it, then. She'd just have to write her own version of the story. Isaveth ran to fetch the box that held her stub of lead-point and the few scraps of paper she'd been hoarding. Then she settled herself on the back step and began scribbling as fast as her thoughts could go.

"Release the men you captured, or die," hissed the thief lord, pointing his dagger menacingly at Auradia. "That is my final offer."

Even tied hand and foot to a chair with a gang of ruffians closing in upon her, Auradia Champion did not falter.

"Never," the noblewoman retorted with a proud lift of her chin. "Kill me if you must, but I shall not release your men. My Lawkeepers will keep them in custody until a new Lord or Lady Justice is appointed, and then they will hunt you down and punish you as your wickedness deserves. You cannot escape! Surrender now, before it is too late!"

"What are you writing there, Vettie?"

She looked up, blinking, as the sights and sounds of Auradia's world faded away. Morra Caverly stood by the fence, a laundry basket balanced against her hip and her blond head tilted quizzically.

"Oh, nothing much," said Isaveth, coloring. Part of her would have liked to show the neighbor girl her story and ask what she thought, but Morra was letter-blind: She could read printed words only with great difficulty and had never learned to write. "Just one of my Auradia stories."

"Another one? What an imagination you've got!" Morra set down her basket and stretched to unpin a bedsheet from the line. "So what's all this for, then? Are you hoping the folk that make the talkie-play will hire you if you're good enough?"

That would be wonderful, but Isaveth hadn't thought that far ahead. She was too young to look for proper work yet, and she still had her schooling to finish. "Maybe," she said, absently twirling the lead-point between her fingers. "I want to be a writer of *some* sort, but I'm not sure what kind. Only . . ."

Morra dropped the folded sheet into the basket. "Only what?"

"Whatever it is, I want to be really good at it. Good enough to make lots of money."

"And be famous, too, I suppose? So you can float off to Uropia and get a ladyship from the regent?"

"Why not?" asked Isaveth, taken aback by the other girl's sour tone. Usually Morra was cheerful and good natured, but now she sounded bitter. "I wouldn't be the first to do it."

"Well, you'd be the first from this place, that's certain." Morra waved a hand at their surroundings: a line of pinched-looking cottages that ranged from run-down to ramshackle, with narrow strips of backyard divided by fences and the coal-lane running behind them. Even the midday sunlight couldn't banish the smog from the nearby factories, nor could the shouts of the neighbor children drown out their relentless din. "I don't blame you for wanting to get out of Cabbage Street. But to do so well by yourself that people forget where you came from? That'd take a miracle of the Sages."

Isaveth liked Morra, but she didn't like it when she talked like this—as though being fifteen and cleaning house for a few merchants' wives made her more mature than Isaveth would ever be. If growing up meant abandoning her dreams, Isaveth wanted no part of it. "But if I did become a noble, I could help people and make the world a better place. Like Auradia did."

"Yes, but she was born noble, and she wasn't a . . ." Morra stopped, made a face, and started over. "Anyway, Auradia lived in another city a hundred years ago. I don't see *our* nobles helping anyone but themselves."

"There's Eryx Lording," Isaveth pointed out, though it was hard not to be distracted by the words Morra had left unsaid: *wasn't a Moshite, like you.* "Everyone says he's the opposite of his father, and that's bound to be a good thing, isn't it?"

"It would be if he was ruling Tarreton right now. But we're stuck with Sagelord Arvis, and Seward says he'll surely ruin this city before his son ever gets the chance to fix it. He's such a misery-miser that other cities scarce want to trade with us anymore, and there's so little work at the box factory, Da might be let go any day . . ." Morra's voice cracked, and she gave a sniff. "Well, never mind that. You've got your own troubles. But you can see why I don't think much of nobles at the moment. Though I'm sure you'd make a fine one."

Now Isaveth understood. Morra's older brother, Seward, had a passion for politics and no shortage of strong opinions about how the city was being run, and if he'd been filling Morra's head with gloomy talk, it was no wonder she was anxious. Yet the Sagelord's greed and callousness had done so much damage to Tarreton's fortunes already, Isaveth found it hard to imagine how things could get much worse.

She thought of her father, trudging the streets with his wheely-cart in search of work. A year ago Urias Breck had been a stonemason, skilled at his craft and respected for it. He'd raised walls, laid drive paths, and built garden follies for the nobles and wealthy Sages who ruled the city. But the project he'd staked all his hopes on had been canceled without warning, and there'd been no more offers since. So now Papa had to make do with whatever small jobs he could find.

Then there was Annagail, bowed over a sewing treadle in the dusty heat of the shirt factory. Until their mother died, she'd been working hard to finish school so she

12

could train as a healer. But the cost of the memorial had eaten up all their savings, and when it became clear that Papa could no longer earn enough to support them, she'd left Isaveth in charge of the younger girls and taken the first job she could get. It was hard work in the factory, with long hours and little pay, and she would have been happier as a nursemaid or even a scrubber. But most wealthy folk were Arcan and preferred not to keep a Moshite girl about the house if they could hire a Unifying one instead. So sewing shirts was the best Annagail could do.

Which was why Isaveth wanted so badly to succeed at *something*, whether that meant becoming a famous writer or merely a good spell-baker. She knew too well the uncertainty and hardship that Morra only feared, the hollow ache of hunger and the bone-gnawing chill of snowy nights without fuel. There had to be a way out of this trap of poverty, both for herself and for her family—and Isaveth was determined to find it, no matter what Morra or anyone else thought of her chances.

"Let's talk about something else, then," she said brightly, setting her writing box aside. "Did I tell you I made spell-tablets today?"

Chapter Two

ISAVETH HAD FINISHED BOILING the potatoes for supper and was doggedly mashing them when the front door creaked and she heard Annagail's step in the hall.

Oh no. Was it that late already? Isaveth had spent only a few minutes talking to Morra, but she'd gone on writing for a good while after that, even while the dinner was cooking. Isaveth shot a guilty glance at Anna, about to ask if she minded fetching the other girls from Aunt Sal's. Then Lilet and Mimmi burst in, squabbling and jostling each other, and she let out a thankful sigh.

"You were supposed to get us half an hour ago," said Lilet accusingly. "It's a good thing we spotted Anna before Aunt Sal started moaning. Ugh, potatoes *again*?"

"There's plenty of air if you'd rather eat that," Isaveth retorted, moving quickly to stop Mimmi from poking at the basket of spell-tablets she'd left by the back door. "Don't touch those. I'm going to sell them."

"They look like candies," said Mimmi with a wistful glance at the basket. Isaveth had torn up some old tissue to wrap the tablets in, hoping it would protect them from crumbling. "What are they?"

"Spells," said Isaveth. She almost added "like Mama used to make," but Mimmi still teared up when anyone spoke of their mother. "Now come and help set the table."

"You made magic without us?" Lilet glared at her. "That's not fair! You didn't even ask!"

"I don't need *your* permission. And Annagail doesn't mind, do you?" Isaveth turned an appealing look to her sister, who shook her head.

"Of course not. I'm glad you thought of it. But will people buy them?"

"Why not? They're better than the factory spells, and they'll last longer too." Factory-made tablets were coated with dampening wax, which was the cheapest way to keep them from breaking by accident. But it also weakened their magical power, and Isaveth's tablets wouldn't have that problem. "Anyway, I'll find out when I go downtown tomorrow. Did you see Papa on your way?"

"Oh. I . . . I think he'll be late tonight," Anna said

distractedly, unpinning her hair and smoothing it before coiling it up at the nape of her neck again. Cropped hair was the fashion for girls, and Isaveth was glad of it, but Annagail refused to cut hers except for a few curls around her forehead. "We should eat without him."

On Duesday evenings, Papa often went to the Workers' Club, where they served soup and bread for only ten cits a plate, so that made sense. Yet Anna hadn't said whether she'd talked to him or not, and it wasn't like her to be so vague. Did she know something she wasn't telling? Was it good news or bad?

Normally, it would have been easy to guess, because Annagail was the most transparent person Isaveth knew. But she always looked strained when she came home from the shirt factory, her eyes puffy and her smile thin with weariness. She might be worried about anything— or nothing.

Perhaps she didn't want to say too much in front of Lilet and Mimmi. Resolving to ask her about it later, Isaveth opened the small hallow cabinet that held their six pairs of blessing candles, a set for each day of the week, and took out the blue ones. Worn and half melted, they still bore traces of the gold coin pattern her mother had painted when she was Annagail's age, preparing for the household she would bless one day.

"All right," Isaveth said, setting the candles in their holders and laying the flint-spark beside them. "Everybody wash up and sit down, so Anna can say the blessing."

The sun was sinking below the rooftops, and Isaveth was about to call Lilet and Mimmi to bed, when Papa came clumping in the door. His face was flushed, his dark hair slick with sweat, but he was smiling. "There's my Vettie!" he exclaimed, and Isaveth ran to embrace him.

"Did you find work today?" she asked eagerly. Usually she didn't dare raise the subject, but a smile was surely a good sign. "Was it a nice meeting?"

Her father's thick brows shot up. "Who told you about that? I only got the message this afternoon."

"What message?" Annagail appeared in the kitchen doorway, half-darned stockings in hand. "Oh, Papa, I'm so glad you're home." She hurried to drop a kiss on his cheek. "I thought you'd gone to the Workers' Club."

So Isaveth had guessed right—her sister *had* been anxious, even if she hadn't wanted to say so. But why?

"No, my Anna," their father said, putting an arm around her shoulders. "I'm not looking for trouble, not with my girls to think about. Is there any supper left for your poor old Papa, or has your boyfriend Merit gobbled it up again?"

Annagail blushed as she always did when Papa teased her, no matter how ridiculous his suggestion might be. Merit was Loyal Kercher's older brother, and he'd left town three months ago to help build the new railway to Vesperia. "I'll warm it up for you," she promised, and hurried to the stove.

Papa had taken his usual seat at the table, and Annagail was scraping the last of the potatoes onto a plate, when Lilet and Mimmi came in. Lilet gave their father a hug, squirmed away from his tickling fingers, and moved on, but Mimmi jumped onto his lap and stole sips of his tea until Isaveth practically had to drag her away. By the time the younger girls were settled and Isaveth returned to the kitchen, her father had cleaned his plate and was filling his pipe with baccy.

"Well, then," he said as Isaveth and Annagail sat down on either side of him, "as you might have guessed, I've got news. Remember that new charmery house Master Orien wanted me to build at the college?"

The girls exchanged startled glances. The charmery was a forbidden subject—had been since before their mother died. That was the project their father had been counting on to save him from ruin, until Orien, the governor of Tarreton College, had canceled the contract with no explanation whatsoever. The shock of it had turned Papa into a different man for a while, short tempered and distant; he'd taken to disappearing at odd times and staying out late, and once he'd come home with bloody knuckles and a great bump on his forehead. It wasn't until Mama took ill that he'd turned himself about and started acting like their papa again.

"Yes," said Isaveth cautiously. "What of it?"

"Well, seems the Sagelord took a dislike to the plan and refused to lend any money to it, and that's why Master Orien had to put a stop to the job. But now Lord Arvis has changed his mind, so it's going forward after all! The master wants me to hire some lads and get to work straightaway. We'll be paid fair wages—not much more than that, not with things the way they are—but . . ."

"Oh, Papa!" The shadow fled from Annagail's face, leaving it radiant. "I'm so happy for you!"

A bubble of joy swelled in Isaveth. If Papa had work again, Annagail could leave her job at the shirt factory and go back to school. They could buy new half soles for their shoes, clothes that actually fit . . . and maybe, just maybe, Isaveth would get an ink bottle and a sheaf of proper writing paper for her birthday.

"That's wonderful news!" she exclaimed, squeezing Papa's hand. "So that was the meeting you went to? With Master Orien?"

"That's right." He leaned back in his chair and took a long, thoughtful draw on his pipe. "I don't mind admitting I misjudged the man—he's a better sort than I took him for. There might be some hope for this city after all."

Which was high praise, coming from Papa. "So what was all that about the Workers' Club?" Isaveth asked. "Why was Anna worried you'd gone—"

"Oh, that's no matter," Papa interrupted with a warning glance at Annagail. "Nothing you and your sisters need to fret about. I won't be going back there anytime soon. All right?"

Annagail lowered her eyes, but she looked more relieved than chastened. "Yes, Papa."

By the time Isaveth and Annagail went up to bed, the younger girls were asleep. Lilet lay sprawled on her back, dark hair snaking out across the pillow, while Mimmi curled neatly as a mouse against the wall.

"Let's not wake them," Annagail whispered. "We can tell them the good news tomorrow."

Isaveth nodded, and the two of them slipped in next to their sisters—though Isaveth had to shove Lilet over first, since Annagail was too softhearted to do it. For a while they lay quiet, until Isaveth said, "I still want to know why you were worried about Papa going to the Workers' Club."

Annagail sighed. "It's not important now. Can't you let it go?"

"No," said Isaveth, propping herself up on one elbow. "I know Papa thinks I'm too young to understand, but I'm not. And I won't tell Lilet and Mimmi, I promise."

She waited, letting the silence grow heavy, until Annagail gave in. "I heard two of the overseers at the factory talking about it," she said. "The City Council's passed a law making it a crime to speak out publicly against the government, or to organize any protests against them. They've ordered landlords to report any political groups that meet in their buildings—"

"The Workers' Club is political?" Isaveth was startled. She'd thought it only a place where Papa went to have a drink and play a few rounds of Gamble with friends. She knew he sometimes came back from their meetings more agitated than usual, but she'd thought it was only a sign that he felt badly for other people's troubles. After all, Anna wasn't the only one in the family with a tender heart.

"Oh, Vettie," said Annagail, sounding more tired than ever. "Did you really not know? Last month they held a big rally on the steps of Council House calling for the

Sagelord to resign, and the Lawkeepers had to break it up. I don't think Papa was there, but if he was, it wouldn't be the first time."

Isaveth stared at the ceiling, trying to digest this new information. She'd heard about the protests that had sprung up in various parts of Tarreton: the Relief Office swarmed by jobless men and women demanding food for their starving families, neighbors stopping a home eviction by blocking the drive and tearing furniture from the movers' hands, angry dockworkers pelting the Sagelord with fish when he stopped by the harbor to make a speech. Not so long ago Seward Caverly had been arrested while taking part in a supposedly violent demonstration—perhaps even the same rally Anna was talking about.

Yet Isaveth found it hard to imagine her papa doing any such things. He might not go to temple the way Isaveth and her sisters did, but he was still a Moshite, and he knew how important it was for their people to stay quiet and keep the peace.

"Please don't say anything to Papa," Annagail pleaded. "He has work now, and he's not going to the club anymore. So there's no need to worry. For any of us."

The tremor in her voice made her sound less than certain, but Isaveth nodded as though convinced. She turned over and pulled the sheet around her, though her eyes stayed open, and it was a long time before she fell asleep.

It was the knock at the front door that woke her, an insistent thumping too loud to ignore. Isaveth sat up and looked around in bleary confusion, to find Annagail doing the same. In unison they scrambled out of bed, pulled blankets around their threadbare nightclothes, and hurried downstairs, leaving the sleeping Lilet and Mimmi behind.

"It's barely dawn," murmured Annagail. "Who could be calling at this hour?"

Isaveth pushed past her to the door, went up on tiptoe to look through the peephole—and sank back onto her heels, feeling chilled all over. Two Lawkeepers, armed and in full uniform, stood on their front step.

"What? Who is it?" Annagail caught her arm, but a curt voice spoke before Isaveth could reply.

"Urias Breck! Open the door or we'll break it down!"

"Papa," gasped Isaveth, clutching her sister in turn. "We have to—"

"All right, I'm coming," grumbled their father from the steps above, dragging his trouser braces up over his shoulders. "Go back to bed, girls. It's me they want."

He sounded resigned, not frightened, so he must have some idea what this was about. Perhaps they only wanted to question him? Isaveth clasped her hands together, willing herself calm. Then she backed up next to Annagail and watched Papa unlock the door.

"Well, then—" he began, but the Keepers didn't give him a chance to finish. They seized him, wrenched his wrists behind his back, and shoved him toward their waiting spell-wagon.

"Papa!" cried Isaveth, rushing after him. Her head felt dizzy and her stomach cramped with fear, but she grabbed the arm of the nearest Lawkeeper and hung on. "Why are you taking him? He's done nothing wrong!"

"That's for the Lord Justice to decide," snapped the Keeper, shaking her off. "Get back in the house, girl."

The Lord Justice! Isaveth stumbled back, aghast. In Auradia Champion's day city justices had ruled on all sorts of legal matters, large and small. But the present ones troubled themselves with only the most serious offenses—crimes that involved large amounts of money, or violence against the government, or . . .

"Out with it, then," said Papa, twisting to look at the Keepers. His brows were knit fiercely, and his dark eyes blazed. "If I'm being arrested, I've a right to know why."

The younger Lawkeeper barked a laugh, but the older

one looked more stern than ever. "Urias Breck," he said, "you are charged with the murder of Governor Orien, who was found dead of Common Magic last night."

The blood drained out of Isaveth's cheeks. Still, that was nothing compared with what the Keeper's words did to Papa. His face crumpled up small, all the pride squeezed out of it, and his knees sagged until the officers had to drag him upright again.

"You will be held in custody until you can be questioned by the Lawkeeper-General," continued the older one, hauling Papa toward the back of the wagon. "If you refuse to answer fully, you may be truth-bound—"

Isaveth's father exploded. With a roar he flung himself against the Keepers' grip, twisting and lunging in all directions. Anna tugged desperately at Isaveth's elbow, trying to coax her inside, but Isaveth couldn't tear herself away.

"Papa, don't!" she cried. "We'll be all right! Just go with them!"

Her father gave no sign of hearing. He kept struggling with the Lawkeepers until the younger man wrenched a sleep-wand from his belt and jabbed her father in the neck with it. Then he dropped like a sack of turnips, and the officers heaved him into their wagon and slammed the door.

"Please, Vettie," whispered Annagail as the Keeper yanked a lever and the spell-wagon juddered to life. "Everyone's watching. And there's nothing we can do."

But Isaveth refused to move, even though she could feel Loyal Kercher's smirk from across the street. She clutched the blanket about her shoulders and watched, sick with misery, as the Lawkeepers took her father away.

Chapter Three

"HE DIDN'T DO IT. He couldn't have."

Isaveth paced around the kitchen table, too restless to eat the porridge Annagail had made for breakfast. Mimmi was eating hers, but slowly and with sniffs between every bite, while Anna kept lifting her spoon, making a face, and putting it down again. Meanwhile, Lilet had pushed away her empty bowl and started on Isaveth's, though her expression made plain she was only building up her strength so she could fight the Lawkeepers and get Papa back.

"Of course he didn't," said Annagail, "but the Lawkeepers don't know that, and it's their responsibility to look into these things. We just have to be patient until this is all cleared up." She retrieved Isaveth's bowl and put it back in place, then slid her own porridge across the table to Lilet. "Vettie, please sit down and eat something. You're making me dizzy."

"I can't eat any more," said Mimmi thickly. "My stomach is too full of sad." She drooped against Annagail's shoulder. "They won't arrest us, too, will they?"

"Don't be stupid, Mimmi," snapped Lilet. "Why would the Lawkeepers want us? We haven't done anything." But she flicked an uncertain look at Isaveth as she spoke. Back when they'd still had a crystal set, Isaveth had listened to all the talkie-plays she could, many of them about Lawkeepers, advocates, and other crime-fighting heroes. She knew more about the justice system than any of them.

"No, they won't arrest us," said Isaveth, trying to sound confident. Her insides were seething and she wanted to cry and smash things, but she had to be calm for her sisters' sake. "They don't put children in jail—we aren't even allowed in court. Anna's the only one old enough, and if the Lawkeepers thought she knew anything, they'd have questioned her already. Or at least told her not to leave the city."

"Vettie's right," said Annagail. "There's no need to worry. The Lawkeepers arrested Papa by mistake, but they'll soon let him go, you'll see. Now both of you get dressed, and I'll take you to Aunt Sal's."

"But we were there yesterday!"

"When Sal hears what happened to Papa, she'll understand. And Vettie and I have work to do, so you'll be better off there than here. Just be polite, and—"

"Don't make any trouble." Lilet gave a gusty sigh. "I know. Come on, Mimmi." She held out a hand to their little sister, who took it reluctantly, and the two of them went upstairs together.

As soon as they were gone, Isaveth dropped into a chair and put her head in her hands. "This is horrible," she whispered. "If Papa goes to prison, what'll become of us? What are we going to do?"

"Pray," said Annagail, equally quiet. "I don't think they'll separate us, not with me being sixteen and working, and Aunt Sal so close by. But it's not going to be easy." She untied the prayer scarf from her neck and veiled herself, then reached for Isaveth's hand.

"I can't right now," said Isaveth hoarsely. "You pray for both of us. I'm going to talk to Morra." Before her sister could protest, she pushed her chair back and hurried out.

The morning sun glared down on her head and shoulders as Isaveth ran to the Caverlys' front door. She knocked and waited, hopping restlessly from one foot to the other, but no one answered.

Could they have gone out? Isaveth rapped harder and pressed her ear to the wood. Floorboards creaked inside the house, while above her muffled voices rose and fell. Yet the door remained shut.

"Morra!" she shouted. "I need to talk to you!" After all, Morra's brother had been arrested not long ago, so she ought to be able to tell Isaveth what to do—or at least what to expect.

A long pause followed. Then the door cracked open, and Morra's round white face peered out.

"I can't—" she began, but that was as far as she got before her mother pulled her aside.

"Morra's got nothing to say to the likes of you. We're respectable folk, and we don't want any trouble. Go back to your own people. Don't come here again."

She started to shut the door, but Isaveth stepped to block it. "Please, I only wanted to ask—"

"How dare you!" said Missus Caverly, kicking at Isaveth's foot. "Morra, get your brother!"

Morra's eyes met Isaveth's, full of fear and misery. "We can't help you," she said. "Please go away." Then she put her shoulder to the door, and Isaveth jumped back a second before it slammed shut.

Until now Morra Caverly had been Isaveth's closest friend in the neighborhood—one of the few people she knew who didn't care that her family was Moshite. She'd thought she could count on the older girl to support her, but it seemed that Morra and her family cared only about protecting themselves.

Shoulders slumping, Isaveth walked down the steps, leaving the Caverlys' house behind her.

Isaveth had to do something. She couldn't bear to lie about, weeping—what good would that be to Papa, or anyone? Yet she was so dazed with the shock of all that had happened, she hardly knew where to turn.

Still, one thing was clear: With Papa gone, the need to make money was more pressing than ever. She had to sell her tablets today, no matter how unhappy she felt. Just as Anna had to go to the factory, or she'd lose her job—and that would be unthinkable.

"I'll sign out at midday and go to the Keeper Station," Anna promised, tying her prayer scarf about her neck. "I'll find out all I can about Papa, and if there's anything we can do." She kissed Isaveth's cheek, whispered, "Be brave," and hurried out.

Isaveth watched her step onto the street, where Lilet and Mimmi were waiting. Her chest tightened and her eyes blurred, but she set her jaw and blinked the tears away. Anna was right: Isaveth had to stay strong, for her sisters' sake. And for Papa's, too.

She climbed the stairs to her bedroom, brushed the tangles from her thick, bobbed hair, and put on the hat and gloves she usually wore to temple. She'd need to

31

look respectable if she wanted people to buy her magic.

When she came downstairs, the Kerchers' dog was barking up a frenzy; Loyal must have got bored and started teasing him again. Not wanting to make herself a target, Isaveth locked the door, slipped through the back garden, and opened the gate to the coal-lane.

The usual gang of neighbor children were playing ticktock-bell behind the houses, and the littlest chirped a greeting as Isaveth walked by. But the older ones shushed him and dragged him away. Isaveth clutched her basket tighter and kept walking.

The lane exited onto Grand Street, where Wellman's Tire Factory loomed with its sooty walls and lingering smell of burned rubber, and wagons rattled over the hard-packed earth. A weary-looking man and two boys were shoveling gravel into the deeper ruts, no doubt hoping some driver would toss them a few cits for the effort. Isaveth recognized the youngest boy at once— only two years ago he'd boasted of being the smartest in their class, so she'd taken a smug pleasure from beating him for the top mark in calculation. But last year they'd both missed more days of school than not, and the prizes had gone to other students. It was hard to keep up if you couldn't afford books, and even harder to concentrate when you were hungry.

Right now, though, the ache inside Isaveth was worse than hunger. She'd managed to choke down the porridge she left at breakfast, knowing she'd need the strength for the forty-minute walk ahead. Yet it sat like a cold rock in her belly, and she felt as though she could never face another meal again. Especially when she remembered the Lawkeepers' terrible accusation—that her father had murdered Governor Orien, one of the most powerful nobles in the city.

Yet why would her father kill a man who'd offered to give him honest work and help him feed his family? It made no sense—surely the Lawkeepers must see that. And it made even less sense if the murder had been done with Common Magic, because Papa had never baked a spell-tablet or brewed a decoction in his life. His hands were too big and clumsy for such work, he said, and there was no need to make a fire with magic when he could do as well with flint-spark and tinder.

Though if Papa had done nothing wrong, why had he been so frightened of being truth-bound? If the Lawkeepers had some kind of Sage-charm that made it impossible to lie, shouldn't he welcome the chance to prove his innocence?

So many uncertainties, so many unanswered questions. She could only hope that Anna would be able to get more information out of the Keepers, and maybe then they'd know how to help Papa and bring him home again.

A bit of paper blew down the street toward her. Automatically Isaveth stooped to retrieve it. AN EQUAL VOTE IS AN EQUAL VOICE, it read. SUPPORT THE REPS' BILL—WRITE YOUR LOCAL NOBLE TODAY!

She had no idea what the Reps' Bill might be, but the other side of the page was gloriously blank. More writing paper! Isaveth tucked the precious sheet into her basket and felt a little better. There was no telling whether anyone would buy her tablets, but at least she wouldn't be going home empty-handed.

A horseless tram rumbled by, whipping Isaveth's too-short skirt in all directions. But she didn't have the two cits for a ride, so she let it pass. She kept walking past the repair shops and factories, crossing line after line of cramped and grubby cottages much like her own, until the dirt beneath her feet smoothed into pavement and the buildings around her grew tall and straight with pride. Now the side streets offered glimpses of sculpted gardens, emerald lawns, and the handsome two- and three-story houses where the wealthy merchants and minor nobles of Tarreton lived.

There were fewer wagons and more carriages in this

part of town, most of them horseless thanks to the latest innovations in spell-power. She even saw a magicycle zooming in and out of the traffic, the driver grinning over the steering bar while the girl in his sidecar squealed and clutched her fashionable hat. Isaveth was nearing the heart of the city.

Soon it would be midday, and the workers in the shops and offices would step outside for fresh air—a good time for selling, Isaveth hoped. She hurried to the next junction and turned right, toward the looming bell tower of Council House.

"Nine injured in power factory explosion!" A rag-boy strode by her, waving a fistful of papers. "Trust the *Tarreton Trumpeter*!"

His voice was high and hoarse, but it carried the full length of the street, as did the cry of "Baccy, baccy, fre-e-e-esh baccy!" from a smoke-peddler coming the other way. Carts selling bread twists and iced pudding lined the pavement, and banners of white and blue— the Sagelord's colors—rippled overhead. Horns blared, lights flashed, and people swarmed around Isaveth in all directions. How could one young girl stand out in such a crowd?

After a little investigation Isaveth found a boarded-up doorway between Sweets' Tea Shop and the two-reel cinema that looked like a good place to start. She paused a moment, dabbing sweat from her face, then stepped to greet her first customer.

"Good day, missus, could I interest you . . ."

But the woman barely glanced at her before walking on. Isaveth tried again with the next passerby, a man, but he, too, brushed past her. Maybe she needed to be bolder.

"Spell-tablets for sale!" she called out, raising her basket high. "Fire and light!"

That got her some curious glances, but still no one stopped. She had to try harder—make them see her wares were worth buying. What did the ad readers on the crystal set always say? "Best quality! Guaranteed or your money back!"

A stocky woman halted to peer at Isaveth. She wore a gray checked suit and matching hat, plain but well tailored—the sort of thing a schoolmistress or a clerk might wear. "Guaranteed, you say? How much?"

"Five cits each," said Isaveth. *Please buy something, please. . . .*

"Hm." The woman plucked one of the tablets out of the basket and sniffed it. "Fresh?"

"Baked yesterday. They'll stay good until harvest if you keep them dry."

"Who made them? Your mother?"

Pride tempted Isaveth to take credit, but the woman might be put off if she did. "It's her special recipe."

"I'll take four, then. Two fire, two light."

Isaveth could have hugged her for sheer gratitude, but she managed to keep her dignity. "Thank you, missus," she said as she picked out the tablets. She'd marked the wrappers with different colors, so it was easy to tell them apart. "You won't be sorry. I promise."

Isaveth hoped the sight of one customer buying would lend boldness to the others, and she'd soon have more people stopping to ask about her wares. But though she called and waved her basket until her arms ached, no one else showed the slightest interest.

With the sun high overhead there was little shade from the buildings around her, and the paving stones shimmered in the heat. The passing trams and spell-carriages peppered Isaveth's legs with grit, and dust filled the sagging creases of her stockings. Not only had shouting left her throat parched, it had also revived her hunger; the delicious smells wafting out of the tea shop were driving her nearly wild. She had to find a better place to stand.

Maybe she'd chosen the wrong half of the street? She might have better luck back at the junction of

Grand and Belltower, where Easson's Cobblery faced Simkin's Category Store. The thought of battling such a large crowd was almost too much for Isaveth's flagging spirits, but she had to try. She tugged up her stockings, straightened her hat, and set off again.

It was the right decision. People had to stop at the corner in order to cross, and the traffic was busy, so they were forced to listen to all of Isaveth's patter instead of only a few words. Within half an hour two factory workers had bought fire for their baccy-kindlers, and one nervous-looking woman had gone away with fifty cits' worth of light in her purse.

As the traffic-minder blared and another stream of people crossed the junction, Isaveth stepped back from the corner to count her money. Sixty . . . seventy . . . eighty cits! She couldn't buy Papa's freedom, but at least she and her sisters would eat a proper meal tonight—

Someone barreled into her from behind, knocking the coins from her hand and sending her basket flying. Tablets spilled over the pavement and into the street. Isaveth cried out in alarm, but too late: A spell-carriage had already turned the corner, crushing several tablets under its wheels. Flames leaped up as the trapped heat escaped, and in seconds the air filled with smoke and the drifting ash of her tissue paper.

The crowd panicked. Some fled into the traffic, bringing carriages and delivery wagons to a squealing halt. But most scrambled back onto the sidewalk, only to step unwittingly on the tablets still scattered there. Men cursed and hopped about, beating at their shoes; women gasped and shielded their eyes from the blinding light. Shouting, screaming, sobbing—the whole junction was chaos, and Isaveth stood in the middle of it all.

In desperation she dropped to her hands and knees and began scooping up all the unbroken tablets she could see. One crumbled into flame as she touched it, searing straight through her glove, and she snatched back her burned fingers with a yelp.

"Miss? Miss!" A big hand seized her shoulder. "Come out of there, you'll be hurt!" But Isaveth shook off his grip and plunged back into the crowd. Her money! She had to save that, if nothing else. Yet after groping in all directions, she found only a few tarnished coppers and one five-cit piece. The others must have rolled into the street or been snatched up before she could get to them. Sick at heart, Isaveth climbed shakily to her feet.

By now the last of the broken fire-tablets had burned out, and the smoke was clearing. There were no more screams, only murmurs and grumbles as people dusted themselves off and moved on. Only a few men and women remained, glaring at Isaveth. She opened her mouth to apologize, to explain. . . .

A whistle split the air, and a Lawkeeper rode up on his magicycle. "What's going on here?" he demanded, raising his goggles. "Who caused this disturbance?"

"This brat dumped fire-tablets all over the sidewalk!" snapped a man with an oily mustache, jabbing his finger at Isaveth. "Right under my feet. See what she's done to my trousers!"

"Trousers?" rose an indignant voice from the crowd. "What about my eyes? I can hardly see for the spots in 'em!" And with that, everyone else started complaining at once.

"My weak heart . . ."

"My baby . . ."

"My parcels . . ."

Isaveth cast a pleading look at the officer, but he didn't even glance at her; he was too busy jotting notes. Fear shivered through her, urging her to drop everything and run—but no, she'd surely be caught, and that would only make things worse. So she stood mute, clutching her battered basket, until the Keeper snapped his notebook shut and the crowd parted to let him through.

"All right, young lady," he said sternly. "You're coming with me."

Chapter Four

IT WAS WORSE THAN a nightmare because there was no chance of waking up. Like her Papa, Isaveth stood accused of a crime she'd had no reason to commit. And no one would listen. Or even give her the benefit of the doubt.

"Please," she faltered as the officer seized her arm, "it was an accident, I never meant—"

"One moment, Keeper." The light, pleasant voice came from behind Isaveth, as did the hand on her shoulder. "I was getting out of my carriage just now, and I saw it all. Some lout of a street-boy came tearing around the corner and crashed into this young lady—knocked her right off her feet and didn't even stop to help her up. He's the one you should be after."

The Keeper's brisk manner melted into deference. He took off his helmet and bowed. "Yes, milord. Of course, milord."

Gasps rose from the crowd, and people began to nudge one another and whisper. Bewildered, Isaveth turned to her rescuer, a fashionably suited young man with the sleek, dark hair and chiseled jaw of a two-reel hero. He smiled and said gently, "Don't worry. I'll set this right."

A noble—but not just any noble. Isaveth had never seen his face before, but between the Keeper's reaction and the way the crowd was staring, there could be no doubt who her rescuer must be: Eryx Lording, firstborn son of Sagelord Arvis and the heir to the city. She bobbed a curtsy, too awed to speak.

The young man's smile deepened, and he patted her shoulder reassuringly. Then he turned back to the Lawkeeper.

"I only saw the boy from behind, so I can't describe his face. But he was wearing a flat cap, brown trousers, and a blue shirt with the sleeves rolled up, and he ran that way." He gestured across the junction. "If you hurry, you might catch him yet."

The Keeper yanked on his helmet, started his magicycle, and whizzed off. The crowd on the sidewalk dispersed with obvious reluctance, and eventually all had gone except for a broad-chested veteran in the uniform of a personal guard, a stylish young woman jotting furiously in her notebook, and a boy with a click-box who kept snapping images of Eryx and Isaveth from every angle until the Lording waved him away.

"No story, please," he said, and the journalist looked up with a red-lipped pout. "I did no more than any good citizen would do." He took Isaveth's singed hand, his expression concerned. "Are you hurt?"

Isaveth lowered her eyes, too shy to return the Lording's gaze. With her hair mussed, her hat askew, and her dress streaked with dirt and ashes, she must look a fright. But though her fingers smarted, she felt strangely light and bubbly inside. She shook her head.

"I'd take you home in my carriage, but I've a speech to give at the Merchants' Union." He dabbed her brow with his handkerchief, then took her other hand and pressed the soot-smudged cloth into it. "Be well, young lady."

Then he was off, strolling up the pavement with the guardsman at his heels and the two reporters bustling in his wake. Isaveth backed against the wall, letting the rough bricks support her as she watched Eryx Lording go.

She'd seen him only once before, and that from a distance: It was at last year's Harvest Parade, and she'd been too entranced by the marching band with its stick-tossing drummers to pay much attention to the two open carriages that followed. But it all flooded back to her now. First Lord Arvis, with his massive body and heavy, petulant features, and next to him his wisp of a wife—Isaveth couldn't recall her face, only the gauzy white scarf that had fluttered out behind her like a flag of truce. In the second carriage rode Eryx Lording, waving to the crowd, but he'd been facing away from Isaveth, so she'd seen only the shining darkness of his head. On the near side of the carriage sat his sister, an icy blonde perhaps a year older than Annagail, while the younger son—the Lilord, as they called him—hunched in the middle seat, as squat and sulky-faced as his father. They hadn't been the least bit interesting to look at, and they hadn't even tossed cits into the crowd like some of the other nobles. No wonder she'd forgotten the incident until today.

But now she'd met Eryx face-to-face, and he'd been every bit as kindhearted and generous as a true noble ought to be. Like Auradia Champion, he'd defended the weak and stood up against injustice; he'd even given Isaveth his handkerchief. Dreamily she pressed the silky cloth to her cheek—and started in surprise. He'd tucked something into the folds. A message? She laid the cloth in her palm, opened it . . .

And the hollow place inside her filled up with joy. He'd given her money, a whole two merches' worth.

Enough to pay for her broken tablets twice over and a taxi home, besides.

What must it be like, to be so rich that two days' wages for her was nothing but pocket money to him? It hardly seemed right, yet at the moment Isaveth was too elated to care. She tucked the note into her sash, then set off down the street to spend it.

When Isaveth left the grocer's stand, her basket was heavy with apples, while the bag on her arm held a half dozen eggs and a fat loaf fresh from the oven. If only Papa were home to share it with them! The best food in the world couldn't make up for his absence, and it pained her to think of him going hungry in his cell. But a good meal would lift her sisters' spirits and give them strength to carry on, and surely that was what Papa would want.

Isaveth's next stop was the butcher's, where she bought sausages and a soupbone. It was tempting to add some minced beef or even a small chicken, but they had no chill-box to keep meat fresh, and it would be reckless to spend all the Lording's money at once. She was standing at the counter, waiting for the butcher to wrap her purchase, when a furtive movement teased the corner of her eye. Someone was peering through the window.

Yet as soon as she looked around, he vanished. Perhaps some passerby had simply paused to glance at the butcher's wares and hadn't been staring at Isaveth at all. But though she'd caught only a glimpse of him, too quick to note his features or guess his age, something about him set off a warning in the back of her mind. A tall, thin boy in a flat cap, a blue shirt with rolled-up sleeves . . . and even more unnerving, a patch over one eye.

No, it couldn't be. Her nerves must be getting the better of her. After causing such a public disturbance and being chased by at least one Lawkeeper, even the cheekiest street-boy wouldn't be reckless enough to show his face so soon. Anyway, there were plenty of flat caps and blue shirts in the world. Determined to stay watchful but not panic, Isaveth tucked her parcel under her arm and headed back out onto the street.

She'd finished her shopping, and was looking for the tram that would take her home, when she passed the Relief Shop and came to a halt so sudden she nearly dropped her basket. There in the window sat a pair of brown leather one-straps, exactly Mimmi's size.

All the Breck sisters needed new shoes, but Mimmi most of all: the ones she'd inherited from Lilet had been in poor shape to begin with, and by now they were little more than scraps of leather held together with twine.

Isaveth bent closer to the window, squinting at the price. One-and-twenty.

That would cost her all the coins she had left, even the two cits she'd been saving for tram fare. And with tired legs and parcels to carry, she could hardly bear to think of walking home. But Papa would want her to take good care of her sisters, and she couldn't let him down. Taking a deep breath, Isaveth opened the shop door and went in.

It was a long, hot journey back to Cabbage Street, and by the time Isaveth reached the coal-lane, her feet were dragging with weariness. The bell tower had rung six, and the neighbors were calling their children in for supper—a meal Isaveth had yet to prepare.

But she had a bag full of groceries, and Mimmi's new shoes, and the pride of having sold some of her spell-tablets, even if most of them had ended up trampled on the street. And despite her gnawing anxiety about Papa, the memory of Eryx Lording's kindness still glowed in Isaveth's heart. She could hardly wait for Annagail to get home, so she could tell her the whole story. . . .

"Well, now," drawled a familiar, hateful voice, and Isaveth stumbled to a halt as Loyal Kercher strolled out in front of her. He was a head taller than she was and nearly twice as broad: There would have been no hope of dodging him even if she weren't exhausted. "Where've you been, eh? Off to visit Papa?"

Isaveth's heart was pounding, but she lifted her chin in defiance. "I'm not playing your game, Loyal," she said, shifting the grocery bag to her left hand and letting the one with Mimmi's shoes in it slide into her right. If he came any closer, she'd clout him with it. "Let me by, or I'll scream."

"So what?" Loyal sauntered closer, his jaw working in circles. His teeth were black with chew, and she could smell his breath from three paces away. "Your papa's a dirty dissenter, and now he's locked up where he belongs. Scream all you want. Nobody's gonna care."

Isaveth's fist knotted in the strings of her bag. "How dare you!" she said hoarsely. "My papa's innocent, and I'm going to prove it. Get out of my way."

Loyal grinned. "Not till I see what you bought me." He feinted left, dodged as Isaveth swung at him, and snatched the grocery bag from her hand. "Ooh, eggs!"

"They're for my sisters, not you! Give them back!"

"I dunno, there's a lot of food here for four scrawny little girls." He pursed his lips, pretending to consider. "But maybe I will, if you tell me where it came from. Who gave you the money? Your Mishmosh friends?"

"I'm not telling you anything, Loyal." Isaveth groped in the bottom of her basket, then set it down by the fence and dropped Mimmi's shoes beside it. "Now give my food back, or you'll be sorry."

He let out a bray of laughter. "Who's gonna make me? You?" He pretended to cringe. "I'm so frightened!"

Paper rustled against Isaveth's palm as she twisted the first tablet open. "You should be," she snapped, and flung her fire-spell straight between Loyal's feet.

She'd expected it to shatter and engulf his shoes in flame. But the tablet only bounced once and settled in the dust, unbroken. She bit her lip in dismay.

Loyal chortled. "You can't even throw a pebble straight." He lifted her bag higher, swinging it teasingly from side to side. "So what'll you do to get this back? Sing a song, maybe? Do a little dance?"

"Please," said Isaveth, hating the tears that sprang to her eyes. "Please give it back."

The older boy moved closer, swaggering with triumph. He pushed back the brim of Isaveth's hat and wound a lock of her hair around his finger. "Tell you what," he said. "I'll give you the bag if you give me two of those eggs . . . and kiss my feet."

The thought of kissing any part of Loyal made Isaveth's stomach heave. She had only one hope left, and that was escape. With trembling fingers she tore the wrapper off her second tablet—and crushed the light-spell right in front of Loyal's face.

"Aaargh!" The boy dropped the bag and staggered back. Isaveth snatched up her groceries with one hand, grabbed her basket and Mimmi's shoes with the other, and bolted.

But she'd only dazzled Loyal, not blinded him, and his legs were longer than hers. She was still struggling with her back gate when he grabbed her and wrenched her around. "You'll pay for that, you little—"

"If you touch her again," came a languid voice from above them, "I will take the greatest pleasure in knocking your teeth down your throat."

Loyal froze, hands braced on Isaveth's shoulders. She craned past him to see who had spoken—and stopped struggling, weak with disbelief.

It was the boy with the eyepatch.

Chapter Five

"YOU RANCID GLOB of pig's meat," continued the boy in a conversational tone, swinging himself over the fence and dropping to the dirt in front of Loyal. "You ought to be trussed up with thorn wire and left for the gorehawks. Who gave you the right to even look at this girl, let alone bully her?"

Uncertainty flickered over Loyal's face. He might be big for thirteen, but the other boy was taller. "None of your business, One-Eye. Why don't you go back to the trash heap where you belong?"

The strange boy looked pained. "Oh, come, you can do better than that." He strolled around Loyal, inspecting him critically. "Though considering the drool stains on your shirt, perhaps not. Pity. If I'm going to thump someone, I prefer it to be more of a challenge."

"Thump me?" Loyal scoffed. "I'd like to see you try."

"Oh, I really don't think you would. But since I abhor needless violence, I'm going to give you a chance to scamper off in, let's see . . ." He gestured at the top of the coal-lane. "That direction. You have fifteen seconds."

"And then what?"

"Then," said Eyepatch, "I thump you. I'm sorry, I thought that was obvious." He put his hands in the pockets of his ragged trousers, relaxed and confident. "Ten. Nine. Eight."

Loyal didn't wait for him to finish. Snarling, he shoved Isaveth aside and hurled himself at the stranger.

What came next happened almost too quickly for Isaveth to see. Eyepatch ducked under Loyal's swing, caught him neatly by the other wrist, and twisted his arm up behind his back. Then he kicked Loyal's feet out from under him, and the other boy toppled.

"Yeeeeeoooooowww!" Loyal writhed on the ground, beating frantically at his trousers. He'd landed on Isaveth's fire-tablet.

"Oh, *well* done," breathed Eyepatch with an admiring glance at Isaveth. He waited until Loyal stopped thrashing and the last glowing crumbs of the spell went out, then stooped over him and said, "Hard luck. Care to try again?"

Loyal lay panting at his feet, eyes glazed with panic. An angry red burn showed through the singed thigh of his trousers, and for a moment Isaveth felt sorry for him. But then he spat a curse, heaved himself upright, and lunged at the other boy again.

This time Eyepatch didn't bother to dodge. He planted his feet, crouched low, and drove his fist up into Loyal's stomach.

The air whoofed out of Loyal's lungs. He staggered against the fence, dropped to his knees, and doubled over, retching.

"We're done," said the boy with the patch, and now he sounded angry—though whether at Loyal or himself, Isaveth couldn't tell. "Get out."

Loyal groaned. Clutching his stomach, he dragged himself to his feet and stumbled down the coal-lane to Mister Wregan's back garden. He wrestled the gate open, lurched through it, and was gone.

Isaveth's knees wobbled. She sank onto the dirt beside her parcels and put her hands over her face.

"Are you all right?" asked Eyepatch, crouching to peer at her. "Did he hurt you?"

Her grocery sack lay in the middle of the coal-lane, a dark stain soaking the fabric. She didn't have to look inside to know that the bread was crushed and every one of her eggs had broken. "Not . . . too much," she said, sniffing. "But thank you."

The boy winced. "Please don't. I'm the last one you should thank. If I'd got here earlier, none of this would have happened." He dragged off his cap, adding heavily, "And here I was trying to make it up to you."

Isaveth wiped her eyes on the Lording's handkerchief and studied her rescuer, unsure what to make of him. He had the look of someone who had done a lot of growing in a short time, with a long face, a cherry-stone throat, and ankles that stuck out past the ragged hems of his trousers. His skin was pale as parchment, with scattered freckles and a touch of sunburn, and the hair that flopped over his forehead was even blonder than Morra's. He looked like an Arcan choirboy, and if not for the patch and the ruthless way he'd thumped Loyal, she'd have thought him too soft to live on the street. But there were all kinds of people living rough these days.

"So it *was* you," she said. "You ruined my spell-tablets and nearly got me arrested. And then you spied on me."

The boy turned red. "I'm awfully sorry," he said. "I was trying to get away from—well, anyway, I was in a hurry. And I was looking over my shoulder, so I didn't see you until it was too late. I wanted to come back and apologize, but it took me a while to dodge the

Lawkeeper, and when I spotted you at the butcher's, the Devaney brothers were sniffing around, so I had to deal with them first—"

"Devaney brothers?" asked Isaveth. "Who are they?"

"Nasty little sneak-thieves, that's who," said the boy with the eyepatch. "And for some reason they had their eye on you. So I chased them off, but by the time I got back, you'd gone." He sat down beside her, pulling his knees up to his chest and folding his arms around them. "Why were they interested in you, anyway? They don't usually steal apples. Or sausages, either."

Isaveth could never have imagined she'd end up chatting to a street-boy about her troubles—let alone the same boy who'd caused half of them in the first place. But it would be ungracious not to answer. "The Lording gave me some money. They must have seen it, before I put it away."

The boy made a disgusted noise. "Eryx Lording needs to stop tossing money about. Not that you aren't deserving," he added quickly, "but it wasn't very bright of him to give it to you in front of everyone."

"It wasn't his fault," said Isaveth, defensive on her hero's behalf. "He did try to be discreet; he wrapped it up in his handkerchief. Anyway, who are you to tell the Sagelord's heir what to do?"

The boy grimaced. "You're right, I'm nobody. S'pose I'm just jealous, what with all his money and people fawning over him everywhere he goes." He kicked a stone across the lane, then went on in a lighter tone, "I'm Quiz, by the way. What's your name?"

Isaveth hesitated.

"You can make one up if you like," the boy suggested, cocking his good eye at her. She'd thought it brown at first, but up close it was a changeable shade of blue. "Call yourself Auradia Champion, for all I care—"

"Oh!" Isaveth sat up, transfigured. "Do you like *Auradia* too? Did you hear what happened this week?"

"Of course," said Quiz. "Simkin's Category Store plays it over the squawker. Brings in customers, they say." He sprang to his feet, sticking out a grubby hand to help her up. "If I tell all, will I be forgiven?"

It was hard not to resent the loss of her precious spell-tablets, even if she couldn't quite blame him for the eggs. But if Quiz hadn't barreled into her, Eryx Lording wouldn't have stopped to help—indeed, he likely wouldn't have noticed Isaveth at all. Loyal would still have been waiting to bully her when she came home, and she wouldn't even have had the satisfaction of seeing him get the drubbing he deserved.

Besides, Quiz really did seem sorry. And she'd feel

better about fetching her sisters from Aunt Sal's if she didn't have to walk alone.

"All right," Isaveth said, and let him pull her to her feet.

"Auradia was sawing through the bars," said Quiz in a dramatic hush as he and Isaveth walked along, "when the door of her cell burst open. And there, silhouetted against the light—"

"Why do you have a patch over your eye?" asked Mimmi, wriggling between them. Unlike Lilet, who was keeping her distance and watching Quiz with the suspicion she reserved for all new things, Mimmi had taken to the strange boy at once. "Does it hurt?"

"I gave it to a raven in exchange for wisdom," Quiz said. "And no, not anymore. Did you know you have dirt on your nose?"

Mimmi squinted and rubbed at the smudge, then tugged his sleeve again. "Did you get it?"

"What?"

"Wisdom."

"Mimmi," said Isaveth, but Quiz held up a hand.

"No, no," he said, "it's a perfectly legitimate question." Then he bent close to Mimmi and whispered, "It was a bad bargain. Never trust a raven."

Isaveth hid a smile behind her hand. Quiz cleared his throat and went on: "Anyway. There in the doorway, tall and proud, stood the last man Auradia Champion had ever expected to see—"

"How do you know he was tall?" demanded Lilet from two paces behind them. "It's a talkie-play. There aren't any pictures."

"The pictures are here," Quiz said, tapping his temple. "And if I say Peacemaker Otsik is tall, he's as tall as I want him to be."

"Otsik?" exclaimed Isaveth, delighted. "Was it really? But didn't he sail to Borealis to make a treaty with the Senguq tribe?"

Lilet groaned, but Quiz ignored her. "Of course. That's why Auradia wasn't expecting him."

"So what did he say?"

"Tune in next week," Quiz intoned, "for another thrilling episode of *Auradia Champion, Lady Justice of Listerbroke*!" And he whistled the closing theme in the sweet, liquid tones of a bird.

Mimmi's eyes grew round. "Teach me to do that."

"Don't be a gobblewit, Mimmi," said Lilet. "That would take ages. And he doesn't live around here."

"Where do you live, then?"

Quiz shrugged, as though he were embarrassed to

answer. And judging by his thin frame and ill-fitting clothes, the truth was probably uglier than Mimmi's innocence could bear. "It's not polite to ask personal questions," Isaveth said hastily. "Now into the house, both of you, and set the table."

Lilet pushed past them and headed up the steps at once. But Mimmi lingered, gazing wistfully at Quiz. "Can't I ask *one* question?"

Quiz squatted next to Mimmi. "Go on," he said in a low, conspiratorial tone. "It'll be our secret. What is it?"

"Have you ever been to jail?"

"Mimmi!" exclaimed Isaveth in horror, but her sister kept talking.

"Because my papa got taken to jail this morning, and we don't know how to get him out. Do you?"

Quiz stood up slowly, gazing down at Mimmi's tousled head. "No," he said at last. "I've never been to jail. I'm sorry."

Mimmi sighed. "Oh well." And she ran into the house, leaving Isaveth and Quiz alone.

Isaveth's cheeks felt hot, and her eyes were stinging. She couldn't bear to look at the boy beside her, couldn't think of what to say. There was an awkward silence, and then Quiz said, "You really have had the worst day, haven't you?"

That startled a laugh out of her, though it broke in the middle and she had to put a hand over her mouth to stop it. She walked to the steps and sat down, and after a moment Quiz followed. "Do you mind if I ask . . . ," he began, but Isaveth shook her head.

"I don't want to talk about it," she said. "Please don't."

Quiz nodded. He picked a twig off the step and turned it over in his fingers, then said in a more casual tone, "Your sisters are charming. Are there just the three of you?"

"There's my older sister, Annagail," said Isaveth. "She's sixteen. What about you? Do you have any family?"

Quiz's face took on a pinched, unhappy look. "None that matters," he said. "None like yours."

Isaveth had suspected as much. He must be one of the many orphaned, neglected, and outcast boys who'd been forced to live on the streets, foraging and thieving to survive. Yet his speech hinted he'd gone to a good school once, and despite the dirt and patches, his clothes were better made than Isaveth's. There was a story here, but she didn't need to ask for details. He wouldn't be the first merchant's or banker's son to see his father's business fall to ruin and his home turn into a black pit of despair and drink.

"Well," she said with an effort at cheerfulness, "thanks for telling me about Auradia. And . . . for scaring off Loyal, too."

"It wasn't all me," said Quiz. "What you did with those tablets was pretty clever. I'd never have thought of using Common Magic to defend myself like that." He shot her a curious glance. "Did you make the spells yourself?"

A blush rose to Isaveth's cheeks, but she nodded.

"You've real talent, then. You ought to keep it up." Quiz swept his blond fringe back and tugged his cap over it, then stood up. "So . . . I'm forgiven, then? You won't gnash your teeth at me the next time I say hello?"

There probably wouldn't be a next time—Tarreton was a big city. But the mental image made Isaveth smile. "I wouldn't know how to gnash my teeth if I tried," she said. "And I'll bet you don't, either."

"Hm." Quiz gripped his jaw and worked it up and down. "Gnash, gnash. No, you're right, that's silly."

Isaveth burst out laughing. "Oh, go away! I have to make supper." Even if all she could do was cut her squashed loaf into pieces, scrape the soggy mess off the bottom of the bag, and dump it all together in a pan. She'd have plenty of lint and bits of shell to pick out, but she couldn't let all those eggs go to waste. "Good-bye, Quiz."

"Wait!" he called as she turned to leave. "You never told me your name!"

She paused, her hand on the door. "It's Isaveth."

"Isaveth." He repeated it softly, as though it were a wonder. "Well, good night, then . . . Isaveth." He touched his cap to her and ambled off up the street.

Isaveth stood in the doorway a moment, watching him go. Then, with a rueful shake of her head, she gathered up her packages and went inside.

The last few pieces of egg-bread were sizzling on the stove top when Annagail came home from the factory. "You've been waiting for me?" she exclaimed. "Oh, Vettie, you shouldn't have."

"It's all right," said Isaveth. "We only got home a few minutes ago. Sit down and I'll get you a cup of tea."

Annagail pulled out a chair, and Mimmi climbed up beside her. "Did you see Papa?"

"I went to the station," said Anna with a sigh, "but I didn't see him." Then her gaze focused on Mimmi, and she managed a smile. "I'm sure he'll be fine, though. The man at the desk said they've put their best officers on the case. And he promised to let us know if there's anything we can do."

Isaveth had hoped for better news, but then, her father had been arrested only that morning. Even Auradia Champion couldn't have solved the murder and cleared Papa's name so quickly.

"Do you want two pieces of egg-bread or three?" Isaveth asked. "There's plenty."

Annagail blinked at the mention of eggs, but then she shook her head. "Only one, please. I'm not hungry."

Isaveth went still. For one moment her sister's voice had been a perfect echo of their mother's. And Mama's illness had begun the same way: fatigue and loss of appetite. "You . . . you're sure?"

"Vettie, don't look like that. I'm fine. It was just so hot in the factory today, I can hardly stand to think of eating." Annagail sighed. "I wish fairweather season were over—it's been more like *fire*weather this year."

"I don't," said Mimmi, kicking her feet back and forth. "Harvest means school."

"It wouldn't if you lived on a farm," Lilet pointed out. "Then you wouldn't have to go until fallowtime. And you'd have eggs to eat every day. Ones that aren't smashed up."

Not long ago Lilet had read a book about an orphan girl who had gone to live with farm folk, and ever since then she'd been set on moving to the country. Isaveth had tried to explain that the farms were all owned by fieldlords who took most of the produce for themselves and that farm life was even harder than life in the city, but Lilet remained stubbornly unconvinced.

"It wasn't Vettie's fault the eggs got smashed," Mimmi said. "It was that Loyal Kercher." She made a face. "He's horrible. I hate him."

"Loyal?" Annagail's brow furrowed in distress. "But he used to be such a sweet boy. Don't you remember him bringing me wildflowers after I broke my ankle?"

"He was probably trying to find out why you hadn't left the house," said Lilet. "The Kerchers are a lot of dirty spies."

"Lilet!"

"Well, it's true. And they hate us for being Moshite, even though they never go anywhere on Templeday themselves. They hate everybody who isn't as mean and miserable as they are."

Annagail cast an imploring look at Isaveth, who busied herself serving the egg-bread and pretended not to notice. It was her older sister's nature to see good in everyone, but for once Isaveth agreed with Lilet. Loyal deserved every bit of the thumping Quiz had given him, and when she remembered how he'd fallen on her fire-tablet . . .

"Why are you smiling?" asked Lilet suspiciously.

"It's nothing," said Isaveth. "I was just thinking of something Quiz said."

"Quiz?" asked Annagail, and then of course Isaveth

had to explain. It was the first time she'd told the full story, and by the time she finished, even Lilet looked impressed.

"You never told us you'd met Eryx Lording," she said. "It's not fair you were out having adventures in the city while Mimmi and I were stuck with a bunch of babies at Aunt Sal's."

"Jory's not a baby," said Mimmi, indignant. "He's seven. That's almost as old as me."

"He might as well be a baby, for all the use he is," Lilet retorted. "Aunt Sal never makes him do anything."

"It's not his fault he was born slow! He's a good boy. You're mean."

"Enough, both of you. It's time to eat." Annagail untied her prayer scarf and draped it over her head and shoulders, then took up the flint-spark Isaveth had left on the table. "With this light we thank the All-One," she said, lighting the first blessing candle. "Giver of life, provider of bread, hope of the world to come."

"We are thankful," the younger girls chorused, but Mimmi pinched Lilet as she said it, and Lilet kicked her in return. "Ow!"

"And with this," Annagail went on loudly as she lit the second, "we remember Moshiel, our guide . . . girls, *stop it*." She pulled off the scarf and dropped back into her seat. "I can't even say a blessing in this house anymore."

Isaveth slid a plate of egg-bread in front of her. "You should be ashamed," she told Lilet and Mimmi. "What would Papa say if he could see you now?"

Which was cruel, and it hurt her even to say it, but it worked. Her younger sisters looked guiltily at each other, and Lilet sat down without another word.

Chapter Six

Iⅼ IT HAD BEEN WARM in the kitchen, it was even hotter in the narrow, slope-ceilinged bedroom that Isaveth shared with all three of her sisters. There was no space for a desk and chair, only the two beds and a battered trunk that held nearly everything they owned. But Isaveth had a solution to that problem. She dragged the trunk to the window, then slipped a rectangle of stiff board from under her mattress and laid it across her knees as she sat down. With the far edge braced against the window frame, it was almost a proper writing desk. Isaveth smoothed the leaflet she'd picked up on the street, turned it to the blank side, and began to write.

She'd meant to make a list of all the things she knew about Papa's case and his relationship with the late Master Orien. Especially what he'd told her and Annagail about the governor offering him a job, and how he'd given up his old grudge against him. But she'd written only a couple of lines before she realized there was no way to prove either of those things. Unless they could find a witness to her father's private conversation with Orien, there was no reason for the Lawkeepers to believe Papa was telling the truth.

So what *did* Papa have in his favor? Four daughters who loved and believed in him, and a reputation for hard work and honest dealing? Put that way, it didn't amount to much. Especially if it came out that Papa was a member of the Workers' Club and had taken part in protests against the government. That he really was what Loyal had called him . . . though to the Kerchers and most other people "dissenter" was just another way of saying "Moshite."

It didn't seem fair to Isaveth that her family should be judged for something their ancestors had done centuries ago, especially since it was no worse than what the various sects that now made up the Unifying Church had done at the same time. They'd all rebelled against the Arcan Temple, with its elaborate, lore-based rituals and charms that only the wealthy could afford, and demanded the right to practice Common Magic and worship as they saw fit. And in the end they'd got what they wanted, but only by agreeing to band together and sign a pact with the Arcans.

The Moshites, however, had refused, saying the treaty went against their beliefs . . . and they'd been feared and despised for it ever since. Even once their leaders were executed, their meeting halls burned, and their traditional day of worship struck from the calendar to enforce one Templeday for all, many still saw the followers of Moshiel as a threat.

But these days most Sagelords allowed Moshites to live and worship freely as long as they kept the peace, and the Lawkeepers were supposed to be above prejudice. That was one of the reforms Auradia had brought to her thirty-year term as Lady Justice, first of the city of Listerbroke and later of the whole province of Upper Colonia. Keepers were sworn to treat all citizens equally and judge them by the same standards, even Moshites.

But would they?

Isaveth stared distractedly out the window, twiddling her lead-point. Then she rubbed out her first few lines and started over.

> "Help me, Lady!" pleaded a voice, and Auradia turned to see a young girl with soulful eyes and dark, bobbed hair standing behind her, hands clasped in supplication. "They've taken my papa

to prison, but I swear to you, he's innocent!"

Moved with compassion, Auradia took out a handkerchief and dried the girl's tears. "Tell me your story," she said. "If my Lawkeepers have acted unjustly, I promise to make it right."

After seeing Annagail off to work and her sisters to Aunt Sal's the next morning, Isaveth counted her remaining spell-tablets and decided she'd soon have to bake more—and find something better to wrap them in. Especially the fire-tablets, for if they broke, tissue paper could do nothing to stop them from bursting into flame. If only she could find some way to protect them that wouldn't affect their potency, yet would be cheap and simple to make. . . .

Isaveth was still mulling over the problem as she set off for the city again, with a sturdier basket to hold her tablets and a couple of tea towels to cushion them. Yet by the time she arrived, she'd come no closer to a solution.

After the commotion she'd caused yesterday it seemed unwise to stand on the same corner, so she crossed the street and walked north to the junction of Grand and College instead. But though Isaveth did her best to catch people's attention and show off her wares, they appeared more annoyed than interested. Some stepped off the pavement or even crossed the street to avoid her; others pushed past with a curt refusal or dismissive wave of the hand. Finally a man leaned out of a window and shouted at her to quit bleating or he'd send for the Lawkeepers.

Maybe she didn't sound professional enough. Maybe her spell-tablets needed a name like the ones from the factories—like Glow-Mor or Fuller's Firelights or Power-Up! Isaveth considered a few possibilities, then decided to stick with a name that was both honest and easy to remember, one that would make people think of home.

"Spell-tablets for sale!" she shouted, holding her basket high as she walked along. "Only the best from Mother Breck's!"

That got a reaction, though not the one Isaveth had hoped for. Several people slowed to stare at her, while others frowned before hurrying on. She repeated her cry a few more times, then trailed off into frustrated silence. What was she doing wrong?

"Latest news!" A rag-boy turned the corner, holding the front page high. "Builder arrested for governor's murder! Breck to stand trial before Lord Justice!"

The words drove like a fist into Isaveth's stomach. How

could she have forgotten that Papa's name would be in all the papers and that by now half the city would know it? And all the while she'd been calling "Breck, Breck" like some silly chicken and wondering why people wouldn't buy her wares!

Even worse, she now knew the Lawkeepers believed her father guilty—so much so that they'd already decided to put him on trial. How could that be? How could they even think of taking him to court, unless they'd found strong evidence against him?

Struggling against tears, Isaveth turned away from the pavement and caught sight of her reflection in a shop window: eyes like coal smudges under thick, straight brows, dark hair frizzing in the heat, her mouth bent into an unhappy shape that looked more sullen than tragic. Even her tawny-brown skin, which normally resisted the sun, was starting to redden and peel in a most unattractive way. No wonder nobody wanted to approach her, especially once they heard her shouting her father's name. . . .

She was still staring miserably at herself when Quiz's face popped up behind her shoulder, and she gave a little shriek.

"Did I frighten you? Sorry." He peered through the glass, his good eye bright with curiosity. "Are garden spades really that fascinating, or was it the washtub you were looking at?"

Last night his silly chatter had made her smile, but Isaveth had no heart for it now. She shook her head and turned away.

"Oh," said Quiz in a softer tone. "It's bad, is it?"

His sympathy was more than Isaveth could bear. She pulled out the Lording's handkerchief and buried her face in it.

"Er . . . well, then," said Quiz, sounding as lost as Isaveth felt. "Maybe . . . yes, right. We should sit down." And with that he steered her over to the steps in front of the Merchants' Union and helped her to a seat.

"I'm sorry," said Isaveth thickly, surfacing from the handkerchief. "It's just been such a horrible day."

"Funny, I was thinking the same thing. It's awfully hot out here, isn't it? Would you like a drink?" Without waiting for an answer, he leaped up, dashed into a nearby café, and returned a few minutes later with two small bottles of bubblewater.

Isaveth felt a twinge of guilt: If he'd found money, he surely couldn't afford to spend it on her. But her thirst was too strong to ignore. She thumbed off the stopper and drank the whole bottle at a gulp.

"I run errands for the shopkeepers sometimes," Quiz

told her, leaning back on his elbows and crossing one bony ankle over the other. "So they don't mind doing me the odd favor. You can have mine, too, if you want. Save it for later."

Isaveth tucked the second bottle into her basket and folded her hands in her lap, feeling suddenly shy. "That's very kind of you."

"Oh, I am positively brimming with kindness," said Quiz. "I keep the cork under my eyepatch. But you also ought to know that I'm terribly nosy. Shall we play questions until I figure out why you're upset? Or would you rather tell me to go and boil my head for a turnip?"

Isaveth gave a faint smile. "You don't look like a turnip."

"Well, a parsnip, then," said Quiz, rubbing his long nose. "Whatever you like. But if you tell me what's wrong, I might be able to help."

"Not this time," said Isaveth. "Not unless you can convince the Lawkeepers that my father isn't a . . . a murderer."

Quiz sat up sharply, the humor vanishing from his face. "You're not serious. That builder they arrested—Breck? *He's* your father?"

So he'd heard the news too. And like all the others, he was horrified. Isaveth closed her eyes and nodded miserably.

"But . . . he can't have done it," said Quiz in a blank tone. "It has to be someone else."

Her eyes popped open. "What?"

"It's not possible, that's all. A man with a family like yours couldn't be a murderer."

Was he teasing her? Surely no one could be that cruel. "Are you—do you really mean it?"

"Sure I do. Besides, you think he's innocent, don't you?"

"Of course!"

"Well, then," he said, as though that settled the matter.

So he really was on her side. She wasn't friendless after all. The ice in Isaveth's chest thawed, and she almost hugged him for gratitude. But he had to be a year older than she was at least, and she didn't want him to think her childish.

"Yes," she said, "but the problem is I can't prove it. I don't even know why the Keepers arrested Papa in the first place. My sister went to the station yesterday, but they wouldn't tell her anything. . . ."

A thought struck her and she stopped, staring into the traffic. Yes, Annagail had talked to the Lawkeepers— her meek, soft-spoken sister, who believed it was her Moshite duty to obey the authorities and not cause any trouble. No wonder she hadn't been able to visit Papa,

75

or find out anything about his case; she'd accepted the first answer the man at the desk gave her, and never dared ask for more. But Isaveth wasn't about to give up so easily.

She was on her feet in an instant, and Quiz looked up in surprise. "Where are you going?"

"To the Keeper Station," Isaveth said. "I'm going to talk to the officers who arrested Papa and find out everything they know."

Chapter Seven

"YOU'RE GOING TO THE LAWKEEPERS?" Quiz looked startled. "I was about to offer to do the same thing. Why don't you let me?"

"He's my father," said Isaveth. A minute ago she'd been close to despair, but now she felt filled with purpose. Like Auradia Champion, setting out on a new quest for truth and justice.

"But I could help." Quiz followed her down the steps. "I'm good at getting people to talk. I might even be able to find out who discovered the . . . body." His voice wavered, but it took him only a second to recover. "Anyway, I want to."

"Why?" asked Isaveth, turning back to him. "You don't know my father—you barely even know me. And if you're trying to make up for yesterday, you've already done that several times over. Don't you have other things to do?"

Quiz reddened and tugged at his eyepatch. "Well, I did say I'm terribly nosy. And I can't resist a mystery. You must have guessed that 'Quiz' is short for 'inquisitive'?"

Isaveth shook her head.

"It's my curse. You might call me an investigative reporter, only I've nobody to report to. Except you. If you'll let me."

He was practically pleading now. Maybe with no work, no school, and no real family, this was how he kept busy—and out of worse kinds of trouble. "But I can't pay you anything," said Isaveth.

"That's all right. I don't mind doing a favor for a friend." He cocked a brow at her. "We are friends, aren't we?"

After all he'd done to help her, it would be rude to deny it. But would he still want to be her friend if he knew everything? After the way Morra had abandoned her, she couldn't bear to put her trust in someone only to be hurt again. Isaveth steeled herself, then blurted out, "I'm Moshite."

"I thought you might be," said Quiz.

"That doesn't bother you?"

"No. Should it?"

Isaveth relaxed. "All right. Friends." She started walking again, and Quiz fell into step beside her.

"Shall we make a list of questions we want to ask? Or

should we start by going over what we already know?"

He really was taking this seriously. "I don't know much yet," Isaveth said reluctantly. "Only what the Keepers said when they came to arrest Papa and . . . a few other things."

"Well, tell me everything you know," said Quiz, pulling a battered notebook and a stub of lead-point out of his pocket. "I can write it down on the way."

The Keeper Station stood at the top of College Street, three square and unyielding stories of gray stone with a central block that looked sturdy enough to survive fire, flood, a siege with battering rams, and possibly a mage-bomb dropped from above. The windows were grilled with iron, and even the doors were barred, which made the building appear impenetrable—though it obviously wasn't, because as Isaveth and Quiz mounted the steps, the left-hand door swung open and a young woman in a sleek gray suit emerged. She tucked a notebook into her purse, then paused to freshen her lip-tint and tidy the black bell of her hair.

For an instant Isaveth wondered why she looked familiar, until she recognized the reporter who'd been shadowing Eryx Lording yesterday. She turned to Quiz, but he wasn't there—he'd dropped to one knee at the far edge of the steps and was retying his bootlace.

"Should we talk to that woman over there?" she asked in a low voice. "I think she works for one of the news-rags. She might know something."

"There's a thought," said Quiz, not looking up. "Wait a second and I'll come with you."

Except his lace must have knotted, because it took him a long time to untangle it. By the time he straightened up, the woman was gone.

"It might be for the best," Quiz said, shrugging off Isaveth's look of reproach. "She'd probably just have squeezed you for information anyway. Besides, don't you think we'll get farther with our investigation if the news-rags don't know who you are?"

Which was a fair argument, but Isaveth was still disappointed. It would have been more pleasant to talk to the woman than to go inside that cold fortress and confront the Lawkeepers. Still, she had no choice now, so she sent up a silent prayer for courage and climbed the steps to the door.

Quiz hurried to open it for her—his way of apologizing, no doubt. She gave him a smile, which brought a tinge of color to his thin cheeks, and the two of them went in.

Inside it was cooler, and their footsteps echoed as

they crossed the polished floor. Smooth granite pillars loomed over them, and the bronze-and-iron crest of the Lawkeepers gleamed high on the opposite wall. Halfway across the chamber stood an imposing wooden barrier, and behind it sat two officers, a man and a woman, stamping papers and stacking them in piles.

"Excuse me," said Isaveth to the female Lawkeeper, but the woman didn't even glance up. She gestured impatiently at her partner, who rose to greet them.

"Well, kids," he said. "What can I do for you?"

Something about his gaze made Isaveth feel as though he were staring straight through her and counting all her bones. "I—I need to see the officers who arrested Urias Breck," she said. "I have . . . information for them."

She'd meant to say "questions" but changed her mind at the last instant. Surely the Lawkeepers would be more likely to talk to her if they thought she had something to offer in return.

"I'm afraid that's not possible," said the officer. "You can fill out a report, and we'll contact you if we have any questions." He took some papers from a pile beside him and slid them toward her. "Name and address here, date and time of the incident here . . ."

"But it's urgent," said Isaveth in desperation. The form was covered with lines and boxes, and looked to be at least three pages long. "Isn't there anyone I can talk to right now?"

The Lawkeeper shook his head. "No public interviews on Trustdays except by order of the Lawkeeper-General. Duesdays and Fastdays by appointment only." He opened his ledger. "You might be able to get in next Duesday, if I put you on the waiting list."

Isaveth hesitated. She could see several names on the list already, and she hated the thought of waiting four more days for an interview that would be brief at best—if she got in at all. What could she do?

Quiz slouched beside her, rubbing his nose and gazing dully about as though he'd never had an original thought in his life. She was about to poke him to get his attention when he muttered, "Advocate."

Of course! Like anyone accused of a serious crime, her father was entitled to a legal adviser. Isaveth turned back to the desk. "We'd like to speak to Mister Breck's advocate. Could you tell us where to find him?"

The officer retrieved a second ledger, opened it, and ran his fingers down the column of names. "There's no advocate listed," he said shortly. "He must have refused counsel."

Isaveth stared at him, disbelieving. Why would her father refuse an advocate? He wasn't stupid, by any means, but he knew no more about the law than most working folk, and he wasn't eloquent enough to speak for himself in court. There was something strange going on here.

"Then I'll have to talk to Urias Breck directly," she said, drawing herself up. "I'm his daughter. Please take me to him right away."

She'd hoped boldness might succeed where Annagail's gentler pleas had failed. But the officer only frowned. "No visitors to the cells today," he said. "Try again Mendday morning, at the Dern Valley Jail. They should have transferred him there by then."

That was three days from now, but the flat line of the Lawkeeper's mouth warned Isaveth that protesting would make no difference. Defeated, she turned away.

"What was wrong with you back there?" asked Isaveth once she and Quiz were outside. "You said you wanted to help!"

Quiz caught her arm, urging her down the steps to the sidewalk. "I did help," he said. "I told you to ask about an advocate." He glanced uneasily over his shoulder, as though fearing the Keeper Station would pick up its stone skirts and chase after them. "Could we talk about this somewhere else?"

Isaveth's lips parted in a soft O. "So that's why. You were frightened."

"I wasn't—"

"Had you met that officer before? Were you afraid he'd recognize you?" She shook free of his grip. "You told Mimmi you'd never been to jail!"

"I haven't!" He hunched his shoulders. "I've just . . . you know . . . come close a couple of times."

"Only a couple?"

Quiz sighed. "All right, I know I wasn't very helpful, but you were doing fine. Anyway," he added more cheerfully, "at least now we know when we can talk to your father."

"Yes, but . . ." Isaveth twisted the basket in her hands. "I can't bear to do nothing while Papa's awaiting trial. Especially if he doesn't even have an advocate. Who knows what sort of evidence they're going to bring against him?"

"We sure don't. And probably neither does he."

"Exactly." Isaveth quickened her stride. "I'm guessing Papa was the last one to see Governor Orien alive, but that can't be the only reason the Lawkeepers arrested him. There must be something else about the murder that makes them think he did it . . . and that's what I need to find out."

"So we're going to forget the Lawkeepers and investigate on our own?" Quiz said, catching up to her. "I like that. Where do you want to start?"

It was a good question. What would Auradia do in a case like this? Well, she was the Lady Justice, so she would have got all the information she needed simply by asking for it. But even so, she always made sure to visit the scene of the crime. . . .

"Quiz," Isaveth said abruptly, "you've read the news-rags. Did they say where Master Orien's body was found?"

"At the college. They didn't say exactly where, but I expect it was in his office."

"And do you know where they took him afterward?"

"Well, if it was murder, they would probably have sent him to the Healer-General for examination," said Quiz, frowning. Then he whirled on her, his good eye wide. "That's it! If I could get into the hospital crypt and take a look . . ."

Isaveth was surprised. "Do you think you can?"

Quiz bared his teeth in a bleak smile. "Oh, I'm sure I can. One way or another."

His usual whimsy had vanished, and it made Isaveth uneasy. She wanted to ask him what he was planning, and what would happen if he got caught . . . but judging by the gleam in his eye, it might be better not to know. Quiz was a street-boy and a fighter; he could look after himself. And while he was sneaking into the hospital, Isaveth could do some investigating of her own.

"Do you know anyone at the college?" she asked, sidestepping a legless veteran who rattled his cup as they passed. She hated to ignore anyone in need, but she had no money, and even one of her tablets would be a poor donation in this heat. "Do you think they'd let me in?"

"Hm," said Quiz, rubbing a knuckle thoughtfully beneath his lip. "I do know someone, though it's too late to introduce you to her today. But if you give me a couple of those spell-tablets and meet me first thing tomorrow . . ." He smiled again, and this time it looked genuine. "I think I can get you in."

Chapter Eight

"LOOK, IT'S QUIZ!" exclaimed Mimmi as Isaveth and her sisters came out of the house the next morning. "What's he doing here, Vettie?"

"It's rude to point," said Lilet, poking her, but Mimmi slapped her hand away and ran to meet the boy waiting in the street.

"Are you going to fight Loyal Kercher again? Can I watch?"

"No duels of honor today," said Quiz. "My schedule's full. Are those new shoes, Mirrim?"

Mimmi turned pink and ducked behind Isaveth, who looked down at her in surprise; it wasn't like her little sister to turn shy, even if she wasn't used to people calling her by her proper name.

"Go on," she said. "He asked you a question."

"Yes," blurted out Mimmi, and then, with renewed

courage, "They don't even flop when I run. Look!" And she took off up the road at a gallop.

"Very fine," said Quiz admiringly when she came puffing back. "You'll be hard to catch in those."

Lilet cast a dark glance at Isaveth, who pretended not to notice. True, Lilet needed a new dress as badly as Mimmi had needed shoes, so her jealousy wasn't surprising. But Isaveth had already spent all the money Eryx Lording had given her, so there was nothing she could do.

"So why do you wear that patch really?" Mimmi asked Quiz, tipping her head sideways. "Are you a lake-pirate?"

"In training," he agreed solemnly. "If I pass my next set of exams, I get to choose between a hook and a peg leg."

"Because Lilet says—"

"Mimmi, *enough*," snapped both her sisters at once, but Quiz only looked intrigued.

"Do tell," he said. "What does Lilet say?"

"She says your eye is lazy, and you have to cover up the other one to make it work better."

Quiz shrugged. "I suppose. If you want to take all the fun out of it."

Which was hardly a definite answer, but Mimmi's face clouded. "I knew it would be something dull," she said, and trudged off across the street. Isaveth would have followed, but Lilet froze her with a glare.

"You don't have to walk us to Aunt Sal's every day, you know," she said. "We aren't *babies*." Then she whirled and stalked after Mimmi.

"I'm sorry," said Isaveth when she had gone. "I'm trying to teach them better manners."

"Not at all," Quiz replied mildly. "Lilet's quite observant, isn't she? And Mirrim's not short on curiosity. Do the detective instincts come from your father's side?"

"My mother's," Isaveth said, and her heart gave that queer sideways lurch it always did when she thought about Mama. But if Quiz was her friend, he ought to know. "She's gone now. She got sick last fallowtime, and she never got better."

Quiz's expression sobered. "I'm sorry. I didn't—I shouldn't have asked."

"It's all right. I miss her, but . . . I have good memories." She took a deep breath and went on, "So, did you have any luck yesterday? Can you get me into the college?"

"I think so, but you'll have to work for it." Quiz dug into his pocket, produced four tarnished cits, and handed two to Isaveth. "Let's catch the next tram, and I'll explain on the way."

From outside, the spell-kitchen of Tarreton College looked plain—a low rectangle of gray stone half covered in ivy, with a glass sunroom on the far end. But inside it was all modern splendor, with a gleaming U-bend of countertop, two enormous ovens, and a spotless mock tile floor; it made Isaveth ashamed of her own small and grubby kitchen at home.

"Hm," said the spellmistress, looking Isaveth up and down. "You're younger than I expected, but with school out of session I suppose there's no reason to turn you away."

Chayla Anandri was a tall, lean-boned woman with eyes so dark as to be almost black, brown skin only a shade lighter, and fog-colored hair cropped close to her skull. She pulled an apron from the peg rack by the door and thrust it at Isaveth. "You remember your mother's recipe? You can make it again?"

Isaveth could only hope so. "Yes, mistress."

When the tram had stopped at the college gate, she'd hoped Quiz would introduce her to the spellmistress in person. But he needed to get to the hospital early, he said, for the best chance of sneaking into the crypt. He'd tried last night, but all the doors and windows had been locked, so he was going to have to get in by a less direct method—and as he'd grudgingly admitted when Isaveth pressed him, it might take him a while to think of one.

So he'd pointed out the spell-kitchen to Isaveth,

handed her a note to deliver to Mistress Anandri, and jumped on the tram again. Isaveth would have liked to know what was in the letter, but the envelope was glued shut. She could only hope Quiz had said the right things to impress this woman . . . and that her own skill and hard work would do the rest.

"Do you have many problems with your spell-tablets?" Isaveth asked as she tied on her apron. Peddling was forbidden on college grounds, but Quiz had dared to show the mistress Isaveth's samples anyway, and once she'd tested them, she'd been quick to ask for more.

"Nothing that common sense wouldn't solve," said Mistress Anandri, folding Quiz's letter and tucking it inside her robe. "It's a waste to buy factory tablets when we could make our own, but I know better than to start baking for the other masters, or they'll never let me stop. The new students will make a few batches come harvest term, but . . ." Her lips pursed in disapproval. "They seldom turn out anything worth keeping."

Isaveth could guess why. Most nobles considered cookery beneath them and would probably be offended to have to begin their learning in the kitchen.

Mistress Anandri strode to the larger of the two ovens and opened the small drawer in its front. There in a narrow chute sat two fire-tablets, all that remained of the samples Quiz had borrowed from Isaveth last night.

"Your spells aren't as smooth or regular as the factory tablets," the spellmistress continued. "And they break more easily, which is unfortunate. But they burn hotter and last longer." She closed the drawer, and with a soft *whoof* the oven kindled to life.

"Make me three batches of fire-tablets," she continued, taking a ring of keys from her belt, "and another three of light—use the sunroom for those. Here are your ingredients." She unlocked a cupboard above the work top and flung it open, revealing a collection of jars, bottles, and tins all labeled in the same clear, decisive hand. "Flours and grains on this shelf, eggs in the rack here, milk in the chill-box . . ."

Still talking, she circled the kitchen, laying out bowls, measuring spoons, and a number of odd utensils Isaveth had never seen before. "There. Is there anything else you require?"

Isaveth hesitated, her gaze traveling over the array of tools and ingredients. It seemed impossible that the spellmistress could have forgotten something so important. "A sifter?"

"Whatever for? This is Tarreton College, young lady. We buy the finest flour available."

Mistress Anandri drew herself up haughtily as she

spoke, and Isaveth's heart gave an anxious flutter. If she offended this woman, she'd lose her chance to investigate the college. Yet her mother's instructions had been clear.

"I'm sure you're right," she said meekly. "But I'd like to sift it anyway. Just to be safe."

Mistress Anandri gave her a hard look, and Isaveth quailed. But then the spellmistress took a sifter out of the cupboard and set it beside the other tools.

"As a matter of fact," she said, "even the best flour sometimes contains neevils, especially in fairweather season. Did you know that neevils have antimagical properties?"

Her posture had relaxed, and her voice held more warmth than before. Had Isaveth passed some sort of test? "No," she said cautiously.

"Most of my students learn that lesson the hard way. Your mother taught you well." She jerked her chin toward the work top. "Go on and get started, then. I'll be back in a few minutes to check on your progress."

Even with two ovens and all the ingredients she needed, it took Isaveth most of the morning to finish the tablets Mistress Anandri had asked for. Though the heat in the sunroom was oppressive, the kitchen stayed pleasantly mild, and by the time she had finished, Isaveth hardly felt tired at all. She was gazing up at the slow rotation of the ceiling fan, wondering if there was a cold-charm worked into its mechanism, when the spellmistress returned for the final inspection.

"Quiz told me you had a gift," she said, lowering the charm-glass she'd been holding to her eye. "I see he was right. This should keep us until the first week of harvest term at least, and I won't have to listen to the other masters squawk about their lamps being dim. Now, then." She drew a chair out from the table and sat down, motioning to Isaveth to join her. "I understand you have some questions about Governor Orien's death?"

Isaveth was startled. Had Quiz actually told Mistress Anandri what the two of them were up to? Even with the offer of free help in exchange for her information, she must be fond of the street-boy to grant such a bold request.

"I . . . yes," she stammered. "I was—er, Quiz was wondering when the master's body was found, and where. The news-rags didn't say."

Mistress Anandri touched her fingertips together, regarding Isaveth shrewdly. "So he sent you to find out for him? You are young to be dealing with such harsh matters."

Which meant she had no idea Isaveth was Urias Breck's daughter. Quiz had kept that secret, at least.

"I know," said Isaveth, gaining confidence, "but ignoring bad things doesn't make them go away. And I know—I mean, we believe that the man the Lawkeepers arrested is innocent."

"I see." The spellmistress's gaze turned reflective. "Well, I suppose it can do no harm to let you look around—as long as you do it discreetly and don't disturb the masters. Keep that apron over your dress, put on one of the kitchen caps, then fill one of those big jars with your light-tablets and take it over to Founders' Hall. If anyone questions you, tell them you've been sent to refill the lamps."

"Founders' Hall? Is that where Master Orien . . . ?"

"The governor's office is there, on the second floor. The cleaning maid found his body when she came in that night, but I don't know any more than that. His secretary might help you, I suppose, if she's in the mood."

"What about the maid? Could I talk to her?"

"I'm afraid not. She gave her notice the next day, saying she'd found a better position. No one's seen her since."

That was odd. Not that the maid would want to quit the college after such a dreadful discovery—Isaveth could understand that part. But how had she found a new post so quickly, when many people were desperate for any work at all?

"Did she say where she was going?" Isaveth asked.

"Not to me, but we never spoke. I only heard about it after she was gone."

Isaveth gave a thoughtful nod. She'd have to ask the other cleaning staff about the maid, then—if she could find an opportunity to do so.

"Thank you," she told Mistress Anandri. "You've been very helpful."

"Not at all." The older woman rose. "I was not close to the governor, but I respected him. I, too, would like to see his murderer brought to justice." She paused, as though debating with herself. Then she opened the chill-box, took out a bottle of milk, and set it in front of Isaveth.

"It will spoil soon, so you may as well drink it," she said, and walked out.

Founders' Hall was only a short walk across the green. It was built from the same gray stone as the kitchen but in a far more ornate style, with pointed towers, haughtily arched windows, and a door so heavy Isaveth struggled to open it.

Inside all was quiet—though not deserted, because the porter glanced up and rustled his news-rag as Isaveth passed, and a youngish man in the lake-blue robe of an undermaster was leaning idly by the foot of the staircase, hands cupped around his baccy pipe. But all the doors she passed were shut, the only voices she heard were murmurs, and as she made her way upstairs, Isaveth cringed at the squeak of her shoes against the stone.

It was equally quiet on the second floor, except here most of the doors stood open. As she tiptoed along, Isaveth glimpsed lecture rooms filled with empty tables and blank slate-boards, tall cabinets displaying trophies and other college memorabilia, and a paneled lounge where two masters sat conversing in low tones. At the far end of the hallway stood a closed door with a window of frosted glass and a brass plate beneath reading GOVERNOR'S OFFICE.

There was a bell-button on the wall. Isaveth pressed it, and the door opened.

A drab-looking blond woman rose as Isaveth entered, hastily smoothing her skirt—but when she caught sight of Isaveth's cap and apron, she frowned and sat down again.

"I didn't call for a maid," she said. "What are you doing here?"

If the governor's secretary was ever in a mood to be friendly, today was not the day. Her mouth was pursed, her eyes narrowed, and the way she glared through her half-spectacles made Isaveth feel suddenly very small, very young, and very foolish indeed.

How could she have thought she could simply walk into the governor's office and get all the information she needed? She'd been so proud of herself for winning over Mistress Anandri, so glad of the chance to get into the college and look around, that she'd dared to imagine the rest of her task would be easy.

But Isaveth knew better now. Getting this cold, suspicious woman to speak to her, let alone answer her questions—that would be her biggest challenge yet.

Chapter Nine

"WELL?" MASTER ORIEN'S secretary demanded. "What do you want, girl? Speak up, or get out!"

Isaveth's mouth felt dry, and her stomach was churning. She could only be grateful for the excuse Mistress Anandri had given her. "I came to fill the lamps, missus. I was told they were getting dim."

"Then you can do it later, when you come back to clean. You are the new maid, aren't you?"

"Yes, missus," Isaveth said, then thought better of it and added, "Or one of them, anyway. I'm sorry I disturbed you, but Mistress Anandri said some of the masters had been complaining, so I thought I'd best get the new tablets put in straightaway."

"Well, you won't hear any complaints from this master," said the woman bitterly. "But I suppose that if the spellmistress sent you, it's not my place to argue." She pressed a button on her desk, and the inner door swung open. "Go on, then."

With ornate moldings, studded leather furniture, and a carpet thick enough to sink into, Master Orien's office was every bit as luxurious as Isaveth had expected—after all, the governor of Tarreton College had been one of the most influential nobles in the city. Bookshelves stretched the length of one wall, packed with volumes on law, history, and magical theory, while the opposite wall held gilt-framed portraits of the founders, past governors, and other patrons of the school. In the center hung the largest picture of all—a painting of the Sagelord himself, seated in a wingback chair, with Eryx standing at his shoulder.

Isaveth glanced at the doorway, fearing the secretary's glare. But the door had shut as silently as it had opened, and Isaveth was alone. Daring, she stepped closer to the portrait, her gaze flicking over Lord Arvis's drooping lids and heavy jowls with distaste before focusing on the young man behind him.

The Lording looked younger here, but no less handsome: His blue eyes gleamed with intelligence, and a faint smile warmed his lips. Isaveth could have basked in that smile forever, but she hadn't come here to sigh over a painting. She gave Eryx a wistful parting glance and turned away.

Now to investigate—and she'd better work quickly, before the secretary got suspicious. Isaveth dropped to all fours and squinted along the carpet, groped around the bottom of all the furniture, then jumped up to inspect the bookcase and look beneath the windowsill. She wasn't even sure what she was looking for, but those were the sorts of things Auradia always did, and if she spotted even the smallest detail that the Lawkeepers had missed, it would be worth it.

Yet she found no incriminating documents, no evidence of struggle, not even a footprint besides her own. The desktop and drawers were empty, and the odd smell in the air turned out to be nothing more than wood soap and fresh paint. The room had been thoroughly cleaned since the Lawkeepers inspected it, leaving no evidence that Master Orien—or his murderer—had ever been here. Disappointed, Isaveth filled the lamp slots with fresh tablets, then returned to the outer chamber.

The secretary sat with her back to Isaveth, arms jerking as she punched the keys of her letter-press. She looked fiercely busy, and Isaveth feared to interrupt her again. Still, if she couldn't get at least a few answers out of this woman, all her efforts would be wasted. There had to be some way to coax her into conversation.

Isaveth's eyes slid to the stack of papers and pile of

envelopes on the desk . . . and all at once she had a plan.

"Is there anything else you'd like me to do for you, missus?" Isaveth asked humbly. "You must have a terrible lot of work just now, with what happened to the governor and all. If there's any way I can make it go smoother, I'd be glad to help."

The woman spun to face her, looking startled—but for the first time not displeased. "Well!" she said. "That's quite an offer, Miss . . ."

"Morra, missus." Isaveth's former friend probably wouldn't be happy to have her name and mannerisms borrowed this way, but since she wasn't talking to Isaveth anymore, it wasn't likely she'd find out. "What about these letters?" Isaveth went on, setting her jar of tablets down on the corner of the desk. "Shall I fold them up for you? I promise I'll do it neat."

The secretary hesitated, glancing at the outer door. Then she sat up decisively and said, "Why not? Yes, you can do that much. Fold them, put them in these envelopes, and seal the flaps with this wax stamper. You know how to use one?"

"Yes, missus," replied Isaveth, pulling up a chair, and she began to fold one near-identical page after another. She worked quickly, not wanting to betray too much interest in the letter's contents, but she was a fast reader and it took her only a minute to grasp its message. It was addressed to the noble patrons and former students of the college, informing them of Governor Orien's passing and inviting them to attend his memorial next Duesday. It also said that a new governor would be appointed as soon as the Sagelord and the board of masters had met to choose the best candidate.

Which was all very well for the college, but not much help to Isaveth. Yes, Governor Orien had been killed, but how? And who else besides Papa could have had the opportunity to do it? The secretary could surely answer at least one of those questions, but she seemed almost as prickly as Lilet.

Yet even Lilet could be won over with a bit of flattery. Perhaps this woman could too? Isaveth was gathering her nerve when the secretary pulled the last sheet of paper from the letter-press and sat back, flexing her bony fingers. If there was ever a good time to speak, it was now.

"You must be awfully brave, missus," Isaveth said, still folding. "You ought to get a rise in pay. Working here all alone after finding the governor dead in this very office, without even taking a few days off to calm your nerves!"

The secretary blinked. "Oh. Well, I wasn't the one who

found him," she said, and privately Isaveth exulted: She *was* like Lilet, unable to resist correcting other people's mistakes. "I didn't learn of his death until the next morning. But yes, it was quite a shock."

"Was he a good master, then? Treated you kindly and all?"

"Certainly. Master Orien was always a fair and decent man. That's why I can't believe anyone would . . ." She cleared her throat. "Well, never mind that. But it was dreadful, what happened to him."

"I heard he was killed with magic," Isaveth said, seizing on the first idea she could think of that was plausible but almost certain to be wrong. "Some nasty 'coction they put in his drink."

The secretary sniffed. "Nasty! I'll say. But it wasn't a decoction. It was a power-tablet."

"The kind that drive spell-carriages?" Isaveth was baffled; she couldn't imagine how that would work.

"No. The kind that . . . explode."

Isaveth's stomach jumped, and she was glad she'd kept her head down. Common Magic or not, exploding-tablets were too dangerous to bake at home and nearly impossible to buy without a license; you had to be a miner, a demolisher . . .

Or a stoneworker, like Papa.

"In his *drink?*" she blurted out, to hide her all too real dismay.

"Of course not! It would have exploded long before he could swallow it. But there's no question it was the tablet that killed him." The secretary touched a hand to her chest, her expression haunted. Then she shook herself and snapped, "Are you here to work or not?"

Isaveth scooped up another pile of papers. "Sorry, missus. I was surprised, that's all." She pressed the remaining pages into neat thirds, then began tucking them into the envelopes. The wax in the stamper was cold, but a tap of the fire-tablet in its head would soon fix that. Though she had to be careful not to press too hard, or the tablet would crack and all its heat would come rushing out at once.

Which must be what had happened to Governor Orien. The murderer had fired the power-tablet at him with a slingshot, or perhaps a modified gun, and it had exploded on impact.

"So that's why they think that Breck fellow did the murder?" she asked, when the secretary's scowl had faded and she dared to speak again. "Because he was a builder?"

The woman flung up her hands. "How should I know? I'd had such a busy day with the new charmery project—patrons and architects and workers stopping in every half hour, it seemed, and no end in sight. So when the master told me he could manage the last few visitors on his own, I was glad enough to get away. If I'd known it was the last time I'd ever see him . . ." She whipped out a handkerchief and began dabbing her eyes furiously.

Isaveth quickened her pace with the envelopes. If the secretary lost patience and threw her out, at least it would be for the right reason. "I'm so sorry, missus! I didn't mean to upset you. I just couldn't help but think . . ."

She let the sentence hang, hoping the woman's curiosity would get the better of her—and it did. "Think what?"

"Well, wouldn't it be dreadful if the Lawkeepers had the wrong man? That builder might be innocent as a lamb, for all we know, and the real murderer still here in the college!"

"Nonsense," said the secretary, but she sounded uneasy. Was she thinking of someone she knew with a grudge against Governor Orien?

"I hope you're right, missus," said Isaveth, picking up the stamper. "But I can't think why a workman would want to kill the governor. Are you sure there's nobody else saw the master that day who might have wished him harm?"

The secretary stiffened, and her hand crept toward her

appointment book. But then she snatched it back and said, "Don't be ridiculous. Now finish those envelopes and be off. I've had enough of your chatter."

As Isaveth left the governor's office, her mind was racing. She understood now why the Lawkeepers felt sure Papa was guilty: If Orien had been killed with an exploding-tablet, it was hard to imagine how anyone else could have done it. Unless the murderer had waited for Papa to leave before making his move. . . .

Which, of course, was what must have happened. And judging by the secretary's reaction, there was at least one person at the college with reason to want Governor Orien out of the way. A jealous rival among the masters, perhaps? Or a servant with a grudge?

Well, as long as Isaveth had a chance to investigate, she might as well take advantage of it. Especially since the two masters she'd seen talking earlier had moved on now, leaving only a pair of half-empty drinks and a lingering aroma of baccy smoke behind. She slipped into the lounge and made a cautious circuit of the room, peering behind the curtains and lifting the cushions off the sofa—a search that yielded a crumpled handkerchief, a broken lead-point, and a slim, battered volume entitled *Elementary Principles of Charm Application*, Fifth Edition.

She also found part of yesterday's *Citizen* lying beside one of the armchairs that featured the headline GOVERNOR'S DEATH STALLS REPS' BILL VOTE. But none of these things seemed to offer any clue to Master Orien's murder.

Resigned, Isaveth was about to leave when she noticed the tall spicewood wardrobe in the corner. It looked more suited to a gentleman's bedroom than a lounge, so what was it doing here? She crossed the carpet to open it.

"WHAT do you think you're doing?" roared a man's voice, and Isaveth jumped and slammed the door shut. Whirling, she shrank back against the wardrobe as her accuser strode into the room.

"How dare you enter this room without permission!" The speaker was a balding, red-faced master with a goatee, whose robe was singed and stained about the sleeves as though he'd been cooking porridge in it. "I'll have your cap for this, you impudent little—"

"Now, Robard," admonished the other master. His eyes met Isaveth's, pale as ice in fallowtime but far more gentle. "She's only a child, and there's no harm done. Let her explain."

"Oh, sir," gasped Isaveth, collecting her wits with an effort, "I'm ever so sorry! I came to replace the light-tablets, and as there was nobody in here, I thought it would be all right. I didn't know you were coming back."

The taller master nodded. "And you were curious about the wardrobe," he said, "as any youngster would be. Isn't that right?"

He'd offered her an escape, and it was tempting to seize it. But if they traced her presence here back to Mistress Anandri, she didn't want the woman to regret having helped her. Isaveth lowered her eyes and said, "No, sir. I know that's not my business. I only thought there might be some of the old light-tablets in there, and if so, I ought to take them away, as I was told they were too dim."

Robard snorted, but his companion relaxed at once. "Of course," he said. "You were only doing your job. But we don't keep extra spell-tablets here." He unlocked the wardrobe and opened the door, revealing an empty rail with one deep-blue master's robe hanging on it. "See?"

"Yes, sir." Isaveth backed away, bobbing curtsies all the while. "Thank you, sir." And before either of the men could stop her, she whirled and fled.

Chapter Ten

ISAVETH HURRIED DOWN the stairs to the ground level, still shaken by her encounter with the masters. She'd hoped to search the other rooms on the second floor as well, but after what had happened in the lounge, she didn't dare take that risk.

Yet she wasn't ready to give up, either. She might still find a clue to Governor Orien's murder if she could steal a look at his secretary's appointment book and find out who besides Papa had visited him the night he was killed. But how could she do that without being caught?

If she were a real cleaning maid, with keys to all the offices, the solution would be obvious. But even if the missing maid's position was still open, Isaveth was too young to apply. If only she were sixteen, like Annagail . . .

Suddenly she knew the answer. She jumped down the last two steps and ran to the porter's office.

"Oh, mister," she said breathlessly, "I've only just started work this morning, and I've got all turned about. Could you tell me where to find the housekeeper?"

The porter gave a disapproving harrumph. "Down the back steps," he said. "But don't come here again. It's your business to know where you ought to be, and keep yourself out of the masters' way."

"Yes, mister," Isaveth said, and dashed off to find the stairs to the basement.

This part of the building looked very different from the oak-paneled lecture rooms and offices above. The walls were bare, the ceiling was low, and exposed pipes dripped moisture overhead. Only one lamp in three was lit, and the steam from the nearby laundry made the air dank as old sweat. By the time Isaveth found the door marked SERVANTS' HALL, she was shivering.

When she opened the door, a fog of baccy smoke enveloped her. She coughed and waved a hand, and the haze parted to reveal a long table framed by benches, where a gaunt, middle-aged man and a stout woman only a little younger sat playing a hand of Gamble. They both looked around, and after a moment the man stubbed out his puffer and got up.

"You're not one of our regulars," he said, though he sounded more puzzled than annoyed. "What are you doing here, miss?"

"Good day, sir," said Isaveth with her prettiest curtsy. "I was helping Mistress Anandri in the spell-kitchen this morning, and she said one of the cleaning maids had given notice. Is the post still open?"

The woman laid down her cards. "That's my department, lovey," she said. "I'm the housekeeper. But you aren't asking for yourself, I hope! You ought to be still in school."

"I am," said Isaveth, "or at least I will be, come harvest. But my older sister's a good worker, missus, very respectful and clean. She's got a job in a factory right now, but she's hoping for something better, and when I heard you needed a maid . . ." She clasped her hands imploringly.

"Hm." The housekeeper pursed her lips, sizing Isaveth up. "The spellmistress asked you to help her? That's a wonder. What have you got in that jar?"

"Light-tablets, missus. Baked them myself this morning." She opened the jar and held it out to the housekeeper, who took a tablet and examined it critically. "Mistress Anandri sent me over to fill the masters' lamps, but the secretary in the governor's office told me to come back later."

"The governor's secretary!" exclaimed the woman. "Bless you, child, you're lucky to have got away with your head. Did she say anything else?"

So Isaveth told her the story, or as much of it as she could without admitting her true motives. When she finished, the housekeeper clucked and shook her head.

"You're a bright thing, aren't you? Clever of you, to smooth down Her Ladyship like that. Oh, she's not a real lady," she added as Isaveth paled, "but she fancies herself one. It'll be a grim day for her when the new governor puts her back in her place—"

"Meggery," warned the thin man, but the housekeeper only huffed.

"It's all very well for you, Mister Jespers. You don't have to put up with her airs. But if it troubles your holy ears to hear me speak ill of my betters, I'll say no more."

"So you know who the new governor's going to be?" asked Isaveth, hoping that Meggery's "no more" meant the secretary, and not upstairs gossip in general. "I thought they weren't going to choose one until after the memorial."

"Oh, that's all fuss and formality," said Meggery with a flap of her hand. "Everyone knows it'll be Master Buldage, unless the Sagelord takes one of his strange tempers and decides to snub him again."

"Snub him?" asked Isaveth. "You mean he ought to have been governor before?"

"Well," said the housekeeper, "certainly Master Buldage thinks so, and he's not the only one. Which is fair enough, I suppose, with him being at the college so long. Not that Master Orien was a bad choice, Sages comfort him, but he was an outsider. So when Lord Arvis named him to the post last year, it came as quite a shock."

"I see," said Isaveth, trying to sound only politely interested despite her quickening pulse. She longed to ask more about Master Buldage, but Jespers was frowning at both of them now, and she sensed he was about to cut off the conversation.

"Ah, well. The cleaning goes on, I always say, no matter who's making the mess." Meggery took a last puff of her baccy stick and ground it out. "Now, about your sister. I've seen a tiresome lot of girls already, but I suppose I can see one more. Bring her here by six bells tonight, and I'll talk to her."

"Oh, thank you, missus!"

"No need for that," the housekeeper warned. "I'm not making any promises. But Mistress Anandri seems to think well of you, and she's no fool." She pulled a notebook from the pocket of her apron. "What's your name, then?"

"M-my name? Don't you mean my sister's?"

"That too." She tapped her lead-point on the pad expectantly. "Well?"

After her misadventures with the secretary and the two masters, it was probably safer to tell the truth. "My name's Isaveth. And my sister is Annagail."

Meggery paused halfway through a loop. "Those sound like dissenter names to me. You aren't one of them Moshite troublemakers, are you?"

Isaveth's palms broke out in a sweat. She'd never lied about her beliefs before. But this was for Papa, and she'd come too far to give up now.

"Oh, no," she said brightly. "We're Unifying."

"Vettie, what are you doing here?" Annagail's face was flushed with heat and weariness, but even as she spoke, her foot continued to work the treadle. "I can't talk now or they'll crop my pay. You know that!"

All around them other women bent over their sewing machines, needles rattling and feet pumping in rhythm. The whole factory sounded like a swarm of angry click beetles, and the air was thick with the smells of dust, oil, and human sweat. If the ceiling fans had ever been cold-charmed, the spell had worn out long ago, and their sluggish turning gave no relief from the stifling heat.

Even the horses in the power factory worked in better conditions than this.

"I know, but this is important," whispered Isaveth, crouching low so the overseer wouldn't spot her. She'd sneaked in while his back was turned, but he was strolling up and down the aisles now, and she might have to duck under the table at any minute. "Keep working and let me tell you what happened today."

Quickly she described her visit to the college and her conversation with the housekeeper. At first Annagail kept her eyes on her work, with only a distracted nod or two to show she was still listening. When she heard what Meggery had said about giving her a chance, however, her treadle slowed to a halt.

"Me, work at the college?" she breathed. "If only I could! But they'd never hire a Moshite—"

"Don't worry about that. Take off your prayer scarf, and Meggery will never know."

Annagail's hand flew to her throat. "That would be lying!"

"No, it wouldn't," Isaveth insisted. Her stomach felt quivery and her cheeks hot, but she couldn't back down—it would be madness to let Anna throw such an opportunity away. "I'm not asking you to *say* anything, only to stop letting people reject you for stupid reasons.

Do you really think the All-One wants you to stay in this horrible place just so you can wear Mama's prayer scarf and tell everyone you're a Moshite? How's that going to get Papa out of prison or keep the rest of us from starving?"

"Don't," said Annagail, near tears. "It's not fair. I'm doing the best I can."

"I know, but you can do better. You don't have to lie, Anna. I'm only asking you not to hang a sign around your neck." Isaveth's foot had a cramp. She shifted uncomfortably. "If Meggery doesn't hire you, there's no harm done. If she does, you'll have a chance to show her that Moshite girls can be as respectful and hardworking as everyone else. Two nobs a week, Anna! Think about it!"

Annagail bit her lip. "I can't, Vettie. Not right now." She resumed her pumping, and the needle flashed into motion. "Please, leave me alone."

It sounded like a refusal, but Isaveth knew her sister too well to take it as one. "Six bells," she whispered as the overseer headed down the row toward them. "I'll meet you at the college." Then she ducked out from under the table and sprinted for the exit.

As the sun dipped toward the horizon, Isaveth waited by the front gate of Tarreton College. It had been a long walk from the shirt factory, and the confidence she'd felt while talking to Annagail had evaporated on the way, leaving only anxiety behind. She leaned back against the gatepost and closed her eyes.

What would she do if Annagail didn't come? It was close to six now, and the traffic on the streets was slowing, but there was no sign of her sister in any direction. Even if Isaveth started back to Cabbage Street at this very moment, it would be dark by the time she arrived. Surely, Anna wouldn't leave her to walk home alone?

"You! Girl!"

Isaveth leaped upright as a short, bullnecked Lawkeeper swung his magicycle up to the curb. "No idling on college property," he growled. "Move on."

Did he think she was a beggar? Her dress was grimy from crawling across the factory floor, but she'd stopped at the public wash-station and scrubbed her hands and face as well as she could. "I'm waiting for my sister," Isaveth said. "She's a cleaning maid here, and I'm going to help her."

"Not at your age, you aren't, and I've heard that song before. Get on with you." He pulled his clouter from his belt, and Isaveth flinched at the sight of its red-banded grip—a warning that it was armed with power-tablets.

Even a light tap of that stick would be enough to

knock Isaveth down. Would he really use it if she didn't obey? Keepers weren't supposed to beat children, or use their clouters except in self-defense. But since Papa was arrested, Isaveth had begun to realize that the Lawkeepers of modern Tarreton were very different from the kindly, truehearted officers in *Auradia*.

"Yes, mister!" she gasped, and ran.

She was huddling in the shrubberies that bordered the west side of the college, wondering gloomily if the Lawkeeper meant to patrol the gates all night, when a battered pedalcycle whizzed around the corner. It was Quiz, his head bowed and his stork's legs pumping. Isaveth jumped out of her hiding place and flagged him down.

"Finally!" Quiz veered across the road, narrowly avoiding a rusty carriage drawn by an even sorrier-looking horse, and pulled up next to her. "Where've you been? We were supposed to meet an hour ago!"

It was true: She'd agreed to wait for him at the fountain in Sage Allum's Park so they could compare notes. But she'd been so caught up with her plan to get Annagail into the college, she'd forgotten. "I'm sorry. I should have left you a note." She cast an anxious glance down the street. "Is the Keeper gone?"

"What Keeper?"

Isaveth relaxed. "Never mind," she said, and started back toward the college. "So did you get into the crypt? Was the governor's—was he there?"

Quiz nodded. "It took a while, but I managed to get a look at him. He was . . ." A greenish tinge came into his face. "Well, let's say he wasn't quite himself. But at least now I know how he was killed."

"An exploding-tablet," said Isaveth, her gaze following a passing tram. If Annagail didn't come now, it would be too late. "I know. His secretary told me."

"Yes, but it wasn't just—"

"Wait." Isaveth grabbed his shoulder. The tram had stopped, and a slim figure was alighting. Could it be?

It was. "Annagail!" she shouted, and ran to meet her sister.

Anna must have left work a few minutes earlier than usual, because she'd combed her hair, tidied her dress, and powdered the shine from her face. And for the first time since their mother died, her neck was bare of all but the tiny heart-shaped pendant Papa had bought for her sixteenth birthday.

"Don't *gallop*, Vettie," she said wearily, and Isaveth faltered: Her sister looked so unhappy. Had Isaveth done wrong, urging her to act against her conscience? But the next moment Anna smiled, and her pretty face came to life again. "You must be Quiz," she said, extending a gloved hand. "I'm Annagail."

Quiz took her fingers and stooped over them. "You're as lovely as your sister. Sisters."

Annagail darted a look at Isaveth. "That's very kind."

Even her eyes were smiling now. Perhaps Isaveth had misread her. She turned toward the college, but Annagail touched her arm.

"I can find my own way from here," she said. "You go home and get Lilet and Mimmi. It's not fair to keep Aunt Sal waiting." Then she dropped a kiss on Isaveth's cheek and hurried away.

"There," panted Quiz, skidding to a halt at the top of Cabbage Street. He held the cycle steady as Isaveth climbed off, then let it drop and flopped onto the grass. "Give me a minute to get my wind back, and I'll walk you home."

"You don't have to," said Isaveth, torn between gratitude and guilt. "It was kind of you to give me a ride this far—I'd never have got home so fast without you."

"But you haven't even heard what I found out at the crypt." Quiz struggled up onto his elbows. "Aren't you the least bit interested?"

"Oh!" She'd been so distracted worrying about Annagail, not to mention struggling to stay on the back of Quiz's pedalcycle, that she hadn't even thought to ask. "Yes, of course!" Quickly she sat down beside him. "I know about the exploding-tablet, but what else?"

"Ah, but it wasn't *just* an exploding-tablet," said Quiz. "The examiner found dust on Master Orien's robe and didn't bother to look any further, but I dug his clothes out of the bin and . . ." He sat up, rummaging in his pocket, then took Isaveth's hand and pressed something into it. "Look at this."

"This" was a scrap of dark, silky cloth, no bigger than Isaveth's palm and ragged around the edges. She was about to ask what was special about it when Quiz took her hand again and turned the fabric to show the other side.

"I cut it from the lining of his robe. See the stain here?"

"Silver?" asked Isaveth, frowning at the mark—more of a blob, really. As though there'd been a tiny piece of metal pressed against the cloth, and it had melted.

"Yes, but not ordinary silver, charm-silver. And you know what that means."

A shiver ran through Isaveth. If Quiz was right, this could change everything. "Sagery," she whispered. "The murderer was a noble."

Chapter Eleven

ISAVETH CLUTCHED QUIZ'S ARM, dizzy with relief and hope. "I'm right, aren't I? Only a noble would use a Sage-charm, so if we show this evidence to the Lawkeepers, they'll have to let Papa go!"

"I wish it were that simple," Quiz said, "but it isn't. The murderer might have stolen the charm and figured out how to use it; anyone with access to the college library could do that. Or it might have been some spell Master Orien was carrying about for his own use, and it has nothing to do with the murder at all."

Crestfallen, Isaveth let him go. "So it doesn't prove anything."

"Maybe not. But it does make it more likely that the murderer wasn't your father."

"How?"

"Well, I don't know a lot about Sagery," said Quiz,

scratching the back of his neck. "Mostly rumors—only nobles really get to study that sort of thing. But I've heard there's a spell that can connect the energy from one charm to another, even over a distance. So when you break one—"

"Then the other one breaks too? Even if it's somewhere else?"

Quiz looked pleased. "Exactly!"

"Which means the murderer could have planted the charm in Master Orien's robe along with the power-tablet, and set off the explosion anytime he wanted." Isaveth wrapped her arms around her knees. "So it needn't have been the last person to visit the governor who murdered him. It could be anyone."

"As long as they had access to the college, knew how to make—or steal—an affinity-charm, and had a reason to want Master Orien dead. That narrows it down a bit. I don't suppose you happened to meet anyone of that sort today?"

"Actually," said Isaveth, "I did. Let's walk down to Aunt Sal's, and I'll tell you what I found out."

"I see," said Quiz when Isaveth had finished. "So you think this, er, Bulfinch—"

"Buldage," said Isaveth. She had no idea what the

master looked like, but she couldn't help picturing the red-faced man who'd accosted her in the lounge. True, the other man had called him Robard, but that could be his first name.

"You think he wanted Orien dead so he could take his place as governor? And he made it look like Common Magic so no one would suspect him of the murder?"

Isaveth nodded. "It was a perfect time for him to get away with it, if he did. The secretary said there'd been plenty of people in the office that day because of the new charmery. Besides, the masters all have those loose robes. . . . I can't imagine they wear them home at night, can you?"

"I'm sure they don't," Quiz said. "Especially in this heat."

The wardrobe in the lounge! That must be where the masters hung their robes when they weren't wearing them. "So," Isaveth went on with growing excitement, "Buldage could have planted the charm and the exploding-tablet in Orien's robe early that morning, or even the night before. That way he could set it off at the end of the day, once everyone else had gone."

"Yes, but he'd have to know Master Orien's schedule down to the last minute and be watching his door like a gorehawk. He'd also have to make a show of leaving and then sneak back into the college somehow, so the porter wouldn't know he was there. And how could he know that the last person to see Master Orien alive would be such a plausible suspect—someone who had access to exploding-tablets *and* an old grudge against him?" Quiz rubbed his chin. "I don't know, Isaveth. It seems pretty unlikely to me."

"If you say so," said Isaveth, a little stung, "but who else could have done it? Or would want to?"

"I don't know. Maybe if your sister gets this job, she can have a look at that appointment ledger and give us some names. . . . Oh, look, it's our friend Loyal." He lifted his hand in cheerful salute, and Loyal Kercher reddened and slunk back into the house.

"You shouldn't tease him," Isaveth said, but she couldn't help smiling. It was nice not to have to worry about Loyal's bullying anymore, even if her other problems were so much bigger now. "Where'd you get the cycle, by the way?"

Quiz glanced down at its rusty steering bar, as though he'd forgotten he was still pushing it. "Oh. Borrowed it from a message boy I know. He's laid up with a broken leg, so I've been doing his work for him."

Which explained how he'd paid her tram fare that morning. "How long . . . ," Isaveth began, but then the front door of Aunt Sal's cottage banged open, and Mimmi came running out.

"Where have you been? Aunt Sal's getting frantic and I'm *starving*." Then she caught sight of the pedalcycle and stopped, openmouthed with awe.

Mimmi was no stranger to exaggeration, but Aunt Sal was no stranger to hysterics, either. Isaveth turned to Quiz. "I'll only be a minute. Would you mind . . ."

"Hop on board," said Quiz, scooping Mimmi up in one arm and plunking her on the seat. "Feet on the pedals, hands on the bar, hold on tight, and *go!*" He took off running, while Mimmi squealed with delight. Conscious of Lilet's silent, accusing presence on the doorstep, Isaveth pushed past her and went into the house.

"I'm so sorry," she said when she found her frizzy-haired aunt, who was banging about the kitchen in a way that showed she was very upset indeed. "I didn't mean to be so late."

"Oh no, of course not." *Slam* went the cupboard door. "At your age it doesn't matter when you eat, or what you eat, or whether anyone else gets to eat at all." *Rattle-crash* as she wrenched a drawer open and snatched up a long-handled spoon. "But I was raised with better manners than to leave two children hungry while the rest of us sit down to dinner, and it's not fair to expect me to conjure more food out of nothing!"

She thrust the spoon into her soup pot and began

stirring with short, furious strokes, while Isaveth clenched her fists behind her back and tried to breathe through her anger. "I don't expect you to feed my sisters," she said when she trusted herself to speak. "I'm grateful you let them come here. I don't know what we'd do without your help."

Never mind that Lilet and Mimmi kept Sal's children busy all day, and gave her plenty of time to ignore her dirty house and lie about reading books like *Magical Beauty Secrets* and *Your Future—Written in the Stars!* The one time Isaveth's mother had dared to point that out, Aunt Sal hadn't talked to her for a month. "Please, Auntie. I promise I won't let it happen again."

Sal sniffed. "It had better not. Bad enough your father's in jail, though I warned Devra something like this would happen. I said, 'Devra, a man who breaks rocks all day isn't going to make daisy chains when he loses his temper,' but oh no, she was in love, and nobody else would do—"

"I have to go," Isaveth cut in quickly. Jory was plodding down the stairs now, and he'd done what he usually did when no one was paying attention to him: taken off his short-pants and draped them over his head. "Thank you, Aunt Sal. We'll see you tomorrow. Good night!"

She rushed out, grabbing Lilet as she went, and

stormed down the steps to the street. How *dare* Sal talk about Papa that way! Who gave her the right—

"Ow!" Lilet swatted her hand. "You're hurting me!"

Flustered, Isaveth let go. "I'm sorry. I just . . ."

"I know," said Lilet, and for the first time in months the two girls shared a look of perfect sympathy. Then Lilet's face soured and she said, "Of course Mimmi *would* get a ride."

Isaveth followed her gaze to the corner, where Quiz was showing Mimmi how to pedal. He'd perched his flat cap on her head, and she looked like a duck treading water.

"It's all right," Isaveth said. "You can have a turn when she's finished."

"You'll stay for supper tonight," Isaveth told Quiz as she came out of the house, wiping her hands on her apron. He was sitting on the front step with Mimmi, watching Lilet pedal determinedly up the street. "It's only soup, but there's plenty to go around."

Mind, what was going around was mostly onions and water. But she refused to be like Aunt Sal, too stingy to feed anyone but her own family. "Mimmi, run inside and set the table."

"But Anna's not home yet."

"I know, but she will be soon. Go."

Quiz got up, furrowing his dirt-smudged brow. "Are you sure? You don't have to, you know. I can manage."

"Of course I'm sure. You want to know if Annagail got the job at the college, don't you? Besides," Isaveth added with a half smile, "if I can't pay you, I can at least feed you."

She'd thought the joke would put him at ease. But when Quiz's shoulders hunched and his gaze dropped to his shoes, it was clear she'd only made him feel even more awkward. "All right," he mumbled. "Thanks."

Lilet came rattling back toward them and nearly fell off the cycle. Quiz leaped out and grabbed the bars as she climbed down. "I want one," she announced. "When I grow up, I'm going to buy a pedalcycle and ride it everywhere."

"How are you going to do that living on a farm?" Isaveth asked, and Lilet huffed and marched toward the house. But when she reached the door, she turned back.

"Thank you," she said to Quiz, her voice low but distinct. "That was very nice of you."

"I think you've won her over," Isaveth said when her sister had vanished inside. "You'll have to teach me that trick sometime."

"You don't think she likes you?" asked Quiz, propping the cycle against the house. "I'd say she admires you more than anyone."

Isaveth chortled, but the tall boy didn't join her. His expression had turned inward, his good eye dark with some emotion she couldn't name.

"Soup's ready," she said at last, to break the uncomfortable silence. She went inside, and Quiz followed her.

"If Anna's not here, can I say the blessing?" asked Mimmi, bouncing up as they entered the kitchen. "Look, I've got a scarf."

She had, too—their mother's second-best prayer veil, gauzy white with blue stars and silver crescents around the hem. Embarrassed, Isaveth snatched it from Mimmi's hand.

"You shouldn't be poking around in Papa's room," she said. "And no, you can't. We've got a guest tonight."

Mimmi went to Lilet, sniffing, and hid her face in her shoulder. "Sillyhead," Lilet whispered, but she didn't push her away.

"I don't mind," said Quiz mildly. "I've never heard a Moshite blessing before."

"I suppose you're Unifying?" said Isaveth, but Quiz only shrugged.

"Oh, I don't bother about these things. I'm just interested. Why do people make such a fuss about Moshites, anyway?"

To Isaveth's surprise, Lilet answered. "Because we

wouldn't join the Unifying Church when everybody else did."

"They think we're fantastic," added Mimmi thickly, and Quiz looked blank until Lilet corrected her: "Fanatics."

Carefully Isaveth removed the red Fastday candles from the table, suppressing the twinge of guilt as she put them back in the hallow cabinet unlit. They'd never eaten without a blessing before, but she didn't feel comfortable veiling herself in front of Quiz. "Please sit," she said.

Quiz had gulped down his bowl of soup, and Isaveth was about to ask if he'd like another, when the front door creaked. She stood up, her chest tightening with hope and dread. "Annagail?"

Anna took off her hat and gloves and came into the kitchen. She looked dazed, her cheeks flushed and her eyes fever-bright.

"Meggery likes me," she said. "I've got the job."

"So that's settled," said Quiz as he and Isaveth stood outside. The evening sky was the deep blue-black of a master's robe, lit by a low silver moon. "All we have to do now is ask Annagail to look at the governor's appointment ledger for us and write down the names of everyone who saw him that day. Do you think she will?"

"I'm sure of it," said Isaveth, smiling. It cheered her

enormously to have that problem solved, even if it was only a small step toward proving her father's innocence. And now that she'd got the job at the college, Annagail seemed happy too. A good cleaning maid was expected to be invisible to her employers, so she'd have to work early in the morning or late into the evening, or both. But no matter what shifts Meggery gave her, it would still be fewer hours and better pay than she'd ever had at the shirt factory.

Isaveth was quiet a moment, listening to the distant thumping and grinding of the factories, and the purr of a night-dove perched on the Caverlys' roof. Then she said, "Tomorrow's Templeday."

"So Anna can't get into the office until next week. I know, but I don't see what else we can do."

"I wasn't thinking about that." Isaveth scuffed her shoe across the step. "I was thinking about going to see Papa. On Mendday morning."

"Oh. Right."

He sounded blank, as though he'd forgotten her father existed. Maybe because he wished he could forget his own?

"Anyway," Isaveth went on, refusing to be daunted, "it's a long way to walk, and . . . I wondered if I might borrow your cycle."

Quiz sucked air between his teeth. "I don't think that's

a good idea," he said. "If anything happened to it—or you—I'd never forgive myself. And my friend the message boy wouldn't be too happy either."

Isaveth deflated. "Oh. I hadn't thought of that."

"It's all right, though. I was about to ask if . . . " His head snapped up like a hound catching a scent. "Did you hear that?"

Isaveth listened but heard nothing out of the ordinary. She was about to ask Quiz what he meant when the faint, familiar music reached her ears at last.

"Auradia!" she whispered in delight. "But where is it coming from?"

"Believe it or not," said Quiz, "I think it's our old friend Loyal's house."

"That's impossible. The Kerchers are on relief—they couldn't possibly afford a crystal set."

"Are you sure? Keep listening."

He was right: It was coming from the Kerchers' cottage. Perhaps Merit had sent some money home from his work on the Vesperia railway, and this was how his parents had spent it?

Quiz nudged Isaveth and offered his arm. "An open window is an open invitation, as the burglar said to the justice. Shall we?"

Chapter Twelve

"GET OUT!" raged a hoarse female voice from the Kerchers' top-floor window. "Out of my yard, and don't come back! Loyal, you get that filthy peeper and make him sorry—"

"Go!" hissed Quiz, and Isaveth shinned down the tree so fast she ripped her skirt. She'd barely touched ground when Quiz jumped down beside her, seized her hand, and dashed off.

"I can't," Isaveth panted, weak with terror and hilarity. "Can't keep up—Quiz!"

Without breaking stride, Quiz snatched her up off the ground, hefted her in his arms, and sprinted around the corner to Aunt Sal's. He practically threw Isaveth over the fence, then tumbled after her, and the two of them landed with a thump in the weedy tangle of Sal's garden.

An instant later the Kerchers' door slammed open. "Bruiser!" shouted Loyal. "Get up, you lazy—"

The dog yelped, and Isaveth winced in sympathy. It wasn't the poor, half-starved creature's fault that he'd gobbled up the sleep-tablet Quiz had tossed him, and ended up snoring as they tiptoed by. And it wasn't Quiz's fault that he'd snapped a dead branch when he tried to get closer to the window, either.

Still, the look on Missus Kercher's face! Isaveth put her hands over her mouth, stifling a giggle. "Peeper," she choked out, and Quiz gave a snort of laughter. They sat with their backs to the fence, quaking silently.

"Find him, Bruiser!" Loyal snapped at the dog. "Go on, hunt him down!"

"Can he?" whispered Isaveth, but Quiz shook his head.

"Not while he's dozy. And it'll be a good half hour before the magic wears off."

They must have been strong sleep-tablets, then. "Where did you get them?"

"Lifted them off a sneak thief." Quiz wiggled his fingers. "In the spirit of fair play, so to speak. . . . Now let's see what Loyal's up to." He half rose, peering through the slats of the fence, and peered out into the night. "Good. He's gone off in the wrong direction."

"Did she get a good look at you? Missus Kercher, I mean?"

"Well, even if she didn't, the patch tends to stick in people's minds. But don't worry." He flashed her a grin. "I doubt she'll call the Keepers on me."

Isaveth hadn't even considered that, since only a few houses on Cabbage Street had a call-box, and the Kerchers' wasn't one of them. But if Missus Kercher described the "peeper" she'd seen to her son, it wouldn't be hard for Loyal to guess who'd been up in that tree. . . .

And with that, what had seemed like a wild lark only a minute ago no longer felt like any fun to Isaveth at all. It was well and fine for Quiz: He didn't live here. But if Loyal decided to take his grudge against the street-boy out on Isaveth and her family, there'd be nothing she could do to stop him.

"But what a story!" Quiz went on, oblivious. "Did you ever think you'd see Peacemaker Otsik and Wil Avenham working together? I only wish we'd caught the last few minutes. . . ." He stopped. "Isaveth?"

Isaveth hugged her knees, queasiness churning inside her. She'd been so pleased with herself for finding Annagail a job, and so eager to hear *Auradia*, that for a few reckless minutes she'd forgotten what really mattered. But this wasn't some grand adventure, even if Quiz had a way of making it feel like one. How could it be, with her papa's freedom and maybe even his life at stake?

"I shouldn't have come with you," she said thickly. "It was stupid. And selfish. I ought to go home."

She started to get up, but Quiz put a hand on her shoulder. "Don't," he said. "Don't let Loyal frighten you. He may look tough, but he's a coward inside."

"It's not Loyal." She rubbed her eyes with the back of her hand. "It's Papa, and—oh, never mind."

Quiz sat back on his heels, and for a long moment he was silent. Then he said quietly, "You don't have to be sad all the time, you know. It doesn't make anything better."

How would you know? Isaveth almost retorted, but then she remembered the patch and held her tongue.

"I just hate that I can't do more for him," she said at last, tearing up a spikeweed and flinging it away. "I hate that he's locked up in a cell right now, when he should be home with us."

Quiz nodded soberly and settled next to her again. "That reminds me. I was going to say it before, but then *Auradia* came on and I forgot. I can't lend you the cycle to go and see your father. But I'd be glad to give you a ride." He glanced at her sidelong. "If you don't mind company."

"Mind? No. I only . . . I didn't think you'd want to go."

"Because I'm likely to end up in jail myself, you mean? Just punishment for my peeping ways?"

Isaveth sputtered.

"I shall never repent," continued Quiz, thumping a fist against his heart. "I would climb the Kerchers' sourapple a thousand times for one glimpse of that divine vision—"

"Of Missus Kercher with her hair in curlpapers?"

"And her robe of snowy white with the egg stain on the lapel. Messy eaters all around, the Kercher family."

The monstrous unfairness of the Kerchers having eggs for dinner, especially after Loyal had smashed all of hers, left Isaveth speechless. But if they could afford a crystal set, why not eggs as well? She supposed she ought to be happy for Merit; he'd always been the best of that family, and he must be doing all right in Vesperia if he could afford to send money home. Still, it was hard to feel anything but bitter about her neighbors' sudden good fortune.

"My love is true!" declared Quiz, leaping up and flinging out his arms theatrically. "Yet I must depart, but verily I shall return—"

Isaveth grabbed the back of his belt and yanked so hard he staggered. "Shh! She'll hear you!"

"Missus Kercher? Surely not."

"No, you neevil-wit, my aunt Sal." Uncle Brom would be home by now as well, but they didn't need to worry about him: Ten years of metalworking had left him mostly deaf anyway.

"Oh. Right." Quiz sank down, chastened. "Sorry."

He really was ridiculous sometimes, but it was nice to be with someone who could make her laugh. Even if part of her still felt guilty for doing it.

"All right," said Isaveth. "I'll take your offer. Thanks."

When the sun came up the next morning, it took all Isaveth's strength to drag herself out of bed. Last night she and Quiz had crouched in Aunt Sal's garden for more than half an hour before Loyal gave up hunting for them, and then they'd had to sneak back to Isaveth's house the long way around. On the way they'd struck up an argument over whether Auradia ought to marry Peacemaker Otsik or Wil Avenham, which left Isaveth with such heated feelings that she'd written a whole new story in her head after Quiz pedaled away. It was past midnight when she finally fell asleep.

Nevertheless, today was Templeday, which meant early rising and baths all around. By rights Annagail ought to wash first, but when Isaveth prodded her, she only mumbled and pulled the sheet over her head, so at last Isaveth gave up and took her place. By the time she'd dried herself and put on her temple clothes, Lilet and Mimmi were up and waiting for their turns. But Anna hadn't stirred.

"Are you feeling sick?" Isaveth whispered as she came back into the bedroom.

Annagail sighed. "I'm just so tired, Vettie. And Meggery asked me to come early tomorrow. You'll be all right without me, won't you?"

It wasn't like Annagail to miss temple, but Isaveth didn't have the heart to argue with her. She nodded and went downstairs to help her younger sisters get ready.

"That was *awful*," Mimmi said fervently as they left the temple later that morning. "I wish we'd stayed home with Anna."

Isaveth didn't have to ask why. Wisdom Hall was the only Moshite congregation within walking distance of Cabbage Street, and so small that all the members knew one another by name. When Devra Breck died, their fellow Moshites had been quick to share food, clothing, and words of consolation—but today they'd offered little but wary glances and uncomfortable silence. Only old Missus Dzato had dared to approach them after the Hour of Remembrance, patting their hands with her soft, wrinkled ones and mumbling that she'd been praying for them.

"It's like we're cursed." Lilet kicked a pebble savagely down the street. "Or infected with some horrible disease."

"They're only frightened," said Isaveth, and she knew

it was true, even if she wasn't sure why. Surely their fellow Moshites weren't afraid that if they showed kindness to Urias Breck's daughters, it would make them look guilty too? Papa had seldom gone to temple before their mother's death and not at all afterward, so it would be ridiculous to claim that he'd killed Master Orien for religious motives. . . .

But somebody had thrown a brick through the window of the hall only a few months ago and painted FILTHY RATS in dripping red letters on the door just because the Gardentown stickball team had allowed a Moshite boy to step in for an injured player and then ended up losing to Willowdell. Some people didn't need a logical reason to blame Moshites for everything that was wrong with the world. Any excuse would do.

"My feet hurt," moaned Mimmi several blocks later. "Can we sit down?"

"Lazylegs," said Lilet scornfully. "We're not even halfway home yet—and you're the one with new shoes. Vettie and I have to walk on boxboard."

It was true: Isaveth had cut fresh liners for both her shoes and Lilet's before setting out, since it was the cheapest way to cover the holes without having them reshod. But their shoes fit and were well broken in, while Mimmi's were stiff and her feet weren't used to them.

"It won't hurt us to rest a little while," Isaveth said, glancing around for a suitable place. They were passing a wealthier neighborhood now, with no benches in sight, but that low stone wall around the corner ought to serve well enough. "Come over here, Mim."

Mimmi limped to the wall, plonked herself onto it with a sigh, and tugged off her shoes and stockings. She hadn't been exaggerating: The back of her right heel was rubbed raw, and there was a blister forming on the left one. Isaveth wished she'd thought to bring sticky gauze, but it was too late for that now. She'd just have to bind up the sores when they got home.

The street was quiet and shady, with big maple trees arching overhead and the soft buzz of humble-bees working the flower beds behind them. As Mimmi poked glumly at her blisters, Isaveth let her gaze wander to the line of houses across the street. These were of the old-fashioned kind owned chiefly by merchants and elderly nobles, peak roofed and stone fronted and slightly taller than they were wide; they all had gardens in the front as well as a longer stretch of lawn behind, and cobbled driveways curving beside them. Even the smallest was three times the size of her own family's cottage, with a glass-paneled door in the topmost peak and a little balcony that would be a perfect spot to write, and Isaveth couldn't help but think how lovely it would be to live in such a place. If she closed her eyes, she could see her grown-up self sitting on that balcony with pen in hand, working on her latest masterpiece. . . .

"This is boring," announced Lilet. "I'm going to explore." Without waiting for an answer, she jumped off the wall and headed down the tree-shaded sidewalk, confident as though she'd been born there. Isaveth watched her go, her thin shoulders proudly straight beneath the faded cotton of her dress, and gave an inward sigh. It was no use arguing when Lilet was in a stubborn mood, and Isaveth supposed her sister couldn't get into much trouble in a well-kept neighborhood like this.

But when twenty minutes had passed and Lilet did not return, Isaveth cursed herself for a fool. "Come on," she said, reaching for her little sister's hand. "We'd better go look for her."

Mimmi whimpered, but she did her best to keep up as Isaveth hurried down the street, glancing from one house to another. There were few walls here and hardly any gates; she could look straight into some of those back gardens and glimpse a stately dowager snipping roses or a little girl playing hoopstick with her governess on the lawn. Lilet, however, had vanished.

"Where would she have gone?" burst out Isaveth in frustration once they'd crossed two streets and looked in all directions to no avail. Lilet might be headstrong, but she was seldom thoughtless, and it wasn't like her to wander off like this. Isaveth was close to despair, and wondering what she would tell Anna, when Mimmi tugged her hand and said, "I hear music."

Sure enough, her sister was right. Either someone on the street had a crystal set turned up loud, or a troupe of string players were performing nearby—and Lilet adored music. "Good ears, Mimmi!" she said, and they set off to find out where the music was coming from.

It didn't take them long. The cross street ended in a little park, and beside it stood the biggest house they'd seen yet, with a sweeping stretch of lawn framed by shrubberies taller than Isaveth. The owner had set up a pavilion at one side of the house, draped with gold ribbons and silvery charm-lights, and beneath its gauzy canopy a trio of musicians was playing. Well-dressed men and women strolled about the grass with flutes of sparkling cider in hand, admiring the flowers and chatting with one another.

"It's a garden party," whispered Mimmi as they crouched behind the hedge. "Oh, Vettie, isn't it beautiful!"

Isaveth had to agree. Even the oldest men looked

handsome in waistcoats and tailored suits, and the women's fluttery dresses and flower-trimmed hats made her ache with envy. Lilet must have been as entranced by it all as they were, but where could she be hiding? Tugging Mimmi with her, Isaveth crept behind the shrubberies, trying to get as close to the pavilion and the music as possible without being seen.

Then she saw it behind the tent curtains, like a vision from some wonderful dream. A table spread with white lace and linen, crowded with sandwich platters and tiered stands of fancy-cakes. And in the shadows beneath the table sat Lilet, shamelessly spying on the party.

"Lilet!" whispered Isaveth, praying the music would cover it. "Come out of there!"

Lilet squirmed, feeling guilty perhaps—but she didn't obey. Isaveth gritted her teeth. "Wait here," she told Mimmi, then dropped to her hands and knees and crawled through the shrubbery to join Lilet.

As soon as she ducked beneath the tablecloth and saw her sister's cream-smeared nose and defiant expression, she knew why Lilet hadn't come out. Somehow she'd managed to swipe a plate of sandwiches while no one was looking, and she was having the feast of her life.

"That's stealing!" Isaveth hissed at her, appalled and envious at once.

Lilet shook her head. "They've all had plenty," she whispered back. "Nobody's come this way in ages—and who's going to eat this food if we don't?" She nudged the plate under Isaveth's nose. "Here. Try one."

Isaveth tried to resist, telling herself it was important to set an example. But she'd been fasting since the night before, and the smell of peppered beef made her stomach cramp with hunger. She took the sandwich, stuffed it into her mouth, and let out a little sigh of pleasure.

The hedge rustled, and Mimmi popped up between them. "Not fair!" she exclaimed—and at that same instant the musicians stopped playing.

Isaveth clapped a hand to Mimmi's mouth, but it was too late. The three sisters sat petrified beneath the table, listening to the awful silence.

That's done it, thought Isaveth wildly. *We'll be caught for sure.*

Chapter Thirteen

ISAVETH CLUTCHED AT HER SISTERS, blood thundering in her ears. Should they run for it? Or should they stay still, keep silent, and hope the guests at the garden party wouldn't guess where the noise had come from?

Then a throat cleared, pages flipped, and the musicians struck up another piece. A shadow fell across the tablecloth, and Lilet dug her fingers into Isaveth's arm—but the guest merely strolled the length of the buffet before wandering off again.

Nobody had heard Mimmi's outburst. They were safe. Isaveth relaxed and helped herself to another sandwich.

Minutes passed while the sisters munched and listened, and snatches of conversation floated back to Isaveth as groups of guests strolled by. Yet they spoke only of lily varieties, fertilizers, and other fine points of gardening, and Isaveth began to grow restless. If this was all rich folk had to talk about, they might as well leave.

". . . wearing the peachiest hat," a girl's voice enthused, and two pairs of spotless heel-shoes stepped into view beneath the dangling skirts of the table. "I'd love to know where she got it."

"Yes, but have you seen her hairstyle?" said her companion. "Positively antique! I must say I'm awfully fond of my new crop, no matter what Daddy thinks. Say, are you going to the dance at the Willtons' tonight?"

Still chatting, the young noblewomen drifted away to the corner of the pavilion. Isaveth crouched and peeked beneath the tablecloth as a third girl, as dark haired and spice skinned as the others were floury pale, crossed the lawn to join them.

"Darling!" gushed the girl with the haircut. "How gorgeous you look in that blue hat. Was the Sagelord's speech very dull?"

The Sagelord was here? Isaveth cast an anxious glance at her sisters, but they were engaged in a silent struggle over the last crab sandwich and didn't notice.

"Stop it!" Isaveth hissed. "Lilet, you've had plenty. Give it to Mimmi and sit still. I'm trying to listen."

Lilet let go of the sandwich and folded her arms, mutinous. Isaveth gave her one last glare and went back to eavesdropping.

". . . as usual, but at least he isn't drunk," the girl in blue was saying. "And I suppose he can't do much harm giving a speech to the Garden Society. If only he'd leave the real politics to Eryx and stop pretending he knows how to run this city."

"Delicia!" gasped the smallest of the girls. "You can't talk that way!"

"Why not? Everyone knows it's true. The man's a wreck, and what's more, he's a disgrace. They talk of dissenters trying to overthrow the council—well, with a fool like Lord Arvis in charge, who can blame them? Honestly, if Eryx hadn't proposed the Reps' Bill, there'd be rioting in the streets by now!"

"Ugh, what a thought!" exclaimed the bob-haired girl. "It won't come to that, I'm sure. Most commoners know their place perfectly well." But the smaller one looked anxious.

"I'm so stupid when it comes to politics," she said plaintively, clutching her necklace. "How is the Reps' Bill going to save us from the dissenters? It didn't stop them murdering Governor Orien!"

Behind Isaveth, Lilet moved abruptly and Mimmi gave a little squeak, but Isaveth was too distracted to care. Did people really believe Papa had killed Orien as part of some dissenter plot?

"We don't know why Master Orien was killed," said Delicia. "It might have nothing to do with politics at all. But the Reps' Bill is really quite simple. Right now we have ten citizens' representatives and fifteen nobles on the council—if all the nobles bother to show up, that is. And a noble's vote is worth twice that of a rep."

"Which is how it should be," said the girl in the middle. "You can't think the commoners are fit to govern themselves, let alone the rest of us!"

"Maybe they would be if we gave them the chance," Delicia retorted. "That's why the Reps' Bill is so important. If it passes, a rep's vote will be worth the same as a noble's, and the council will split the two biggest voting wards in half and elect a new rep for each. Then ordinary folk will finally have a real say in council—and since there are so many more commoners than nobles, surely that's only right?"

An equal vote is an equal voice. That was what it had said on that leaflet Isaveth found the day Papa was arrested. And Eryx Lording was the one who'd proposed the Reps' Bill? That was as unselfish as anything Auradia might have done, and it made Isaveth admire him more than ever.

"Well, I don't think it's right at all," said the crop-haired girl. "I can't imagine what Eryx was thinking. Why bother changing the council? The Sagelord's already in poor health and once he steps down, the commoners won't have anything to complain about."

"Steps down!" Delicia breathed a laugh. "Have you met Lord Arvis? He won't retire short of his deathbed. And he'll never support the Reps' Bill, either—it's a wonder Eryx managed to bring it to a vote at all."

But now that vote had been postponed because someone had killed Master Orien. Could that have been the murderer's plan? Isaveth eased herself into a more comfortable position, watching the young women all the while.

"Oh, do keep your voice down!" the littlest noblewoman pleaded, with a nervous glance over her shoulder. "Civilla's over there, and it would be mortifying if she heard us. You know how frosty she gets when people gossip about her family."

Isaveth squinted past them, and sure enough, there was the icy blonde she remembered from the Harvest Parade: Civilla Ladyship. She wore a hat trimmed with white roses and a flowing dress that softened her angular figure, and her smile made her look less haughty than before. But if she'd brought her sulky-faced younger brother, the Lilord, there was no sign of him.

"There's nothing I've said that Civilla doesn't know already," Delicia retorted. "And we should all be talking about the future of this city. What with this new law they've passed in council, and the Keepers arresting anyone who even looks like a dissenter—"

"Can you blame them?" asked the girl with the haircut. "Someone's got to protect us from the radicals! Why, if they could murder the most powerful Sage in the city, they might be capable of anything!"

"Really, Priss, you make it sound as though Master Orien had a whole arsenal of charms at his fingertips. Why would he? He was a scholar, not a soldier." Delicia shook her head. "Poor man. I know what everyone said when he took the post, but it does seem unfair."

"What did they say?" the short girl asked. "I always wondered why there was such a fuss."

"Only what you'd expect when the Sagelord promotes his children's old magical tutor to governor of Tarreton College . . . oh!" The severity vanished from Delicia's face. "It's Eryx! He's made it after all!"

Isaveth's heart skipped. She leaned sideways, straining to see past the edge of the pavilion to the spell-carriage pulling up outside.

The door opened and Eryx stepped out onto the lawn, every bit as handsome as she remembered. He doffed his hat to the matron bustling up to greet him, and his teeth flashed in a welcoming smile.

"Such lovely manners," Priss sighed. "You'd think Lady Marcham was his favorite aunt, instead of the nasty old harridan she is. Well, it's true," she added defensively as the other girls stared at her. "Just because she puts on a nice garden party doesn't make her any less horrible the rest of the year."

Delicia frowned and walked out of the tent. "Well!" said Priss, glaring after her. "*Someone* thinks very well of herself, I must say. But if she thinks she's going to impress Eryx with her nose-up airs, she's going to be sorry when she finds out he's going to the Willtons' dance with *me*."

"Is he really?" exclaimed the small girl, clutching Priss's arm, and the two of them strolled off together. The music continued, but no one was listening anymore—not even Lilet, who had managed to steal yet another platter and was fending off Mimmi with one hand while she crammed tarts into her mouth with the other.

Isaveth snatched the tray out of Lilet's reach. "What are you doing?" she whispered fiercely.

"She took *all* the tarts." Mimmi sniffed. "And she wouldn't let me have a single one."

"That's because you're a spoiled brat," Lilet shot back, and Mimmi turned crimson. Before Isaveth could catch her, she wriggled backward and jumped to her feet.

"Thief!" cried a woman at the edge of the crowd, and Mimmi bolted. But her shoe buckle snagged the trailing lace of the tablecloth, and as she lunged forward, the whole table's worth of sandwich platters and dessert stands came crashing after her.

The music stopped and a gasp rose from the crowd. Lilet shamelessly scooped up one last tart, yanked the tablecloth off the wildly kicking Mimmi, and shoved her through the hedge into the neighboring garden. For a second Isaveth crouched beneath the table, too shocked to move—but as the guests surged forward, fear spurred her into motion. She stumbled over the ruins of the buffet, leaped through the shrubbery, and ran.

"Ooooh," groaned Lilet as she crouched over the basin, her face flushed and shiny with sweat. "I'm going to die."

Isaveth sat beside her sister in their bedroom, rubbing her back as she doubled up and retched again. In the other bed Mimmi slept peacefully, her raw heels wrapped with rags and healing salve. But Lilet had started to feel sick soon after they escaped from Lady Marcham's garden party, and she'd been increasingly miserable ever since.

"You're not going to die," said Isaveth. "You just ate too much, that's all."

"But it was so good," Lilet moaned. "You would have

done it too, if you hadn't been busy making goop-eyes at Eryx Lording." She wiped her mouth on her hand and slumped against the pillows. "Ugh."

Isaveth made a face at her. "Goop-eyes?"

"Anyway, I think that Priss girl lied about him taking her to the dance," Lilet mumbled. "I don't think he cares a cit for her, and she was only trying to impress her friend."

So Lilet had been listening too. No wonder she and Mimmi had kept so quiet, even while they were fighting. "You're probably right," said Isaveth. "But I liked Delicia. I hope . . ."

She stopped, heat creeping into her cheeks. She'd almost said she hoped Delicia would make a good impression on Eryx Lording, but that wasn't really what she wanted. The truth was that even as Isaveth had pelted across the grass after her sisters and scrambled over a stone wall to safety, even as they'd crept through back streets and coal-lanes all the way home, she'd been imagining herself grown up and elegant in a wine-colored gown, being introduced to the Lording as the famous author Isavera Brecon. Eryx would ask her, "Are you sure we haven't met before?" and she would toss her head and laugh merrily because he'd never guess she was the poor little girl he'd met selling spell-tablets on the street only a few years ago. . . .

"I'm sorry I was so greedy," Lilet whispered, her voice slurred with weariness. "But Mimmi got shoes, and . . . I wanted something too."

Guilt twisted inside Isaveth. Even if Lilet had behaved badly, she had reason to feel slighted. She'd waited months for a dress that would fit her, and it wasn't fair—or even decent, given how fast she was growing—to make her wait any longer. Yet it would be at least another week before Annagail got her first pay from the college. Somehow Isaveth had to earn enough money to buy Lilet that dress.

Lilet had fallen asleep, her wan face turned to the window and one hand hanging limp over the edge of the bed. Isaveth got up gently, so as not to disturb her, and carried the basin downstairs to the kitchen to empty it out.

"Is she any better?" asked Annagail, glancing up anxiously from her mending. "We don't need to call for a healer, do we?"

"No," said Isaveth. "She's resting now. I'm sure she'll be fine." She rinsed the basin and set it aside, then took down the Book of Common Magic from the shelf and began leafing through it. Fire- and light-tablets might be easy to make, but there wasn't enough demand for them in this weather. She had to be bolder, think bigger—and find the courage to try selling her magic again.

Chapter Fourteen

"TAKE THIS NOTE WITH YOU to Aunt Sal's," said Isaveth, folding it up and tucking it into Mimmi's pocket. "Tell her I need to borrow some magical ingredients, but I'll pay her back as soon as I can."

Mendday morning had come at last, and Annagail had already left for her first day at the college. The sky outside the kitchen window was woolly with cloud, and a light drizzle pattered the glass—the first rain Tarreton had seen in nearly three weeks.

"Where are you going?" Mimmi asked, wrinkling her nose at Isaveth. "Nobody's going to buy spell-tablets in this weather."

Isaveth sighed. She'd hoped her sisters wouldn't figure that out. "To see Papa."

"What?" exclaimed Lilet. "That's not fair! Why can't we come too?"

"Because I need to talk to him in private." The conversation she'd overheard at Lady Marcham's garden party had left her with more questions than ever, but Papa would never speak about politics, let alone Master Orien's murder, with her little sisters listening in. "Besides, Quiz is driving me, and there isn't enough room on the cycle for all of us. Anna will take you some other day. Now go."

Her sisters trudged out the door, grumbling. Isaveth waited until they had passed the Kerchers' house, then reached for her hat and cardigan. Quiz had promised to meet her in the coal-lane, and she didn't want to keep him waiting.

"Lovely weather for it," Quiz called cheerfully to Isaveth as a spell-carriage whizzed past, spattering them with muddy water for the tenth time that morning. The rain was falling harder now, soaking through the thin knit of Isaveth's sweater. "Wishing you'd taken the tram?"

"I've never been in this part of the city before," she shouted back. "Are you sure this is the way to Dern Valley?"

"Course I am!" He stood up, leaning his weight on the pedals as the road slanted upward. "This is the shortcut."

Doubt pricked Isaveth, but a street-boy would probably know better than she did, so she held her peace. Yet the road grew narrower and steeper every minute. Soon Quiz was puffing, his wiry muscles knotted beneath the wet fabric of his shirt. Isaveth was about to poke him and tell him to slow down when a last grunting effort brought them over the crest, and the cycle slowed to a halt.

"Well," Quiz said breathlessly. "There's a view."

Dern Valley sprawled below them, all tight-clustered cottages and smoke-belching factories with an emerald ribbon of parkland winding through it. Quiz had been right about the shortcut—except that the path into the valley was dauntingly steep and as full of sharp bends as Isaveth had ever seen.

"We can't cycle that," she said in dismay. "We'll have to go by the tram route."

"Oh, that's too slow." Quiz's face was flushed, his good eye glittering with excitement. "We'll get to the jail much quicker this way. Hang on tight . . ." And before Isaveth could stop him, he kicked off, crouched forward, and shot straight down the hill.

Isaveth's muscles locked with terror. A scream bubbled into her mouth, but she gulped it back and flung her arms around Quiz's waist, pressing her face desperately against his spine. If only she didn't look, it might not be so bad . . .

Or so she hoped until they hit the first bend. The

cycle skidded sideways, spray hissing from the tires, and Isaveth nearly fell off her seat. She wanted to yell at Quiz to slow down, but the wind was rushing past at terrific speed, and she knew he'd never hear. All she could do was hold tighter, squeeze her eyes shut, and pray they made it to the bottom in one piece.

The cycle jerked, Quiz whooped, and for one horrible instant the wheels lifted clear off the road before landing with a sickening thump back down again. Isaveth dug her fingers into his stomach, hoping he'd take the hint— and mercifully, the cycle slowed a little as he leaned into the next turn. Still, she'd barely caught her breath before they hurtled down the slope again.

"Stop!" she screeched, pounding Quiz's shoulder. "Stop, stop, *stop*!"

"Can't!" yelled Quiz. "Don't worry, we're nearly there."

Isaveth cracked one eye open and immediately regretted it. Yet the same glimpse showed her the grin on Quiz's mud-streaked face, and she thought numbly: *He's going to kill us both. And it doesn't frighten him at all.*

They veered around two more corners, and Isaveth felt sure her heart would explode at any moment, before they shot out of the trees and whizzed onto level ground. Quiz stomped on the brake, and Isaveth wilted as the pedalcycle ground to a halt.

"That was horrible," she gasped, tumbling off and collapsing by the side of the road. "Never ever do that again!"

Quiz twisted to look at her, his good eye wide. "Really? You didn't like it? Isaveth, that's the best hill in the city!"

Isaveth put her hands over her face, calling on all the patience she possessed. Clearly, Quiz was insane, so there was no point shouting at him. But she wouldn't soon forget what he'd put her through. Or how happy he'd looked while doing it.

"I think," she said, "I'd prefer to walk the rest of the way."

"Got a girl here says she's Urias Breck's daughter." The officer at the gatehouse spoke brusquely to the charmband on his wrist. "And her boyfriend. I've searched them, and they're clean. All right to let them in?"

After a long, wet walk past several factories, a brick works, and a gravel pit, they stood at the entrance of the Dern Valley Jail, with its iron gates and towering wall crowned with thorn wire. Isaveth was uncomfortably conscious of being soaked through and muddy from knee to ankle, but it wasn't until Quiz took her hand that she realized she was trembling. Still, she didn't want to seem babyish, so she withdrew her fingers and gave him a thin smile instead.

"Go on, then." The officer jerked his head toward the

gates. "Up the steps, through the front door, and show yourself at the visitors' station. Leave the cycle here."

The Dern Valley Jail had the same unassailable appearance as the Keeper Station, its stone facade inset with twisting pillars, and rising four floors to the peaked, templelike roof above. Yet the prison block behind it was plain by contrast, more like a livestock barn than a place for human beings. And when Isaveth saw the stern, bearded face of Sage Armus carved above the entrance, and the fierce-looking serpents that formed the arch of the door, part of her wished she'd hung on to Quiz's hand after all.

The receiving area inside was more gloomy still, floored in black granite and lit by globe-lamps hanging on chains from the ceiling. Once Isaveth and Quiz had presented themselves to the woman at the desk, she unlocked a heavily barred door behind her and led them through.

Stark gray walls surrounded them, the plaster cracked in places to show the concrete beneath. The corridor opened into a rotunda ringed with metal catwalks, where more guards paced and swung their red-banded batons. A gallows beam jutted out from the wall, its frayed noose dangling over emptiness. Isaveth shuddered.

"In here," the officer said, opening a second door.

Hesitant, Isaveth stepped through into a dim, stale-smelling room, a little wider than her outstretched fingertips and perhaps four times as long, with a double-paned window across the center. And behind that wall of glass, his shaggy head bowed and his cuffed hands in his lap, sat her father.

The sight of him, so familiar and so dear, choked Isaveth speechless. She started forward, but the officer stopped her.

"Sit there," the woman said, pointing to a chair on the near side of the window. "Don't get up until you're finished." Then she turned to Quiz and added, "One visitor at a time. You want a turn, you wait with me. Either way you get ten minutes with the prisoner, no more. Understand?"

Quiz's jaw tightened, but he nodded. He followed the officer out, and the door swung shut behind them.

Isaveth tried to drag the chair closer to the window, but it was bolted fast. She could feel the guard watching them through the eye-slot in the door. "Papa?" she whispered.

Slowly her father raised his head, and Isaveth clapped a hand to her mouth. His cheek was purple with bruises, and one eye had swollen nearly shut.

"My Vettie." His voice sounded hoarse, but it held all

the tenderness she remembered. "How did you get here? Don't tell me you came all this way alone."

"No," she replied shakily, unable to tear her eyes from his battered face. "A friend gave me a ride. Papa, what happened to you?"

"Ah, it was only a foolish accident. Nothing worth talking about."

A lie so obvious could mean only one thing: He didn't want Isaveth to know what had really happened.

Unless it was the guard he feared, because she knew and had warned him not to tell anyone. . . .

Sickness crawled up Isaveth's throat. Did she dare ask Papa the questions that were burning inside her, or would it only make things worse for him if she did?

"How are my girls?" her father went on. "Are you getting along all right without me?"

Isaveth's eyes pricked with tears. "Oh, Papa, we miss you. But we're doing fine. You don't need to worry about us."

"Good, good." He scratched his beard awkwardly with his manacled hands. "Well, you needn't worry for me, either. I've had a talk with the Lawkeeper-General, so he knows where I stand. And I'm sure the Lord Justice will do the right thing, when the time comes."

This was horrible—more like talking to a friendly

stranger than the father she knew and loved. How could Isaveth help him if all they could do was tell cheerful lies to each other and act as though nothing was wrong?

"That's wonderful," she said, trying to sound as though she believed it, and leaned closer to the glass. Maybe if she lowered her voice and spoke quickly, the guard at the door wouldn't hear. "Papa, I'm trying to prove you didn't kill Master Orien. But there are a few things I don't understand. Please, can I ask you some questions?"

Her father stiffened, his gaze flicking to the door. Then he sat up, and the false smile vanished. "Ah, Vettie. You're a brave girl, but you shouldn't be mixing yourself up with all this. It's a bad lot of trouble I'm in, and I couldn't bear to think of you getting hurt."

Startled, Isaveth twisted around. The eye-slot was empty, and no sound or movement came from the other side. Had the guard been called away on some errand? Or had Quiz distracted her somehow?

Either way this might be her only chance to talk freely, so she'd better make the most of it. "It's all right, Papa," she said, turning back to him. "I'm not doing this alone." Quickly she explained about Quiz and the things they'd discovered about Orien's murder. "Do you think the governor suspected someone was plotting to kill him? Did he act nervous or worried at all?"

"He did seem a bit distracted," Papa mused. "Though it was late and he'd had a busy day, so I didn't make too much of that. I was a bit gruff with him at first, not being best pleased over the way he'd treated me before, so that might have had something to do with it. But once he apologized and explained himself, we got on all right."

"Explained?" asked Isaveth. "What did he say?"

"Well, we talked about a lot of things that won't interest you, but the sum of it was that he thought I was the right man for the charmery job, Moshite or not. Seems the Sagelord had recommended some other fellow, but Orien didn't like the look of him—said there was something shifty about his eyes. So he sent a message boy to track me down instead."

Had the shifty-eyed man guessed that the governor planned to reject him and hire Urias Breck in his place? If so, that might be a motive for him to murder the one and frame the other. "Do you know who the other man was?"

"Well, of course I asked, being curious. I thought I might know him, or at least have heard something about his work. But the governor wouldn't say."

That was a shame, but presumably the man's name would be in the appointment book, so she and Quiz could always look him up later. "Was there anyone else in the college when you left?" Isaveth asked. "Another workman, perhaps, or one of the masters?"

Papa chewed his lip thoughtfully. "I met a cleaning maid coming up the stairs as I was going down. And I spoke to the porter on my way out."

"All right," Isaveth said, trying not to sound too disappointed. She'd hoped he might confirm her suspicions about Master Buldage. "Is there anything else you can think of? Something that could help prove you didn't do it?"

"If I did, Vettie, I'd tell you." Papa heaved a sigh. "I'd have been glad of a good advocate to help me make my case. But the fellow they sent me made no secret of how he felt about Moshites, and I feared he'd be more harm to me than help."

So that was why he'd declined counsel. It hurt Isaveth to think of Papa having to face this man's contempt, on top of everything else.

"One more thing, then," she said. "When the Lawkeepers came to arrest you, you didn't resist them at first. Until they said you might be truth-bound. . . ."

He winced. "Ah, sweetling, don't make me speak of that. It was a foolish thing I did, fighting them, and I fear I'll pay for it yet. But whatever you may think of me, I swear I didn't kill the governor—"

"Oh, no, Papa!" Isaveth burst out. "I didn't mean it like that! I was only trying to understand!"

His expression softened. "My Vettie," he said, stretching his cuffed hands to the window, as though he could reach through it and touch her face. "So like your mother."

He didn't want to tell her, that much was clear. "Please," Isaveth urged. "It could be important. Why don't you want to be truth-bound? What are you afraid of?"

Papa was quiet, his head bent. At last he said, "Truth-binding's not a gentle thing, Vettie. Still, I'd not fear their questions if I could be sure it was only me they meant to ask about. But there's a difference between giving up your own secrets and betraying someone else's."

"You mean . . ." Isaveth was aghast. "The Workers' Club? They're the ones you're protecting?"

A heavy rasp and click echoed through the room, and the door swung open. Surely it hadn't been ten minutes already? Isaveth turned to protest—but it was Quiz standing in the doorway, his cap clutched humbly in his hands.

"Sorry," he said. "Time's running out, and the guard'll be back any minute. I wanted to have a word, if that's all right."

Reluctantly Isaveth rose and backed away, still searching Papa's face. She was almost to the door when she got her answer: a single nod and a sad twitch of a smile.

Emotion welled up inside her. She wanted to run to him, bury her face in his chest, and hug him. But a wall stood between them, and she had to be brave, for both their sakes.

"Don't worry, Papa," she said, though her lips were trembling and her throat ached with unshed tears. "I'll keep looking, and I won't give up. We'll get you out of here, you'll see."

Chapter Fifteen

"WHAT DID YOU SAY TO PAPA?" Isaveth asked as she and Quiz walked away from the gatehouse. She'd hoped to linger by the door of the visiting room and eavesdrop, but the guard had returned as soon as Isaveth came out. So Isaveth had paced the rotunda, shuddering at every muffled clang and curse from the cells above, and praying that the prisoners—or guards—who'd hurt Papa would leave him alone from now on.

"Oh, not much," said Quiz, scrubbing a fleck of mud off the pedalcycle's seat. The rain had dissolved into mist now, and the thunderclouds were rolling eastward, grumbling as they went. "I only wanted to tell him who I was and that I'd be looking out for you." He glanced at her. "Are you all right?"

Isaveth drew a slow breath, letting the rain-washed air drive the sour prison smell away. "I'll be fine. It's Papa

I'm worried about. If the Lawkeepers think he was part of a conspiracy, I suppose it makes sense that they'd ask him for names. But if they put him under a truth-spell, why can't he just tell them he didn't kill Master Orien and have done with it?"

"Well," said Quiz, still picking at the mud, "I don't know whether they're going to truth-bind your father or not. But I found out a bit more about how the spell works, and . . . it's not what you think."

"What do you mean?"

"I mean the decoction they give people doesn't really make it impossible for them to lie. It only forces them to talk, and keep talking, until the Lawkeepers get tired of asking questions and give them the antidote."

Isaveth stopped walking and stared at him. "But they could say anything, then. How do the Keepers know it's the truth?"

"They don't," Quiz said. "But if a prisoner starts to ramble or avoids the question, they poke him with a shock-wand. And it's hard to make up a convincing lie when you're talking as fast as you can."

A chill ran through Isaveth. Papa wasn't stupid by any means, but his thoughts worked slowly, and he seldom spoke without weighing his words first. "What happens if they stop talking? Or can't they do that?"

"Oh, they can. But if they don't talk, they don't breathe. That's how the spell really works."

Isaveth's throat went dry. "That—that's horrible."

"Yes, and it's also illegal in most provinces, including a good part of this one. Tarreton is one of the few cities in Upper Colonia that allows truth-binding, and it's only supposed to be used on the most dangerous dissenters—the kind of people who lead riots or threaten to blow up the council."

Or murder the governor of Tarreton College. Did the Lawkeepers think Papa had been trying to scare the other nobles into supporting the Reps' Bill, or merely stop Orien from taking part in the final vote? Either way it seemed like a reckless scheme, more likely to harm the reps' cause than strengthen it. Papa surely didn't believe anyone in the Workers' Club would do such a wicked, foolish thing, or he wouldn't be so anxious to keep their secrets.

Yet if the Lawkeepers truth-bound him, what choice would he have? He'd either have to betray his friends or suffocate. . . .

"They can't bind him yet, though," Quiz said, putting a reassuring hand on Isaveth's shoulder. "Even if they want to. The Lord Justice has to sign the order first, and he's in Uropia."

173

The knot in Isaveth's chest eased. Uropia was clear across the Eastern Ocean, a week's journey by steamship and at least three days by floater. "How do you know all of this?" she asked. "Affinity-charms, truth-binding, the Lord Justice's schedule . . ."

"Oh, people love to tell me things," said Quiz cheerfully. "I expect I have that sort of face."

Someone had left a bundle of wet news-rags outside the tram station. Quiz blinked when Isaveth asked him to stop so she could pick them up, but he didn't hesitate to oblige. Once she got home, Isaveth tore the damp pages into tiny pieces, added some beetroot juice and puff-weed petals for color, and left the pinkish glop in the washtub to soak. She'd screen it and press it dry, and then she'd have paper to wrap her next batch of spells in.

Her heart still ached for Papa, and Isaveth feared for his safety more than ever. But worrying wouldn't help him, or her sisters, either. She'd done all she could for Papa today; now she needed to work on getting that new dress for Lilet.

It cost Isaveth a nerve-racking dash past the Kerchers' house and a shameful amount of begging to get Aunt Sal to lend the ingredients she needed. Mimmi, of course, had forgotten to deliver Isaveth's note. But in the end her aunt gave in, and Isaveth returned to her own kitchen triumphant. She tied on her mother's apron, opened the Book of Common Magic, and set to work.

She'd sifted all the flour she needed and was about to toss the neevils outside when a thought came to her. What had Mistress Anandri said about neevils? On impulse she dumped the wriggling bugs onto the pulp soaking in the washtub, then mashed them in. If it made her wrappers even a little more resistant to magic, it would be worth it.

Isaveth spent the next two hours in a frenzy of mixing, stirring, and pouring, and she had one bad fright when the decoction she'd left on the stove burst into flame. But she slammed the lid down in an instant, and when the liquid cooled, it was exactly the color the book said it ought to be. She poured it carefully into pill bottles—they had a lot of those left over from her mother's illness—and bent to take her last batch of spell-tablets out of the oven.

"More spell-baking?" asked Annagail from behind her, and Isaveth jumped. She'd been so absorbed in her work, she hadn't even heard the front door open. Quickly she dropped the pan onto the table and wiped her hands. "Anna! How was your day?"

Annagail didn't answer. She circled the kitchen table, studying one decoction and batch of tablets after another. "You've been awfully busy," she said. "What's it all for?"

"Well, these ones are cleaning-tablets," Isaveth said, pointing to the spongy-looking squares on the far end. "You can rub them on your hands or clothes, even if you don't have water. Those are dark-tablets—I thought I could sell them to people with headaches or who work at night and have trouble falling asleep during the day. And this decoction is called Mother's Helper because—"

"That's not what I meant," said Anna. "I only wondered why you were making them. I thought maybe Mistress Anandri had asked you to do some more spell-baking for the college."

"Oh," said Isaveth. "No. I just thought that if people weren't interested in my other spells, maybe they'd want these ones." Not to mention that measuring ingredients and stirring pots was better than brooding over Papa's battered face or her fear that he might be truth-bound. "But what about you? Did everything go all right at the college?"

"Oh . . . oh yes, it went fine." Anna toyed with her necklace, her gaze unfocused and a little troubled. Then she recollected herself and pulled a notebook from her pocket. "I did what you asked," she said.

Isaveth took the notes eagerly and flipped through

them. Sure enough, her sister had written down all of Master Orien's visitors on the day he died—and the times they'd come to the office as well. "Thank you, Anna!" she exclaimed.

"Do you recognize any of the names?" Annagail asked. "I didn't."

"No," admitted Isaveth. "But Quiz might." Carefully she tore out the pages and handed the book back—Anna probably needed it for her work. "Anyway, I'm sure it won't be hard to find them."

Annagail nodded, but she still looked distracted. Clearly something was weighing on her mind. "What is it?" asked Isaveth.

Anna hesitated. Then she reached into the bodice of her dress and pulled out their mother's prayer scarf. "I . . . want you to have this."

Her sister treasured that scarf, and with good reason: Mama had draped it around Anna's neck with her own hands only a few minutes before she died. "B-but I'm not thirteen yet," stammered Isaveth as her sister pressed the scarf into her hand. "And you're the oldest. It's yours to wear, not mine."

"Wear it where?" Anna asked tiredly. "Vettie, I can't risk anyone seeing me in a prayer scarf, at the college or not. I'm scared even to go to temple now, because who knows who might spot me on the way? And if word got back to Meggery . . ." She shook her head. "It's too dangerous."

Guilt stabbed at Isaveth. She'd been so determined not to let Annagail's faith keep her from getting the job at the college, she'd scarcely thought about what it would cost her sister to hide it. "I'm sorry."

"Don't be. It's not forever, it's only for now. And the All-One knows what's in my heart, even if I can't show it." She laid a hand on Isaveth's shoulder. "But I would feel better if someone was wearing Mama's scarf. Will you do it? For me?"

Isaveth folded the silky cloth and draped it about her neck. It felt strange to have a knot sitting in the hollow of her throat. Or maybe that was just the lump inside it.

"All right," she said quietly. "For now."

The next morning Isaveth was in the kitchen, ironing her newly made wrapping paper, when a tentative knock sounded at the door.

"Come in, Quiz," she called. After all, who else would it be?

"What are you doing?" asked Quiz, doffing his cap as he came in. He must have bathed in the lake last night, because his face was clean, his patch all but hidden beneath the silky fall of his hair. "Making paper?"

"Neevil paper," said Isaveth. "I don't know how useful it'll be, but I thought it was worth a try."

Quiz blinked. "Come again?"

"Mistress Anandri said neevils have antimagical properties, and that's why you have to be careful not to let them get into your spell-baking. But once the cooking's finished, the magic's sealed until you let it out. So I thought if I mashed up some neevils in my batch of paper and then wrapped my spells in it . . ."

Quiz's brows shot up. "Clever! Does it work?"

"I'm about to find out," said Isaveth, reaching for the scissors. She cut off a strip of her first page, wrapped up one of her old fire-tablets candy fashion, then flung the little parcel onto the table.

Nothing happened. Isaveth picked up the meat mallet and gave the tablet a rap—not hard enough to crush it, but enough that it ought to crack. Still nothing.

"Maybe it's a bad one," said Quiz, and before Isaveth could stop him, he'd pinched the package open. "Ow!"

The fire-tablet flamed up, then subsided into glowing crumbs. The neevil paper, however, was scarcely blackened at all. "It works!" exclaimed Isaveth in delight.

Quiz sucked his singed fingers, looking aggrieved. "You didn't tell me it was a *fire*-tablet."

"Well, you didn't tell me you were going to touch it.

Here." Isaveth soaked a cloth in pump water and handed it to him. "Better?"

"I'll live," said Quiz. He waited until Isaveth had sat down and picked up her scissors again, then pulled out the chair across from her. "How was Annagail's first day at the college?"

It didn't take Isaveth long to tell him all her sister had said, even the details that had come out after Anna gave her the prayer scarf—she'd been more at ease then, willing to answer all Isaveth's questions about her duties and what she thought of the other people at the college.

"So she's got keys to the governor's office and the rest of that floor as well?" Quiz leaned back, stretching his long legs under the table. "Perfect! Now we can get in anywhere we want."

"I don't know about that," said Isaveth, shifting uncomfortably as his feet brushed hers. Why did boys always have to take up so much space? "She was willing to get me that list for Papa's sake, but she doesn't like prying into other people's things, and I don't think she'd want to help us do it, either. She did promise to ask about the cleaning maid who found Orien's body, though, and to find out as much as she can about Master Buldage."

"We could find out a lot more by searching his office,"

said Quiz glumly, "but I suppose it'll have to do. Where's that list, then?"

Isaveth took the pages from her pocket and handed them over. Quiz adjusted his patch, then brought the pages close to his nose and squinted.

Was his vision really as poor as that? The thought made Isaveth's skin break out in turkey-flesh, especially when she remembered that wild ride down the hill into Dern Valley. Yet he'd always dodged Mimmi's questions about his patch, so he wouldn't be likely to give Isaveth a straight answer about his eyesight, either.

"That's disappointing," Quiz said at last, lowering the papers. "I was hoping there'd be at least one master on the list."

"So was I," Isaveth admitted. "But if the murderer was one of the masters, why would he make an appointment? There'd be no need to visit the governor's office if he'd planted the charm and tablet in his robe the night before."

"True," said Quiz. "Well, then, let's look closer to the time of the murder. Who were the other people on Master Orien's schedule that day who might have had access to exploding-tablets?"

Isaveth leaned across the table, scanning the pages. "Well, in the afternoon there was Alv Nowatcz and Tomias Rennick—they're both listed as 'builder.' Oh, and

Errol Yeng, the architect, but he came in the morning."

"And Alv came next, early in the afternoon. I'll bet he's the man the Sagelord picked to oversee the charmery project," said Quiz. "The one Master Orien didn't like. I think we should start with him." He started to rise, but Isaveth tapped his hand.

"Wait. If one of these men was the murderer, he'd have had to slip the charm and the tablet into Orien's pocket while he was talking to him. How would he do that without him noticing?"

"Easy," Quiz replied. "Disguise them as something innocent. Wrap them up and make them look like . . . I don't know, a packet of candies. Or pipe-baccy."

"But how could they know Master Orien would accept the gift, let alone put it in his pocket? What if he'd left it on his desk or given it to his secretary instead?"

Quiz made a wry face. "You're right, it would be a chancy way to kill someone. So you've still got your eye on Master Buldage?"

"Or someone else inside the college," Isaveth said. "Like that cleaning maid Papa saw coming up the stairs when he was going out. What if she killed Orien for some reason we don't know yet and then fooled the Lawkeepers into thinking she'd stumbled onto his body by accident?"

"I suppose," said Quiz, "but in that case we might as well suspect everyone else on the staff. If the cleaning maid, why not the porter? He was there at the time too."

"Yes, but he's still at the college. He didn't vanish and not tell anyone where he was going." Isaveth tugged at her prayer scarf—she was still self-conscious about wearing it, and the knot always felt a little too tight. Yet Quiz hadn't even seemed to notice. "But I'm not saying we shouldn't look into these other men as well. Let's go to the city records and find out as much about them as we can."

Chapter Sixteen

ONCE ISAVETH HAD PACKED her father's old lunch satchel with her newly wrapped spells, she and Quiz cycled into the city. There they spent the next two hours in the dusty heat of the Records Office, peppering the bemused clerk with questions and hunting through business directories until they found the information they needed. While Quiz scribbled down addresses and sketched maps on his notepad, Isaveth leafed through a copy of last year's Governor's Report—which gave her a better sense of Master Orien's character, as well as a few more insights into Master Buldage.

"His great-grandfather was one of the founders of Tarreton College," she explained to Quiz as they left the building. "And his father was governor for nearly twenty years. So of course Master Buldage would have been upset when the Sagelord appointed Orien instead of him. It was an insult to his whole family."

"That's a good motive for wanting to kill the Sagelord," said Quiz, "but not so much for wanting to kill Master Orien. After all, Buldage couldn't be sure that Lord Arvis wouldn't just snub him again." He flipped the notebook shut and stuffed it back into his pocket. "I've got an idea. Instead of both of us going to Alv Nowatcz's workshop, why don't I go there on my own? Then you can check out the architect's office at the same time. Maybe sell some of those spell-tablets you're carrying too."

It wasn't a bad idea—after all, Quiz could always pretend to be looking for work, and he'd have a better chance of getting Mister Nowatcz's workers to talk than she would. Besides, Alv's workshop was a fair distance away, and Quiz could pedal faster if he didn't have to carry Isaveth as well.

"All right," she said as Quiz swung himself onto the cycle. "Good luck."

Unfortunately, Isaveth's visit to Errol Yeng turned out to be a disappointing waste of time. Not only was the architect out of his office, but his secretary had no patience for Isaveth's questions, and shooed her away with a stern warning not to come back.

Still, now that Isaveth had seen Yeng's spare, modern,

and fastidiously neat workplace, she was even less inclined to suspect him than the college porter. Certainly Yeng worked in building construction, but only in the planning stages, so there was no reason he'd have any more access to exploding-tablets than the average citizen. He appeared well off, and most of his clients were nobles, so why would he want to murder Master Orien? He had even less motive than Papa, as far as Isaveth could see.

As she walked away from the office, the bell tower tolled for midday, and soon the sidewalk was crowded with workers streaming out of the shops, offices, and nearby factories. She'd never find a better time to sell her magic. Isaveth peered into her satchel, checking the tablets and bottles to be sure none of them had broken. Then she stepped up to the corner and launched into the speech she'd been silently rehearsing since that morning.

"Spell-tablets of all kinds! Clean your clothes, soothe a headache, find a wandering child! Homemade is better made!"

At first Isaveth feared her mother's prayer scarf would put off customers, as surely as her father's name had driven them away before. But she was soon approached by a woman wearing a healer's cap and a scarf similar to her own, who bought a generous handful of cleaning-tablets and traced a blessing sign on Isaveth's palm before continuing on her way. And not long after, a young mother with a pair of squabbling twins stopped to ask Isaveth about her child-finding decoction and ended up buying two bottles.

Isaveth kept calling and waving until the crowd began to thin, but no one else approached her. Quiz hadn't come back, either, and the heat was growing unbearable, so at last she shouldered her satchel and walked on. Still, she'd made nearly half the money she needed to buy Lilet's dress, which buoyed her spirits a little.

She was standing at the junction of Long Street and Ellsley, waiting to cross with the rest of the crowd, when a flash of color caught her eye. Striding past was the fashionably dressed woman she'd seen twice before, wearing a bright orange hat that set off her black hair and russet skin.

This time Isaveth didn't hesitate. "Excuse me!" she said, running up to her. "I don't mean to be rude, but . . . are you a reporter?"

The woman turned, sculpted brows arching in surprise. "Why, yes, I am. What can I do for you?"

She didn't say "little girl," but she might as well have. Isaveth's cheeks flamed, but she swallowed her pride and pressed on. "I saw you with Eryx Lording last week, making notes of . . . of whatever he was doing."

"Oh, yes! I recognize you now." A half smile curved the reporter's lips. "The little tablet seller. And didn't I see you by the Keeper Station the next day as well, waiting for your boyfriend to tie his shoe?"

So she had noticed. "Yes," Isaveth said. "I was wondering . . . if it wouldn't be too much trouble, could I ask . . ."

The words came awkwardly, as she had no idea how to explain her interest in the details of Papa's case without admitting Urias Breck was her father. Fortunately, the woman didn't wait for her to finish the sentence.

"You want to be a journalist yourself, of course! Well, my dear . . ." She took Isaveth's arm, leading her away from the crowd. "I'm not going to lie to you, it won't be easy. Without the right connections you'll have to work twice as hard as anyone else. Still, it can be done if you've got the will and the talent. Plus a nose for news, of course!"

"Oh, thank you!" Isaveth gushed, making her eyes wide. If it flattered the woman to think she was an admirer, it only made sense to play along. "But how do you get important people like the Lording, or even the Lawkeepers, to talk to you? It seems like every time I ask questions, people tell me to go away."

"It's a matter of reputation," said the reporter airily.

"The leaders of this city know they can count on the *Trumpeter* to print the facts, not rumors and made-up nonsense." She cast a scornful look at a rag-boy waving copies of the *Citizen*, then breezed on, "Of course, it's also important to cultivate the right sources. The Sage-lord, for instance, tends to be very closemouthed, and most of the other lords on the council are too stuffy and self-important to talk about anything but themselves. But even when Eryx was still at college, I could see how committed he was to making Tarreton a better place, and I knew that if I stuck close to him, I'd soon find out what was really going on." She smiled proudly. "It's paid off, as I'm sure you've noticed. He's given me more exclusives than any other reporter in the city."

"What about Governor Orien?" asked Isaveth. "Did you ever talk to him?"

The woman looked surprised. "Well, yes. Not that he was as frank or forthcoming as Eryx—he was a more reserved sort of man. But a decent one." She gave a little sigh. "Such a loss, really."

First her father, then the secretary, and now the repor-ter: They all agreed that Orien had been a good person. Which made it unlikely that the murderer had acted out of personal hatred or a desire for revenge, and more likely he or she had done it as part of some greater plan. . . .

"Was that why you were at the Keeper Station that day?" asked Isaveth. "To find out more about the murder?"

"Naturally. A good reporter always goes to the most reliable source."

"Do you think he really did it, then? That man they arrested?"

Until that moment the woman's manner had been casual, even relaxed. Now her gaze focused sharply on Isaveth. "Why would you ask a question like that?"

"It's just—I mean—how can they be sure? What if they made a mistake, and the real murderer's still out there planning to—well, who knows what he might do?"

She was talking too quickly, stumbling over her words. But she couldn't let this woman suspect she was Urias Breck's daughter, or she'd end up in the news-rags next.

The reporter's face softened. "You poor kid," she said. "You're too young for this ugly stuff. Don't worry, though. I've talked to the Lawkeepers, and I'm sure they've got the right man."

"You think so?" asked Isaveth, trying to look relieved even though she felt the opposite. "But why would a builder kill the governor of Tarreton College?"

"To stop him voting against the Reps' Bill, of course," said the woman. "Governor Orien had a lot of influence on the council, especially over the older lords and ladies. If he decided it wasn't in the best interests of the city to give the reps more power, they'd most likely follow his lead."

"That's all?" asked Isaveth, screwing up her nose the way Mimmi did when she was puzzled. "Politics? That doesn't seem like a very good reason to kill someone."

The woman gave a little laugh. "I'd agree with you there. Still, I'm afraid it's true. Urias Breck was a member of the Workers' Club, a radical group of dissenters that the council declared illegal a few days ago—and Orien had voted in favor of that law. Besides, Breck was known to have a personal grudge against the governor."

Shock rippled through Isaveth, and it took all her strength to hide it. How could the Lawkeepers know where her father had gone on Duesday evenings or how he felt about Master Orien? Unless they had a spy inside the Workers' Club . . . or else they'd been watching Papa long before they arrested him.

"Anyway, even if the Lawkeepers did arrest the wrong man, which I doubt," the reporter continued, "there are some good officers working on the investigation, and they'll soon get to the bottom of it. In fact"—she leaned closer, her tone confiding—"I have reason to believe that Eryx Lording has taken a special interest in the case himself."

When Isaveth's eyes widened this time, it wasn't an act. If Eryx was looking into Master Orien's murder—which made sense, with Orien being his old tutor and a family friend—then there might be a chance to save Papa from being truth-bound after all. If she could get to the Lording and tell him what she and Quiz had discovered . . .

"So you see, my dear, there's no need to worry. The Lawkeepers know what they're doing." The journalist opened her handbag, took out a cream-colored card, and handed it to Isaveth. "Now I have to run off to the memorial, so I can't stay any longer. But I can see you've got a journalistic mind. If you spot something newsworthy, drop me a message, won't you?"

SU AMARAQ, INVESTIGATIVE REPORTER, it read, with the address and call-code of the *Tarreton Trumpeter* beneath it. Isaveth tucked the card into her satchel and put on her brightest smile.

"Thank you," she said. "I will."

After her conversation with Su, Isaveth could hardly wait for Quiz to get back so she could tell him what she'd found out about the Lording. But when he finally returned, he seemed tired and short tempered, and not impressed with Isaveth's news at all.

"He'd be better to keep out of it," he said. "It's none of the Lording's business, whether he knew Orien or not."

"Well, you're investigating, aren't you? And it's even less of your business than his." Isaveth folded her arms. "Besides, Eryx is the heir to the city, and the Lawkeepers respect him, so he might actually be able to make a difference. I think we should talk to him."

"No!" Quiz nearly dropped the pedalcycle. "Isaveth, you can't bring him into this. It could ruin everything."

"How? I know you don't think much of him, but just because he's a noble doesn't make him the enemy. He may be wealthy and good looking, but—"

"Good looking!" Quiz gave a bitter laugh. "Oh, he's certainly that. And charming. And clever. And he's got half the city in love with him—including that Su woman, who takes down everything he says like it's the wisdom of the Sages." He made a sour face, then muttered, "I knew this would happen if you talked to her."

Isaveth's mouth dropped open. "You knew who she was all along! You knew Su worked for the *Trumpeter*, you knew she'd talked to the Lawkeepers about Papa's case, and you deliberately stopped me from meeting her!"

"I didn't stop—"

"You might as well have. 'Wait, let me tie my boot-lace. Whoops, she's gone.' And why? Because she thinks highly of Eryx Lording and you don't? Well, in that case, you might as well give up on me, too!"

"I didn't mean it like that." Quiz closed his good eye, looking miserable. "I meant—oh, curse it. I'm sorry. I was only afraid she'd find out Breck was your father."

"Well, she didn't." Isaveth let her arms drop, her anger fading as she studied his face. He didn't merely look unhappy, he looked unwell. "What's wrong with you, anyway?"

"I've got a beast of a headache, that's all. It happens sometimes." He propped the cycle against a lamppost and rubbed his temples. "Anyway, I found Alv's workshop, and I was wrong. I don't think he's the one we're looking for."

"Why not?"

"For one thing, he and his men were building roof trusses. They work mostly in wood and metal, so they wouldn't have much use for exploding-tablets. Besides, it turns out that at the time Master Orien died, Alv and his foreman were having a friendly boxing match, while the rest of his men were laying wagers on which of them would win."

"Why does that matter?" asked Isaveth. "He could have hidden the affinity-charm in his pocket and set it off while nobody was . . ." She stopped as Quiz gave her a pitying look. "What?"

"Affinity-charms aren't like spell-tablets: You can't set one off by bumping it. You need a charm-breaker, or at least a hard surface and a hammer." He pulled off his cap and ran his fingers through his sweaty hair. "Besides, Alv was being watched by at least ten other people during the fight, and not one noticed him doing anything unusual."

"Unless they're all lying."

"That's exactly the sort of thing I knew Su would get you thinking," said Quiz, whacking his cap against the lamppost in disgust. "That's what the nobles who banned the Workers' Club want you to think. 'See how dangerous these common folk are when they stick together? Good thing we outlawed their meetings, so they can't plot to murder the rest of us!'"

"So you don't think it was political?"

Quiz blew out his breath in frustration. "I'm not saying that. I just don't think it was some big dissenter conspiracy, like Su and the Lawkeepers do. I also don't think Alv could be the fellow Master Orien mentioned to your father, because he's got a smile like a big baby and the brightest blue eyes you've ever seen. He couldn't look shifty if he tried."

"That leaves Tomias Rennick, then," said Isaveth. "Did you ask Alv's men if they knew him?"

"I did. Turns out he's a stonemason, like your father.

But that was all I got out of them before they stopped being friendly and told me to take myself elsewhere."

"You mean they're protecting him?" asked Isaveth, but Quiz shook his head.

"No. I just think they don't like him very much."

Rennick must have a bad name among his fellow builders, then. And since he was in the same trade as her father, they probably knew each other. Could he be the spy in the Workers' Club?

The easiest way to find out would be to talk to one of the other club members. But besides her father, the only person Isaveth knew who might belong to the club was Seward Caverly, and she didn't dare knock at *that* door again. She'd have to wait and talk to Papa.

"Well," she said, resigned, "it's too late to do anything more today. I promised Annagail I'd be home by four, and it's almost three now."

Quiz glanced up at the clock tower—and turned ashen. "Oh no! I'm an idiot, I'm dead, they're going to kill me!" And with that he leaped onto the cycle, hopped the curb, and pedaled frantically away.

"Wait!" cried Isaveth, but Quiz didn't look back. He swerved past the iced-custard stand, cut in front of a dairy wagon, and crossed two lanes of screeching, whinnying traffic. Then he veered around the corner and was gone.

Chapter Seventeen

ISAVETH EXPECTED QUIZ to drop by her house the next morning, full of apologies and explanations—or at least a funny story about whatever trouble he'd got into. But when hours passed with no sign of him, she slung her satchel of spells over her shoulder and headed to the city on foot. Perhaps she'd find him there.

Isaveth paced the streets the rest of that morning and into the afternoon, hawking her spells along the way. By the time the bell tower tolled four, her satchel felt lighter and she'd earned a small handful of coins, but she was too anxious to take much comfort in her success. She needed Quiz's help to hunt down Tomias Rennick and save Papa from being truth-bound, and she couldn't believe he'd willingly abandon her with so much at stake.

Something bad must have happened to him, then. What if he'd been arrested for reckless cycling, or beaten up by a gang of his fellow street-boys? What if he was trapped in a cell at the Keeper Station right now, or lying in a dark alley somewhere, too weak to move?

The thought was too dreadful to contemplate. Isaveth had known Quiz for only a week, but he'd already become a better friend to her than Morra had ever been. True, his reckless impulses and sudden shifts of mood unnerved her, but he'd proved himself trustworthy, and she'd come to rely on his help. If he didn't come back, how would she manage without him?

Isaveth wasn't merely worried for her own sake—she was concerned about Quiz as well. He acted so confident, it was easy to think of him as a natural loner. But she'd seen the wistfulness in his face as he watched Isaveth with her family. And when she'd invited him to dinner, he'd turned so shy that it seemed he wasn't used to such kindness from anyone. How dreary must his life have been before they met that he'd been glad to help Isaveth solve a murder just for something to do?

Isaveth touched the knot of her scarf, silently begging the All-One to keep Quiz safe. But her faith wasn't as strong as Annagail's, and it felt like a futile gesture. She hugged her satchel to her side, for comfort as much as protection, and turned her weary feet toward home.

* * *

The sun set on Worksday and rose high on Trustday, yet Quiz did not appear. By afternoon Isaveth had earned all the money she needed to buy Lilet a dress, but she felt little joy in her achievement. How could she be happy, even for her sister's sake, when Quiz was missing, Papa was still in jail, and the Lord Justice might return from Uropia at any moment?

She hadn't told anyone in her family, not even Annagail, what she'd learned about truth-binding—no more than she'd confided in them about Papa's bruised face or her fear that someone inside the Workers' Club had betrayed him. Lilet and Mimmi were too young to carry such heavy burdens, and her older sister was already bearing too many. So when Annagail exclaimed and hugged Isaveth at the sight of the money, Isaveth put on a smile and hugged her back.

"I'll take Lilet to the Relief Shop tomorrow," said Anna, dropping the coins into her pocket. "And now I have good news for you. I found out a few things about that cleaning maid you've been looking for."

As it turned out, the maid's name was Ellice. The other servants at the college remembered her as a plain-faced woman about ten years older than Anna, with thin brown hair and a stammer; Mister Jespers had thought her a slow worker, but reliable enough once she knew her duty. But the juiciest details, as usual, had come from Meggery.

"She said Ellice had been married once," said Annagail, "but her husband died. So she went back to live with her mother."

If Ellice was only in her midtwenties now, she must have been widowed unusually young. "What did her husband die of?" Isaveth asked.

"I don't know. Meggery thought it was an accident, but she couldn't remember the details. It happened a few months after Ellice first came to work at the college."

Definitely strange. Perhaps the death of Ellice's mister wasn't as accidental as it appeared. "Did Meggery know anything about the husband? What sort of man he was?"

"I didn't ask. Anyway, that's all I could find out. Does it help at all?"

"I'm not sure," Isaveth admitted. "I wish Quiz . . ." She sighed. "Never mind."

Anna's face softened. "Don't despair. There's bound to be a reason he's stayed away, and it needn't be a bad one. You don't know who else might be relying on him."

It would have been nice to think so, but Isaveth doubted it. If Quiz had merely been late to visit his friend with the broken leg or to run an errand for one of the shopkeepers, he wouldn't have acted so panic stricken the other day. And he wouldn't have been gone this long, either.

"Well," Isaveth said, "I can't sit around and wait forever. If I don't hear from Quiz by tomorrow, I'll have to find Tomias Rennick myself."

Annagail's brow furrowed anxiously. "Vettie, I'm not sure that's a good idea. Have you thought about this?"

"Of course I have. I still think Master Orien was killed by someone at the college, but perhaps the murderer bought the exploding-tablets from Rennick, and if I can get him to—"

Anna seized her hand. "This is about *murder*, Vettie. You're chasing someone who plotted to kill the governor in his own office and make it look as though Papa had done it. If this person is that cruel and that cunning, what makes you think you can catch him without getting hurt?"

Isaveth opened her mouth, then shut it again. Yes, Papa's life was more important than her own safety, and she'd gladly risk anything to help him. But Anna had a point too. Even Quiz's fighting skills, impressive as they'd been against Loyal, wouldn't be a match for a grown man with a weapon. How did Isaveth expect to defend herself all alone?

Yet she couldn't afford to worry about such things, or she'd lose her nerve. "I know it *sounds* dangerous," she said soothingly, patting Anna's hand in return. "But it's not like I'm going to charge into Tomias Rennick's house, yelling, 'Stop, murderer!' I'm only going to ask him a few questions. And in plain daylight, too."

Annagail sighed. "I'd still feel better if you had some kind of protection. Like a dog or . . ."

"We can barely feed ourselves, and you want to get a dog?" Though the Kerchers kept Bruiser, but they weren't much of an example. The poor beast would surely have starved by now if Loyal didn't turn him loose in the factory yard every night to hunt rats.

"Vettie, you know what I mean. You ought to have something."

She looked so distressed that Isaveth relented. "All right. I'll see what I can do."

Isaveth was sitting on the back step, sorting through her unsold spells and setting aside a few she thought might come in handy when the door creaked open behind her.

"I'll be there in a minute, Anna," she said, without turning around.

There was a brief, uncertain pause. Then a throat cleared, and an absurdly high-pitched voice replied: "All right, darling!"

Isaveth scrambled to her feet, aglow with joy. "Quiz!"

"The very same." He swept off his cap and bowed. "My abject apologies for dashing off so rudely the other day. I'd forgotten something that landed me in quite a boggy hole, and it's taken me this long to climb out."

"What kind of trouble?" Isaveth asked, but Quiz went on as though he hadn't heard.

"Nonetheless, here I am, at your service. I've already asked your sister if she can spare you, so I thought we might squeak in a visit to our Mister Rennick before it gets dark. What do you say?"

There could be only one answer to that. "Yes, of course!" exclaimed Isaveth, stooping to collect her arsenal of spells. "Let me pack these up, and we'll go."

The address they'd found for Tomias Rennick took them to the most run-down part of the city, only a few blocks from the rail yard and the harbor front running behind it. The houses here had been stately once, when Tarreton was new. But over the decades they had gradually decayed, merged, and subdivided into rows of narrow tenements, grime-caked windows staring blindly out at the heaved and crumbling cobbles of the street.

No trees or even grass grew here, only the occasional patch of weeds, and the alleyways were heaped with broken bricks, rusty metal, and other old rubbish. A page from a discarded news-rag skittered in front of them, and something lithe and dark wriggled under a nearby fence—a small dog, Isaveth thought, until she saw its whiplike tail and realized it was the biggest rat she'd ever seen.

"Ugh!" she said, pressing closer to Quiz as he cycled along. "Are you sure we're in the right place?"

"Well, there's only one Gentian Lane on the map," said Quiz. "So I'm afraid so. But it does seem odd. I know everyone's struggling these days, but if Rennick was a good enough stonemason for the Sagelord to recommend him, he shouldn't have to live in a place like this."

Isaveth was tempted to point out that her papa was an even better stonemason, and they still had to live in a tiny rented house on Cabbage Street. Though Papa was Moshite, a widower with four daughters to support, and had gone for months without steady work. As far as she knew, Rennick had none of those troubles.

"There it is," Isaveth said, pointing. "Forty-eight C."

Quiz stopped the pedalcycle a few paces from the house, where a cluster of grubby, raggedly dressed children were climbing on one of the scrap piles. They darted for cover as Quiz and Isaveth dismounted, peering out from the shadows with bruise-dark, suspicious eyes.

"I've got a cit for every one of you," said Quiz, showing them the coins on his palm, "if you watch my cycle and don't let anybody touch it. Can you do that?"

The children exchanged looks, and all four heads bobbed at once. "Right," Quiz continued, "it's a bargain. Now, is this the house where Mister Rennick lives? The stonemason?"

"He's my da," piped up the smallest girl. "But he's not home right now."

"Do you know where he is?" asked Isaveth, but the girl shook her head.

"You can talk to my mum, though." She pushed between Quiz and Isaveth, ran up the steps, and shoved the door open. "Mummy! There's a boy and girl here to see you!"

"Please send them away," came a weak, unhappy-sounding voice from inside. "I don't want to buy anything."

"Missus Rennick," Quiz called back, "we're not peddlers. I have a message for your husband. About an important business matter."

His tone was courteous, but there was an authority in it Isaveth had never heard before. "Oh—oh, I see," said the woman, cowed. "Well, then, you'd . . . better come in."

Quiz stepped through the doorway, and Isaveth followed. Dim light revealed a staircase running up the wall to their left, and beside it a corridor so narrow that they had to walk in single file. A door to their right stood open, and there in a tiny parlor lay Missus Rennick, stretched out on the faded sofa with a blanket over her lap and pillows propped around her. Her skin was pale as watered milk, her cheeks sunken, and her hair so lank and thin that the scalp showed through.

"I'm sorry I can't get up," she said, with a wan smile.

Isaveth gripped the strap of her satchel, shaken. For months she'd tried to forget it, but toward the end her mother had looked just like this. She tried to speak, but her throat was dry, and words refused to come.

"You can give me the message if you like," Missus Rennick continued. "I'll see that Tomias gets it, whenever . . . when he comes home."

Quiz stood straighter at that, and Isaveth could tell he'd caught the woman's slip. She wasn't sure when to expect her husband, if he came home tonight at all. "I'm afraid I can't do that," he said in an apologetic tone. "The sender told me to give the message only to Mister Rennick, and that it was urgent. Do you know where we might find him?"

The woman wilted, her outstretched hand falling to her side. "I . . . I wish I could help. But he left early this morning, and he didn't tell me where he was going. If it was Duesday, you might try the club, but . . ."

A tingle ran up Isaveth's spine. Her guess about

Rennick had been right. But Quiz must have missed that particular clue, because he was scratching the back of his neck and looking puzzled. "I don't mean to be rude," he ventured after a moment, "but is Mister Rennick fond of drinking?"

"Oh, no!" The woman's heavy-lidded eyes flew open. "Tomias would never—well, he did drink once, but that was a long time ago. He hasn't touched a drop since I fell ill."

Suddenly Isaveth understood, or thought she did. Yet she had to be certain. Her eyes prickled and her chest felt sore, but she swallowed the pain and forced herself to speak.

"Mister Rennick sounds like my papa," she said. "When Mama was sick, he worked every job he could get his hands on, and all the extra money he made went to pay for medicines and the best healers he could find. He loved her too much to spend any of it on himself."

"Yes," whispered Missus Rennick with a smile that was pitifully sweet. "That's my Tomias. He'd do anything for me."

Chapter Eighteen

"SO MUCH FOR THAT," said Quiz as he and Isaveth left the tenement. "I thought we might find Rennick at his favorite watering hole, but if his wife says he's not a drinker . . ."

"No," said Isaveth, "but she as good as said he was a member of the Workers' Club."

"Are you sure? She mentioned a club, but there's plenty of—"

"She also mentioned Duesday. That's the day Papa always used to go." Isaveth wrapped her arms around her stomach, a fresh wave of grief surging over her. She'd imagined herself confronting Rennick the way Auradia stood up to the petty villains in the talkie-plays, all firmness and righteous anger, refusing to back down until she got the truth. But now that Isaveth had met Rennick's missus and little girl and heard all he'd done to provide for them, it was hard to see him as wholly corrupt.

"Well," said Quiz, rubbing his lower lip thoughtfully, "I suppose we could look for him at the next Workers' Club meeting. Not that it's likely to be Duesday, and it definitely won't be in the usual place, but there's bound to be a gathering somewhere."

"Even with the antidissenter law?"

Quiz gave a short laugh. "Especially with the law. They may lose a few members, but that'll only put more fire into the rest of 'em. It's not that easy to stop a revolution."

As they came down the steps, the urchins who'd been guarding the cycle jumped to attention. Quiz dropped a cit into each dirty palm, and they vanished like smoke. Only the Rennick girl remained, her hand stubbornly outstretched.

"I let you in to see Mummy," she said. "That's worth two."

"So it is," he agreed, and dug out an extra coin. She flashed him a gap-toothed grin and scampered back into the house.

"Are you all right?" Quiz asked Isaveth, holding the cycle steady for her. "You look a bit pale." He lowered his voice. "Was it Missus Rennick?"

Isaveth gave a wretched nod. She didn't have the words to untangle all the emotions inside her, but Quiz seemed to understand. He put a hand on her shoulder and left it there a moment. Then he swung himself onto the cycle in front of her and kicked off.

Such a small gesture, but it was enough. The ache in Isaveth's chest eased, and she slipped her arms around Quiz's waist as they pedaled away. "So how do we find the club?" she asked. "If their meetings are illegal, they're not exactly going to put up signs or give out leaflets on the street."

Quiz snorted. "I should say not. I bet I can find out from the Devaneys, though. Even if they don't have the answer, they can point me to somebody who does."

"Devaneys? Weren't they the brothers you—"

"Thumped for trying to pick your pocket, yes. But don't worry, we have an excellent relationship now. Built on mutual respect and understanding."

"The understanding that you'll thump them again if they don't respect you?"

"You make it sound so harsh," said Quiz in an injured tone, and Isaveth hid a smile against his spine. She leaned with him as they turned the corner, and they sped up the street toward home.

"I'll come back for you tomorrow," said Quiz, stopping in the coal-lane behind Isaveth's house. "Probably in the afternoon—it might take me that long to find out where the Workers' Club is meeting. Think you'll be able to get away from your sisters if you have to?"

Anna did most of her work in the early mornings, so she could look after Lilet and Mimmi if need be. "I'll be ready," said Isaveth, and turned to go.

"Wait." Quiz took off his cap and hung it on the steering bar, his expression serious. "I wasn't sure how to tell you," he said. "But you ought to know. The Lord Justice is back from Uropia."

Isaveth felt as though the air had turned to stone. She stood motionless, staring at nothing, until Quiz stepped forward and took her hands in his own.

"I know it's a shock," he said softly. "It rattled me when I found out too. We don't know he'll sign the truth-binding order, though. He may decide there's not enough evidence that Master Orien's murder was political. Or he might leave it up to your father to decide if he's willing to be truth-bound or not."

"But . . . why would Papa do that? If it's so—"

"As a sign of good faith. Besides, they're not allowed to shock him if he volunteers."

Would Papa take such a risk? Obviously he'd been unwilling at first, but now Isaveth feared he might. He must be as anxious about his daughters as they were about him, and the jail was a brutal place. Perhaps by now he was ready to take any bargain the Lawkeepers offered, just for the chance of convincing them they'd arrested the wrong man. . . .

Quiz was still holding her hands, lightly enough that Isaveth could pull free if she chose, but not so carelessly that she could mistake it for an oversight. His fingers were callused but surprisingly smooth, like a polished instrument or one of her father's finer chisels, and it was hard not to wonder what he did when he wasn't helping her. Was he a pickpocket, like the Devaneys? Was that how he'd got the cits he gave to Rennick's daughter and the other children?

Quickly Isaveth discarded the thought. If Quiz was a thief, he was surely the kind who only robbed people with plenty to spare. Never mind what trouble he'd got himself into the day he bolted off; all that mattered was that he'd come back.

"It's all right," Isaveth said gently, drawing her hands away. "I'm not going to faint, or cry, either. Thank you for telling me."

"I'm taking Lilet and Mimmi to the Relief Shop," Annagail called from the front door. "We'll be back in an hour or so."

Isaveth nodded, so absorbed in her writing that she forgot her sister couldn't see the gesture. Not until Anna repeated herself did she look around. "Oh—yes, that's fine. Have a good time."

"Bet she's writing a love story," said Lilet, and Mimmi giggled. The door shut, and the house was quiet once more.

Lilet's guess was more right than she knew, but Isaveth hadn't planned it that way. She'd spent the morning with her younger sisters, catching up on all the household chores she could bully or coax them into doing until Anna returned. Then, since Quiz hadn't turned up yet and she was restless to pass the time, Isaveth had started making a list of the clues they'd discovered so far, and all the people who might have been involved in Master Orien's murder.

It was possible, for instance, that Tomias Rennick had killed the governor for some reason she didn't understand yet, and questions about the cleaning maid Ellice's disappearance and her husband's untimely death still niggled at Isaveth's mind. Nonetheless, her thoughts kept going back to the first and most obvious suspect: Master Buldage.

Buldage had a clear motive, plenty of opportunity, and—if he was the same little man who'd accosted Isaveth

213

in the masters' lounge—a fiery enough temperament for murder. He'd been enraged to find her poking around the wardrobe, which hinted at a guilty conscience. What if his scheme to kill Orien with an affinity-charm and make it look like Common Magic had led him to Rennick, a builder desperate for money so he could care for his dying wife?

Perhaps Rennick had sold the exploding-tablets to Buldage without knowing why the master wanted them. Or perhaps Rennick *had* known but chose to go through with it anyway because he belonged to the Workers' Club and saw Master Orien as a threat to their cause. . . .

Yet Rennick had come to Governor Orien with the Sagelord's approval. And Meggery had hinted that Lord Arvis and Master Buldage weren't on friendly terms, so the Sagelord would hardly have recommended Rennick because Buldage had asked him to. Was there a connection between Rennick and the Sagelord that Isaveth didn't know about? Or had Lord Arvis simply taken one of his "strange tempers," as Meggery had called them, and decided that any builder who wasn't Moshite would do?

Isaveth mulled over the question until her head ached, but it brought her no closer to an answer. So at last she'd given up and started working on her latest Auradia story instead.

Otsik took Auradia's hands in his own strong brown ones, lamplight gleaming in the black pools of his eyes. To a stranger his face might have appeared impassive, but Auradia knew the peacemaker too well not to see that he was deeply moved.

"I am not a man of many words," he said in his deep, rich voice, "for often the greatest wisdom is found in silence. But now that I know the answer you gave Wil Avenham yesterday, I cannot be silent any longer." He lowered himself to one knee. "Auradia Champion, I have loved you since I met you. If you will not have him, will you have me?"

Auradia's face lit up with joy. She moved forward...

"Please tell me she's not going to kiss him," said Quiz, and Isaveth shoved back her chair so fast it nearly tipped over.

"What—how could—who let you in?" she gasped, clutching the page to her chest.

"Well, I knocked, but you didn't answer, and the door was unlocked, so . . ."

Isaveth's hands shook and her cheeks felt like she'd rubbed a fire-tablet on each one, but she kept her chin up as she tucked the story away in her writing box. "It's rude to look over people's shoulders," she said coldly.

"Sorry." Quiz had the grace to look sheepish. "I was only curious at first, but when I saw you were writing about Auradia, I couldn't help reading a bit. You write very well, you know."

If he'd been Su Amaraq, that sentence would have ended with "for your age." But there was no superiority in Quiz's tone, only admiration. The heat ebbed out of Isaveth's face, and she managed a smile. "Even if you think Auradia ought to marry Wil Avenham instead?"

"Oh, I don't mind that so much," Quiz said. "The real Auradia never married anyone, did she? So we're equally right. Or wrong." He leaned back on his heels and added wistfully, "I don't suppose you'll let me read it when you're done?"

Flattering as it was to be asked, Isaveth couldn't imagine trying to finish that particular story now. Every word she wrote, she'd imagine Quiz looking over her shoulder.

"What about the Workers' Club?" she asked, to change the subject. "Did you find out anything?"

"Cruel lady," said Quiz. "I shall go to my grave unsatisfied. But yes, I did. They're meeting tonight."

Though it was only one of many docks jutting out into Lake Colonia, Goodram's Wharf was instantly recognizable by its size and the enormous grain elevator behind it. Its great doors were shut now, the last shipload packed away and the workers sent home for the weekend, and at first the wharf appeared empty. But as Isaveth and Quiz crouched in the shadow of a packing crate, furtive shapes emerged from the side streets and alleys around them. One by one the members of the Workers' Club crept toward the side door of the elevator, murmured a few indistinct words, and slipped inside.

"How are we supposed to get in?" whispered Isaveth. "It sounds like there's a pass-phrase, and I don't know what it is. Do you?"

"No, curse it," muttered Quiz. "If the Devaneys knew, they didn't tell me. No wonder I didn't have to thump them to find out where the club was meeting—they're probably still sniggering about it."

Isaveth knelt down, tugging her satchel into her lap. If she crushed one of her dark-tablets, it would hide them, and perhaps then they could sneak up close enough to overhear. But would they still be able to see? There wasn't much point shrouding themselves in darkness if they ended up tripping over a pile of fish boxes or falling into the lake. . . .

Better not to risk it. There had to be something else. She was rummaging through the other tablets and decoctions she'd brought, wincing at every clink and rustle, when Quiz nudged her arm. "That girl looks familiar," he said, jerking his chin at the newest arrival stealing along the dockside. "But I can't think why. Do you know her?"

Isaveth peered into the half darkness. The flickering dock lights made everything uncertain, but even so, it took only a glance to be sure. Those wide shoulders and strong bones, the plait of yellow hair escaping from her kerchief . . .

Bitterness soured Isaveth's stomach, and she clenched her hands. She'd been rejected once already; did she really want to put herself through a second humiliation? But this might be their only chance to get into the grain elevator, and she couldn't let it pass. Isaveth set her satchel aside and climbed to her feet.

"Morra!" she whispered. "Over here!"

Chapter Nineteen

THE GIRL ON THE DOCKSIDE spun around. "Who's that?" she hissed.

Isaveth stepped out from behind the crate, hands spread to show she meant no harm. "It's me, Isaveth. I know you don't want to be friends anymore, but . . ."

Morra's jaw dropped. "Vettie! Thank the Sages!" And to Isaveth's astonishment, she rushed over and hugged her.

"I'm ever so sorry," she said in a rush. "I wanted to talk to you when the Lawkeepers took your da, but Mam wouldn't hear of it—she was that sure they'd be coming for us next. I knew it was no use fighting her, so I had to play along. I thought I'd catch you later and apologize, but you know how stubborn Mam is; she stuck to me like tree sap wherever I went. It was days before I got a chance to sneak over and rap on your door, and then nobody was at home."

Isaveth's resentment melted. It was true that since Papa's arrest she'd been out of the house more often than not. And with Morra's letter-blindness there was no way she could have left a note. Despite Isaveth's fears that the other girl had abandoned her, she really had done her best.

"It's all right," Isaveth said, hugging her back. "I'm just glad to know you tried. But what are you doing here?"

"I might ask the same," said Morra, cocking a hip and planting her fist on it. "Hanging about the harbor front at this late hour? I'm not afraid of a tussle, and I've got Seward watching for me, but who's looking out for a little slip like you?"

"I came with a friend." Isaveth nodded at Quiz, who rose and stepped out to join them. He doffed his cap to Morra.

"Pleasure to meet you," he said, and Morra gave the little snort that meant she was amused.

"I heard the Workers' Club was meeting here," Isaveth told her quickly, "but we don't know the pass-phrase to get in. Can you help?"

Morra frowned. "I don't know if that's a good idea, Vettie. It's bad enough for me, with Mam crying fit to drown because I wouldn't stay home once I found out Seward was going. But with the stew your pa's in over that dead noble, and everyone saying the Workers' Club put him up to it—"

"I know," said Isaveth, "that's why I'm here. I'm looking for someone who can help prove Papa didn't do it. Do you know a builder named Tomias Rennick? Lives down on Gentian Lane with a sick wife and a little girl?"

Morra considered this. "Don't think so. Though I'm new to the club myself, so that doesn't say much. I'll ask Seward after the meeting, if you like."

She started to move away, but Isaveth caught her arm. "Please, Morra. We won't cause trouble, I promise. Just give us the pass-phrase."

The older girl glanced back at the shadowy bulk of the grain elevator. "All right, but if anyone asks, it wasn't me who told you." She lowered her voice. "Once I've gone in, wait a few minutes and let a couple more folk go past. Then knock twice at the door and say, 'Mister Syme sends his regards.' That'll do it."

"Thank you, Morra," said Isaveth, squeezing her hand. "You're a true friend."

Morra's cheeks darkened in a blush. "Not as true as I ought to be. It's taken me this long to stand up to Mam, and no doubt she'll make me sorry for it. But I'm glad I could help. Good luck, Vettie."

* * *

Inside the grain elevator it was dim and dusty, with sacks of hop-grain and red maize piled up high on every side and a throng of rough-dressed workers packed into the center of the floor. Here and there someone had placed jars with flickering candles in them, cheaper than light-tablets and easier to snuff out; but instead of brightening the room, they only made its shadows darker and people's faces harder to see.

"It would help if we had any idea what Rennick looked like," Quiz whispered to Isaveth as they slipped into the back row of the crowd. "We should have asked his wife to describe him."

All around them groups of men and women were talking. They kept their voices low, but the tone of their murmurs and the gestures that went with them were anything but sedate. Isaveth's skin prickled with apprehension. She'd never been to any kind of political meeting before, especially not an illegal one.

What would happen if she introduced herself? Would the workers sympathize with her for Papa's sake and lend her the help she needed? Or would they notice her Moshite scarf, the dark hair and thick, straight brows that were so like his, and cast her out of their meeting in disgrace? They'd surely heard the rumor that the Workers' Club was behind Master Orien's murder. What if they, like Missus Caverly, decided that turning their backs on the Breck family was the only way to protect themselves?

Perhaps she'd better search for Rennick on her own. Isaveth stretched up on tiptoe and scanned the audience. Rennick was a stonemason, so his arms and shoulders must be well built; his sickly wife was young and their only child was small, so he probably wasn't much older than thirty; and Master Orien had described him to Papa as shifty looking. . . .

"Excuse me, miss," said a gravelly voice, and Isaveth dropped to her heels as a handsome, broad-shouldered man with deep brown skin thrust past her, striding to the front of the crowd. He stepped up onto the makeshift platform, which creaked beneath his weight, and raised his hands for silence.

"Brothers and sisters," he began, so quietly that everyone had to lean forward to hear. "We are here tonight in defiance of the Lawkeepers, against the will of the Sagelord and his council, and at the risk of our own safety and freedom. We are here because we care too much about the future of our city to be put off by unjust laws or slanderous rumors aimed at destroying us. We are here not to promote anarchy and bloodshed, as our enemies claim, but to declare the truth and fight for the justice Tarreton's citizens deserve!"

His last words cracked through the air, and the crowd jumped. But then heads began to nod all over, and approving murmurs rose around Isaveth as the speaker continued.

"The Sagelord and his noble friends call us dissenters. They say we are dangerous, because we are not content with their rule. They tell us we are not wise enough to know what is best for us and our children, especially in these hard times; they ask us to trust in their experience and have faith that their guidance will see us through. But I ask you, my friends"—he stretched out his hands to them, appealing—"what kind of wisdom have they shown us? Our children go hungry, our young men are jobless, our women toil in factories for a beggar's wage—while the nobles of Tarreton live in luxury, guzzling wine and gorging themselves on sweets!"

"That's right!" shouted a woman from the back of the room, and the crowd stirred restlessly as others took up the cry. The speaker let the clamor build a moment, then lifted a hand to quiet them again.

"And now they accuse us of conspiring to kill Governor Orien—of sending Urias Breck, one of our own members, to murder him. Why? Because they want to discredit the Workers' Club, defeat the Reps' Bill that would give us power, and turn our fellow citizens against our cause.

But we are neither murderers nor fools, and we had no reason to wish Master Orien harm. In fact, I have it on the very highest authority that before the governor died . . ." He paused, his dark eyes sweeping the room. "He was planning to join Eryx Lording and our other allies on the council and give the Reps' Bill his full support."

Isaveth's heart thumped against her ribs. She grabbed Quiz's arm. "Did you hear that?"

"I heard," said Quiz in a thick-sounding voice, as though he were trying not to sneeze. His eye looked red too; he must be sensitive to the dust. "That changes a few things, doesn't it?"

"It changes everything." Dazed, Isaveth backed away and sank down on a pile of grain bags. The speaker kept talking, but she was too distracted to listen. "If Orien planned to vote with the reps instead of against them, and the weaker nobles were likely to follow his lead . . ."

"Then that would give anyone who wanted to defeat the bill a motive for killing him." Quiz sat down beside her, his hands on his knees. "Which means we have a few more suspects than we thought."

Isaveth gave a shaky nod. It seemed almost certain now that Rennick had sold the exploding-tablets to some noble buyer, but which one?

"Although," Quiz continued slowly, "that's assuming

all the other nobles on the council knew about Orien's intentions. Are we sure they did? Because if I'd been handpicked for an important position by Lord Arvis, and I was planning to turn around and vote against him, I don't know that I'd want to go blabbing about it. At least not to anyone I wasn't absolutely sure was on the same side."

Isaveth looked sharply at him. "Are you saying . . . ?"

"I don't know," said Quiz, his expression as blank as his patch. "What do you think I'm saying?"

"That he was betrayed by someone he trusted. So either that person murdered him . . ."

"Or that person told someone else who did. Exactly."

Sickness burned Isaveth's throat. She'd thought Master Buldage had the best motive for killing the governor, but now it was clear she'd been overlooking the prime suspect all along. Someone powerful, wealthy, and used to getting his own way; someone who'd been counting on Orien to help him vote down the Reps' Bill, and who'd had every reason to feel offended—even threatened—by the governor's change of heart.

"The Sagelord," she whispered. "Lord Arvis killed him."

Chapter Twenty

QUIZ GAPED AT HER. "The Sagelord? That's not who I . . . where did you get that idea?"

Isaveth hugged her elbows, too overwhelmed and miserable to reply. If the Sagelord had murdered Master Orien—or hired someone else to kill him, which was more likely—what hope did they have of saving Papa? Lord Arvis might be unpopular with the common folk, but he was still the ruler of Tarreton, and both the Lord Justice and the Lawkeepers were under his command. No matter how much evidence she and Quiz found against him, it would take a lot more than one Moshite girl and a street-boy to bring him down.

A cold, bitter fury rose inside Isaveth. Now she understood why Papa had joined the Workers' Club, and why Morra wanted to join too. The Sagelord wasn't just incompetent, he was evil—and he'd abused his power too long.

"Isaveth?" Quiz asked urgently, but she ignored him. As the speaker climbed off the platform to the sounds of clapping and cheers, she got up and marched across the floor to join the others.

One of the older men broke out into a loud, defiant anthem, something about the workers' pride being unbroken and justice marching on. Other voices rose around him, and soon the whole crowd was swaying with their arms about one another's shoulders, singing.

Isaveth had taken her place at the back of the crowd and was humming along with the third verse when she caught a movement out of the corner of her eye. A young-ish man with a pinched face and a shock of red-brown hair was creeping through the shadows at the edge of the room, shoulders hunched as though trying to make himself smaller. No one else seemed to have noticed him, not even Quiz, but he was heading for the door.

He wasn't as muscular as Isaveth had expected, but she didn't dare waste time second-guessing. She darted after the stranger, and tugged his sleeve. "Tomias Rennick?"

The man whirled, his small eyes darting over her. His face looked gray in the half-light, and sweat glittered on his brow. "What do you want?"

"I need to ask you some questions," Isaveth said. "Do you think—"

She got no further, because at that moment Rennick's eyes focused on something behind her, and his face contorted into a mask of horror. He let out a yell, shoved Isaveth aside, and plunged out the door into the night.

"Come on!" shouted Quiz, sprinting past her. Isaveth reeled, dizzy with surprise, then picked herself up and raced after him.

The sky was black now, the wharf lit only by the dock lamps' sallow, wavering light. Isaveth's legs shook from the violent push Rennick had given her, but she did her best to keep up as Quiz pelted along the harbor front, dodging crates, nets, and coils of ship's rope as he went.

Ahead of them Rennick staggered through the darkness, moaning like a man in pain. For some reason the sight of Quiz had frightened him practically witless. But what could be so terrifying about a grubby-faced boy with an eyepatch?

Uncertainty flickered inside Isaveth. How much did she know about Quiz really? She'd accepted him into her life without much question because she was lonely and needed all the help she could get. When he'd disappeared, she'd been worried, but she hadn't pressed him to explain. Had she been too trusting? Might the life he'd lived before her, the things he'd done when they were apart, have been more sinister than she ever guessed?

After all, there *was* something suspicious about how readily Quiz had volunteered to help her investigate Master Orien's murder—not to mention how often he'd managed to come up with exactly the right contacts, tools, and information they needed to do it. And it was hard not to wonder at the reckless way he threw himself into danger, or his refusal to admit what had really happened to his eye.

Yet he'd fought Loyal Kercher for Isaveth's sake, and he loved *Auradia Champion, Lady Justice of Listerbroke* as much as she did, and she'd never have found the Workers' Club—or Tomias Rennick—without him. Quiz might not exactly be a messenger from the All-One, but he surely wasn't her enemy, either. Isaveth gritted her teeth, shoved her doubts to the back of her mind, and kept running.

They chased the fleeing stonemason past a row of warehouses, then up a narrow lane—which stopped, to Rennick's obvious alarm, at a dead end. He twisted about, glancing wildly in all directions, then snatched something from his pocket and brandished it.

"Don't come any closer!" he shouted. "Or I'll break it!"

Quiz skidded to a halt, flinging out an arm to stop Isaveth from running past him. "Rennick," he panted, "don't be a fool."

Isaveth stared at the small white object on the stone-mason's palm. The sputtering wharf lights made it hard to see clearly, but it looked factory made, with a round shape and the fading mark of a stamp. Still, it could have been a fire-tablet or even a sleeping-spell, for all she knew. Would Rennick really have come to a crowded gathering with explosives in his pocket?

"We only want to talk to you," Isaveth said in her most soothing voice. "About what happened to Master Orien. We don't mean any harm."

Rennick backed against the fence, trembling so hard the wood rattled. "I didn't know," he groaned. "I swear I didn't."

"You didn't realize that Orien was planning to vote with the reps instead of against them?" Isaveth asked. "You thought it would help the Workers' Club if he was out of the way?"

The young man nodded, his features sagging with misery.

"And you needed the money," said Quiz softly. "Because you'd already spent everything you had and more, trying to save your wife."

Rennick made no answer, but the tears dripping down his face said everything. He closed his hand around the tablet and bowed his head.

So that was why he'd crept out of the meeting tonight. He'd learned the truth about Master Orien's plans, and he'd been stricken with guilt and shame. But what part had he actually played in the murder?

"Tell us who hired you," Isaveth said, stepping closer. "Maybe we can help."

Rennick rubbed his eyes, as though seeing her clearly for the first time. His gaze dropped to the prayer scarf at her throat. "Moshite," he rasped. "You're Breck's daughter."

Until that moment, Isaveth had felt sorry for him. But when he spoke her father's name, there was no mistaking the loathing in his tone. "And you're the spy who betrayed him to the Lawkeepers," she said coldly. "Aren't you?"

A keening noise broke from Rennick, like the scream of a wounded rabbit. He flung the tablet—

"Isaveth!" Quiz shouted, and tackled her out of the way. They crashed into a stack of fishy-smelling pallets, which cascaded around them, burying them both.

For several seconds Isaveth lay gasping, crushed beneath Quiz's protective weight. Then she started to wriggle and push, but the street-boy didn't move. Was he unconscious? Please the All-One, let him not be dead!

Desperately she squirmed until she could turn over and shove the fallen pallets aside. Rennick had vanished: Either he'd bolted back down the alley, or he'd climbed the fence. The spell he'd thrown at her had disappeared among the shadows, but Isaveth was fairly sure it hadn't been an exploding-tablet anyway. She pulled her legs out from under Quiz and rolled him over, feeling his neck for a pulse.

He was alive. Isaveth let out the breath she'd been holding, then opened her satchel and rummaged for a light-tablet. She was unwrapping it when Quiz stirred and gave a feeble groan.

"Stay still," she ordered, laying a hand on his chest. "You might be hurt." She stuffed the neevil paper back into her satchel, then crushed the tablet in her hand.

Sunlight burst between her fingers, banishing the shadows and leaping up the walls on both sides. Quiz sprawled beside her, an ugly bump on his forehead. The fall had knocked off his cap and twisted his patch askew, and for the first time Isaveth could see his other eye. The closed lid showed little damage, but a red, puckered scar slanted across the socket, slashing from cheek to eyebrow like a cut from a whip—or a knife.

Gingerly Isaveth began to probe his skull for damage, but Quiz pushed her hand aside. He sat up and said thickly, "Where's Rennick?"

"Gone," said Isaveth. She hesitated, hand hovering over the open mouth of her satchel, then palmed another tablet and shut it again. Moving like an old woman, all stiff muscles and aching bones, she retrieved Quiz's cap from beneath the pile of fish boxes, tugged it into shape, and handed it back to him. "But we know where he lives, and that's probably where he's going, don't you think?"

"Maybe, but we can't be sure. And it's too dark to chase him all over the city." Quiz adjusted his patch, then carefully pulled the cap over his bruised forehead. "Ow."

"Does it hurt very much?" Isaveth asked. "I have a decoction that might soothe it." She paused, then added quietly, "Thank you. That was very brave."

"It was nothing," said Quiz gruffly. "I'm fine. Let's go."

"So," Isaveth began as the two of them walked back toward Goodram's Wharf. A breeze was gusting off the lake now, cool enough to make her shiver. "Do you have any idea why Rennick was so frightened of you?"

"Me?" Quiz said. "I haven't the slightest." But his shoulders hunched and his eyes slid away from hers as he spoke. Isaveth caught his arm.

"You've met Rennick before, haven't you? Why didn't you tell me?"

She expected anger, or at least another lie. But this time Quiz met her gaze without flinching. "I'd never seen him until tonight," he said. "I swear. Maybe he thought he recognized me from somewhere, but I'm not sure how."

"Not sure" was hardly the same as "haven't the slightest," but Isaveth let it pass. For a little while they walked in silence, and then she said, "You don't think I'm right about the Sagelord murdering Orien, do you? You think it was one of the other nobles who did it. Who?"

Quiz stared out at the lake. At last he said flatly, "It doesn't matter. You wouldn't believe me anyway."

Isaveth halted midstride. There was only one noble he could be talking about. "You aren't serious. You can't actually believe—"

"I told you, it doesn't matter!" He rounded on her. "Leave it, Isaveth."

She'd left the crumbs of her light-tablet behind in the lane, but not even the feeble glow of the dock lamps could disguise the hectic color in Quiz's cheeks. He was shaking all over, his lips twitching and his good eye glazed and unfocused. She'd never seen anyone look like that who wasn't ill . . . or insane.

"You really hate him, don't you?" she said, slow with disbelief. "Even though it makes no sense at all, you want Eryx Lording to be the murderer."

"I don't hate him." His voice was rough. "I just don't trust him. I don't think you should, either."

"Why shouldn't I? What possible reason could the Lording have to kill Orien? Even if he didn't know the governor was on his side, he's not stupid. Besides, if he was really so obsessed with making sure his Reps' Bill would go through, why didn't he kill the Sagelord instead?"

Quiz gave a cracked laugh. "How do you know he hasn't tried?"

Clearly it was no use arguing with him. It might not even be safe when he was in this mood. Isaveth inhaled slowly to calm her nerves and started walking again.

Quiz followed in sullen silence, and for a little while the only sounds were the distant clang of a ship's bell and the waves lapping against the harbor wall below. Then Quiz seized Isaveth's arm, wrenching her to a stop.

Half angry, half alarmed by the strength of his grip, she tried to pull away. But he only held her tighter. "Wait," he said curtly. "Listen."

Isaveth stood still, and now she could hear it: a muffled pop and crackle, like wheels rolling over crushed stone. She was glancing about, wondering where it might be coming from, when the square black front of a spell-wagon nosed out of the lane ahead of them.

Quiz dashed behind the base of a loading crane, drag-ging Isaveth with him. As they crouched in the shadows, the back of the wagon swung open and a swarm of dark-clad Lawkeepers poured out onto the dockside. They fanned out around the wharf, sleep-wands and clouters at the ready, then advanced with silent purpose toward the grain elevator.

Isaveth started to rise, but Quiz held her back. "Don't. There's nothing we can do."

"How can you say that?" Furiously she pried at his fingers. "Morra's in there, and her brother. I have to warn them!"

"It's too late for that. And we're not going to help anyone by getting arrested." He glanced in the opposite direction. "We have to get out of here."

"But the pedalcycle—"

"We can come back for it later. Come on!"

Keeping low, he darted off toward the warehouses. Isaveth backed after him, her gaze on the grain elevator. The Keepers had reached the door, and the officer in the lead was pouring something over its hinges. He nodded to one of his companions, and with a single powerful kick the bigger man smashed it down. Light erupted from inside as the Lawkeepers stormed in, and shouts of terror echoed through the night.

Until this moment Isaveth had dared to hope that Auradia's principles of justice and compassion had not been wholly forgotten, and that the Lawkeepers of Tarreton were only doing their best to keep the peace. No doubt there were cruel and heartless officers among them; she might even have been unlucky enough to meet one or two herself. Still, surely they were more the exception than the rule?

But as she watched one worker after another being dragged out of the elevator, women shrieking and young men begging for mercy as the clouters struck again and again, Isaveth could feel nothing but horror. These people were unarmed, and most of them weren't even attempting to fight. Yet the Lawkeepers were treating them like wild animals who had to be beaten into submission.

"Isaveth!" hissed Quiz from the shadows. "Get out of there!" She'd frozen in the middle of the dockside, and the light was shining full upon her. With a sob, Isaveth turned and fled.

A shout from the wharf warned her she'd been spotted, but she didn't dare look back. She dashed between two rows of shipping containers, then veered behind them to plunge up the dark, fishy-smelling lane beyond.

It was wet here, and she nearly fell as her broken-down shoes skidded on the cobbles. The light above her flickered and went out, and suddenly Isaveth could see nothing at all. She flailed at the blackness until her hand hit wood, and she let out a yelp as a splinter jabbed her skin. She could have sworn Quiz had run this way, but she must have been mistaken—and now she was trapped.

Panicked, Isaveth groped along the fence one way, then the other. The Lawkeepers' boot steps pounded after her, and their light-beams sliced the dark . . .

A hand shot out of nowhere, grabbing Isaveth's wrist and dragging her around the fence to safety. She had only a second to gasp her thanks before Quiz took off running again, and she had to follow.

They burst out of the dark mouth of the lane into the dazzling moonlight of the railway yard. Dodging among the shipping cars, they hopped the tracks and climbed a stony embankment to the street beyond.

"I think we've lost them," panted Quiz. "Are you all right?"

Isaveth put her hands on her knees and bent double, partly to get her breath back but mostly to hide the tears that blinded her eyes. By now Morra and her brother would be crammed into the back of that spell-wagon with the rest of the Workers' Club, and who knew what would become of them after this?

"I'm sorry," Quiz said softly. "But there was no way you could have warned them in time."

Now that she'd seen the brutal efficiency of the

Lawkeepers, Isaveth couldn't deny it. Still, she felt ashamed of herself for running away. How must it have looked when she and Quiz bolted out of the meeting, only to have the Lawkeepers turn up a few minutes later? Yet when she said as much to Quiz, he shook his head.

"I doubt they'll blame us, especially since Rennick left the meeting before we did. I'm pretty sure he's been selling out the Workers' Club for a while now—that's probably why the murderer approached him in the first place. He was only there tonight because he didn't want the other workers to get suspicious." Quiz put an arm around Isaveth's shoulders. "Come on. We'd better get you home."

Chapter Twenty-One

A HUNDRED YEARS AGO Harbor Street had been a fashionable thoroughfare, but now it was one of the grimiest parts of Tarreton, with broken sidewalks, rusty lampposts, and rubbish clogging the gutters on both sides. Every third storefront stood vacant, with boards nailed across the windows in a feeble attempt to keep squatters from breaking in, and even the ink-parlors and baccy-shops had closed for the night. The only lit windows in the neighborhood belonged to a tavern, whose faded and creaking sign read THE SAILOR'S KNOT.

As Quiz and Isaveth passed the tavern, a roar rose from inside, followed by a tinkling crash. They both jumped back as a man in dockworker's slicks reeled out of the tavern, one hand clapped to his bleeding scalp, and stumbled off down the street. A second man burst out after him, yelling and waving a broken bottle, while the other patrons crowded eagerly into the doorway to watch the fight.

Alarmed, Isaveth started to cross to the other side of the road, but Quiz caught her. "Better not," he muttered. "Too dark over there. Just walk faster."

They passed one junction and then another, glancing nervously in all directions for signs of danger or pursuit. The next block held a few more lit buildings, their windows unmarked except for the occasional pair of gauzy red curtains or a battered playing card tucked into one corner, but none of them looked any safer or more welcoming than the tavern. The smell of stale beer and baccy-smoke hung heavy here, mingled with an odor of rotting fish, and Isaveth had to pinch her nose and cover her mouth tight to keep from retching.

"Not much farther now," Quiz said, taking her other hand. "Once we get to Long Street . . ." All at once he stopped, his fingers clenching around hers.

"What is it?" Isaveth asked, but Quiz didn't answer. He was staring at the next junction, where a lone spell-carriage, its lamps muted to a dull yellow, sat by the opposite curb. The rain top was closed and its windows were tinted dark, so there was no way to tell whether the car was occupied. But it was the wrong shape for a taxi.

"Keepers?" Isaveth whispered, but Quiz shook his

head. He turned, gazing back the way they'd come. And at that moment, as though by magic, a broad-chested man in coveralls materialized from the shadows and strode toward them.

"Run!" yelled Quiz, and the two of them dashed for the corner. But every step took them nearer to the darkened carriage, and Isaveth prayed fervently that it might be empty. She had no idea who was chasing them, but she'd never seen Quiz look so frightened.

Then came the cough of a spell-engine sparking to life, and with a squeal of tires the carriage pulled out from the curb and veered to block the road before them. A second man leaped out, leaner but no shorter than the first, and planted himself on the sidewalk in their path.

There was no escape. All the shops on this side of the street were closed, and the alley to their right was piled high with rubbish. Isaveth dug frantically in her satchel, searching for a spell, but it was so dark she couldn't tell which of her tablets was which.

"Get out of here," said Quiz rapidly as the men closed in. "Don't worry about me, I can sort this. Go."

"I can't leave you—"

"Yes you can!" He tore off his cap, his face white and desperate. "Isaveth, please!"

The men lunged. Isaveth ducked, unwrapped the first

spell-tablet she could find, and hurled it to the pavement at their feet.

Magic billowed up, plunging them all into a blinding fog of shadow. One of the men cursed and swiped at her, but he missed. Isaveth backed up hastily, groping sideways along the wall until the blackness frayed and she could see again. Her dark-spell wouldn't confuse the men for long, but if it bought Quiz even a few seconds to escape . . .

A flash of green lit the darkness, and her spell vanished. The lean man shoved a slim wand back into his pocket, while the bigger one seized Quiz by the collar and hauled him toward the carriage. He kicked and struggled with all the strength in his slim body, but his captor was twice his weight, and he opened the door and tossed Quiz into the backseat as though he weighed no more than a sack of feathers.

Quiz's street-boy cap lay crumpled on the sidewalk. Frantic, Isaveth raced to snatch it up. She had only an instant to fling it after him before the carriage door slammed shut. Then, without so much as a glance at Isaveth, the two men climbed into the front and drove away.

Isaveth watched the spell-carriage until it disappeared, her heart thumping painfully in her chest. Then her knees gave out and she crumpled onto the sidewalk, exhausted.

Quiz had been kidnapped, and Morra arrested. Isaveth had no way to contact Anna and no money for a cab. Which left her alone and friendless in one of the worst parts of Tarreton, with nothing more than a satchel of homemade spells to protect herself.

Tears pressed at her eyelids, but Isaveth gritted her teeth until they went away. Frightened though she was, she had no time for self-pity—there were too many people counting on her. She had to put her terror aside and *think*.

What would Auradia do? Something brave, no doubt, because Auradia was always courageous. She'd also deal with the most immediate problem first and go where she could do the most good.

Where was that? Not home, to be sure. Isaveth's sisters might be worried about her, but they were safe enough. There was no point chasing Rennick, either: Now that he knew she was Urias Breck's daughter, he'd never tell her anything.

But if she could get back to Goodram's Wharf, she'd find Quiz's pedalcycle . . . and if the spell-tablet she'd slipped into his cap worked, she'd soon find him as well.

Isaveth rummaged through her spells and tucked a

couple into the pocket of her skirt so they'd be ready if she needed them. Then she got up, slung her satchel across her shoulder, and started back toward the harbor.

By the time Isaveth reached Goodram's Wharf, the grain elevator was dark, with no sign of the Lawkeepers anywhere. Fortunately, Quiz's cycle was still propped behind the crates where they'd left it. She wheeled it out onto the dockside and climbed on.

It had been a long time since Isaveth had driven a pedalcycle, and at first her progress was wobbly. But the cycle worked well despite its battered appearance, and soon Isaveth felt confident enough to urge it to full speed. She pedaled up the hill to Fore Street and turned east, following the route Quiz's captors had driven some twenty minutes ago.

Her journey began smoothly enough, especially once she'd passed the last few blocks of squalor and entered the open, brightly lit area of the power factory complex beyond. There was little traffic at this hour, so she could ride straight down the middle of the street, and the light-tablet she clutched against the steering bar made it easy to see her way. Soon, however, she'd traveled as far as her memory could take her. She stopped the cycle at the next junction and pulled out her little bottle of Mother's Helper.

Even as she'd packed it with her other defensive spells, she'd doubted she'd have the need—let alone the chance—to use it. But Quiz had behaved so oddly tonight, especially after she suggested the Sagelord was behind Master Orien's murder, that Isaveth had no longer felt comfortable not knowing what he was up to. Which was why she'd taken the chance to slip the source-tablet into Quiz's cap while he lay half-conscious on the dockside . . . though she'd never imagined she'd have to use the tracking-spell so soon.

Isaveth uncorked the decoction and raised it toward the light, watching the purple liquid closely. For a few seconds nothing happened, and she feared Quiz might be too far away. But at last the potion's grainy depths stirred, and the particles drifted to the left side of the bottle.

North, then. Isaveth tucked the potion into her satchel, jumped back onto the cycle, and pedaled doggedly up Council Street, toward the heart of the city.

Chapter Twenty-Two

TRACKING QUIZ through the streets of Tarreton was a maddeningly slow process, since Isaveth had to check the decoction every few minutes to make sure she was going in the right direction. She cycled past factories and warehouses, the great gray bulk of Sage Johram's Hospital, and parks full of wandering homeless looking for a place to spend the night. She swerved to the edge of the road as a late tram rattled by, then back into the middle to avoid the ranks of milk wagons outside the City Dairy. By the time Isaveth passed the massive Arcan Temple with its glittering spire, every muscle in her legs ached and she felt she couldn't pedal one street more. But with every junction the particles in her bottle moved more sluggishly, and she feared that if she paused to rest even for a moment, the spell would stop working altogether.

Soon the road narrowed, winding lazily into smooth-cobbled bends, and the factories and office buildings receded as gated mansions and walled gardens took their place. Even the streetlamps had a decorative look to them, slender trunks of iron dangling light-globes like ripe, tempting fruit. She had reached Rollingdale, the wealthiest neighborhood in the city.

Only days ago Isaveth had envied Lady Marcham her house and garden, and dreamed of one day living in such a place. Now, as she rode past one sprawling estate after another, with their twinkling rows of lit windows and gleaming spell-carriages parked along the drive, that ambition seemed positively modest. Here lived the true nobility of Tarreton, the families that had held power for generations. And this, Isaveth now felt sure, was where Quiz's captors had taken him.

The road branched, and Isaveth stopped to consult her decoction. The particles moved eagerly now, as though sensing their spell-tablet counterpart was near—though this time the grains drifted back the way Isaveth had come. She retraced her route to a brass gate flanked by towering maples, where a cobbled drive wound between banks of ornamental shrubbery. There, in the distance, stood the most magnificent house Isaveth had ever seen.

It was two stories high and ten windows wide, pearl

white and pillar fronted, with a glittering crystal of a conservatory on one side and a handsome three-door carriage house at the other. By its front steps rose a fountain like an enormous fancy-cake, iced with falling water and tinted rosy gold by a ring of underwater lights. It was so beautiful it took Isaveth's breath away—but it also made her horribly thirsty.

Whoever lived here must not have much fear of intruders, because the gates were open and she could see no guard. Licking her dry lips, Isaveth wheeled the pedalcycle inside the grounds and parked it in the shadows of an enormous fairy bush, where it couldn't be seen from either the drive or the roadway. Then she crouched and sneaked across the lawn toward the carriage house.

One of the bays stood open, light slanting out onto the drive. As Isaveth crept closer, she spotted one of the men who'd kidnapped Quiz—only now his rough coveralls were gone, replaced by the brass-buttoned coat and peaked cap of a personal driver. With leisurely confidence he paced about the carriage, pausing here and there to buff a headlamp or wipe a smudge from its gleaming side. It was the same vehicle she'd seen speeding away with Quiz—but the rain top was scrolled back, and the backseat lay empty.

It was just as Isaveth feared: Quiz had been kidnapped on the orders of someone in this house. But surely, if Master Orien's killer wanted to keep them from getting to the truth, the sensible thing would have been to abduct Isaveth as well?

Unless this wasn't about the murder investigation. Could it have something to do with the "boggy hole" of trouble that had kept Quiz away for two days? Had he been secretly spying for some powerful noble all along and made the mistake of disappointing him?

Well, whatever the answer, Isaveth wouldn't find it lurking in the shrubbery. She had to get inside that house. Isaveth waited with growing impatience until the driver finished his polishing and closed the bay door behind him. Then she darted behind the carriage house and peered around the corner, waiting for the driver to come out.

But though she watched the side door for what seemed ages, it never opened. Either there was some powerful Sagery going on here and the man had magically transported himself to the house, or—more likely—there was another exit. Isaveth sent up a quick prayer for safety, then tiptoed down the stone path to the door.

The handle felt stiff, and she feared it might be locked. But when she squeezed harder, the latch clicked open.

Silent as a shadow, Isaveth slipped through and shut the door behind her.

The darkness inside the carriage house was absolute. Step by cautious step Isaveth felt her way toward the back wall—until, without warning, her right foot dropped into emptiness. She would have plunged headlong if she hadn't caught herself in time.

That decided her. Risky or not, she had to make a light. Still shaky from her near-fall, Isaveth fished the remnants of her light-tablet out of its wrapping and squeezed the crumbs in her palm. The magic was almost exhausted, but its faint glow was enough to reveal what lay at her feet—a stairwell leading to a tunnel whose gray walls and exposed pipes reminded her of the basement of Founders' Hall.

There was an underground passage between the mansion and the carriage house. Isaveth had never imagined such luxury, but it wasn't hard to guess its purpose: so the nobles who lived here could easily get to their vehicles in bad weather. Was this the way the men had taken Quiz as well? Raising her luminous palm, Isaveth searched the walls and floor of the tunnel for signs of struggle. But she found no scuff marks, nor even a grimy handprint.

Perhaps they'd threatened Quiz with a weapon, so

that he'd had no choice but to go quietly. Or else they'd knocked him out with a sleep-wand and carried him in. Treading softly in her worn shoes, Isaveth followed the passage to its end, then up another set of steps to ground level.

The landing held two identical doors set at right angles, which puzzled Isaveth at first, until she realized that one must lead to the servants' wing and the other to the main part of the house. Judging by the noises coming from the left-hand door—a distant clatter that sounded like someone dropping a tray, followed by two female voices raised in furious quarrel—she'd be safer trying the other one. She eased it open, scanned the semidarkness on the other side, then slipped through.

She found herself in a handsomely tiled passage with a staircase slanting down from the ceiling on her left, and a spacious foyer spreading out beyond. Isaveth edged along the side of the staircase, past the end of its curving banister, and peeked out at the archways that flanked the house's front entrance. One opened onto a parlor, though the curtains were closed and its spell-lamps turned so low that she could only guess at its opulence. The other revealed an equally darkened library. Neither room held Quiz, tied to a chair or otherwise. Indeed, there was no sign of anyone in this part of the house at all.

So far Isaveth had been fortunate, but she reminded herself not to get overconfident. If she was caught sneaking about a noble's house, there was no telling what he might do to her. Pulse beating in her throat, Isaveth darted across the brightly lit foyer to the corridor on the other side.

The first door she found was mostly glass, but so thickly etched and frosted that even when Isaveth pressed her face against it, she could make out only shadows. She could hear no sound from inside, which made it tempting to move on. But what if Quiz had been gagged silent or knocked out, and she walked past him without knowing it? Gathering courage, Isaveth turned the handle.

She found herself in a gaming room, surrounded by dark wood paneling and tables for everything from Gamble to Crock-in-the-Hole. There was a lingering aroma of baccy. An enormous drinks cabinet stretched the length of the wall beside her, while at the opposite end of the room a fireplace gave off its wavering light. Two leather armchairs faced away from her, so broad and high-backed that at first Isaveth thought them empty—until she spotted the hand draped over the arm of the right-hand chair, and the signet ring glittering upon it.

Fear iced through Isaveth, freezing her in her tracks.

For a few dreadful seconds she stood motionless, gaze locked on the drooping hand. Then a snore rose from the depths of the armchair, and for the first time Isaveth noticed the empty wine bottle lying on the floor.

Her terror melted away. He'd drunk himself into a stupor and wouldn't notice Isaveth if she did a stomp-dance on top of the card table. Curiosity prodded her, and she tiptoed over to study the sleeping man.

Heavy jowls, a florid nose, and a flap of thinning gray hair. One look was all Isaveth needed to be certain: She was in the presence of the Sagelord of Tarreton himself.

But did that mean he was Orien's killer, or Quiz's master, or both?

Whatever the answer, she'd better get out of here quickly. Eyes fixed on the snoring Lord Arvis, Isaveth backed away, turned—and bumped straight into the broad, uniformed chest of a personal guard. She was staring at his buttons, too shocked to cry out, when something cold poked her neck and the room furled up like a black umbrella, taking her consciousness with it.

Isaveth woke slumped in an armchair in a gentleman's study she'd never seen before, with Tarreton-blue curtains and silver wallpaper patterned in the latest geometric style. Plush carpet spread beneath her feet, and the tea-table in front of her was polished to mirror sheen—like the enormous tray that sat upon it, close enough to touch. She rubbed her eyes and sat up, half convinced she was dreaming.

Yet the tray remained, laden with a steaming silver teapot and matching service, three gold-rimmed cups and saucers, and a plate of cakes and sandwiches as tempting as anything at Lady Marcham's garden party. And there was no one else in sight.

Isaveth's mouth felt dry as a tomb, and her stomach groaned with hunger. Yet she couldn't start eating without even trying to escape. She rose and tugged at the door.

Unsurprisingly, it was locked. The study window was not, but the wall outside was a smooth expanse of plaster with a stone pavement two stories below; she'd never get out that way. If she'd still had her satchel of spells, she might have created a diversion, but the big guard had taken it.

Isaveth pressed her palms to the glass, gazing hopelessly out into the night. Then she drew the curtains, walked back to the tea tray, and helped herself to a sandwich. After all, if her host had wanted her dead, he'd have killed her already, and if he wanted her unconscious, he only needed to poke her with the sleep-wand again. So it seemed unlikely the food would do her any harm.

She'd finished off half the plate and started on her second cup of tea when the door opened and Quiz stumbled in, blond hair flopping over his eyepatch, and his clothes even more ragged than usual. He looked like he'd wakened from a nightmare—or a double dose of the sleep-wand, more likely—and when he saw Isaveth, he turned a delicate shade of green.

"No," he breathed, and rounded on the guard standing behind him. "Let her go! It's a mistake—she's got nothing to do with this!"

The guard didn't argue, only stepped sideways and took up a position by the door. Isaveth studied the man's blunt, square-boned face, then set her teacup down and rose. She was beginning to think she understood what was going on, even if she wasn't sure about the reason—and so she was barely surprised at all when the door opened for the second time and Eryx Lording walked in.

"Good evening," he said mildly. He gave his hat to the guard, then crossed the room to the desk and peeled off his leather driving gloves. "Sorry to have kept you waiting, but I was out this evening and only learned of your arrival a few minutes ago. Please . . ." He gestured to the armchairs that flanked the table. "Sit down."

"Our *arrival*." Quiz spat the word with venom. "Is that

what you call sending your thugs to accost us and drag us halfway across the city? I'm not interested in playing word games, Eryx. Whatever punishment you think I deserve, that's one thing. But Isaveth's done nothing wrong. Let her go."

"Actually," said Eryx, "according to Hulton, she broke into the house, snooped all around the downstairs looking for you, and nearly woke Father from one of his refreshing naps. But I'm not inclined to hold that against her." He flashed Isaveth a smile. "How was she to know you were never really in danger, let alone that you were coming h—"

He never finished the sentence. Isaveth barely had time to realize Quiz was moving before the street-boy grabbed Eryx by the throat.

Eryx staggered back, clawing at the younger boy's grip. "Hulton!" he wheezed, but the big guard was already in motion. One hand hauled Quiz off the Lording, while the other ripped the sleep-wand from his belt.

"No!" Quiz howled, writhing like a garden snake. "Isaveth, don't let him . . ." Then he crumpled, and the guard scooped him up and carried him out of the room.

"I apologize," said Eryx hoarsely once the door had shut. He smoothed his hair, straightened his collar, and walked to the tea tray. "I'd hoped to avoid any unpleasantness. But Esmond can be . . . difficult, sometimes."

Isaveth felt light-headed, her mind reeling from one shock after another. She said feebly, "Esmond?"

"He didn't tell you. I'm sorry. I should have realized." Eryx poured a cup of tea and sipped it, wincing as he swallowed. "The boy who was here just now is Esmond Lilord. My younger brother."

Chapter Twenty-Three

ISAVETH GAZED AT THE LORDING, speechless. She backed up to the armchair and sank into it.

"I don't . . . ," she faltered, then swallowed and tried again. "But he doesn't . . ."

"Look like me?" asked Eryx. "Not especially, no. He looked like a smaller and not very flattering copy of our father until he turned thirteen. Then he shot up like a puff-weed, and now he looks like Mother and Civilla. I'm the odd man out in this family, I'm afraid. Take after my uncle Calvius instead."

Isaveth pressed her fingers against her eyes, appalled by her own stupidity. She'd seen the Lilord slumped between his siblings at last year's Harvest Parade and thought him ugly, fat, and self-centered. She'd never imagined a boy's appearance could change so dramatically in a matter of months, or that the sulky expression he'd worn that day might not be typical.

But blind as she'd been not to notice the straight nose and high forehead he shared with Eryx, or the similar quirk in their smiles, the next thought hit Isaveth even harder: Quiz had been lying to her from the start.

"I know this must come as a shock," said Eryx, hooking a leg over the corner of the desk and sitting down across from her. "You must be a very good friend to him, to have followed him all this way. I'm only sorry Hulton didn't tell you straight off why he'd come to fetch Esmond, and save you the trouble."

Isaveth looked up sharply. "He didn't *fetch* him," she said. "He and that other man—the driver—grabbed him and dragged him away."

Eryx sighed. "I'm afraid they had no choice. Esmond would never have gone with them willingly. Especially not if he was with you."

"I don't understand."

The Lording studied his polished shoes. When he raised his head again, his expression was both apologetic and grave. "We don't talk about private matters outside the family," he said, "so I must ask you to keep this in the strictest confidence. But since you seem close to Esmond, and you've shown such concern for his welfare, you ought to know that my brother is . . . unwell."

Isaveth's heart beat faster. "What do you mean?" she asked.

"His troubles began last year, when he started growing." Eryx rose and began to pace the room, hands clasped behind his tailored jacket. "He complained of headaches, and blurred vision in one eye."

I've got a beast of a headache, Quiz had told her only a few days ago. *It happens sometimes.* Isaveth sat motionless, waiting for Eryx to go on.

"Naturally, my parents took him to the best healers in the city, but after months of treatment Esmond was no better. He became moody, suspicious, even violent at times, and the pain grew so intense that one day he . . . injured himself, trying to relieve the pressure. The surgeon did his best to save the eye, but he's been blind on that side ever since."

Isaveth's nails dug into her palms. "Did it help?" she whispered. "Even a little?"

"With the pain, yes," said the Lording. "But not his condition. He began to experience hallucinations, delusions, gaps in his memory . . . sometimes he seemed to forget he had a family, while other times he was convinced we were all trying to kill him, or one another. Then he started disappearing for hours, even days, at a time. Yet he always came home in the end, so we did our best to be patient. My mother couldn't bear to have him locked up, you see. None of us could."

"You must have tried to find him, though," said Isaveth, and Eryx nodded sadly.

"Of course. But we were looking for the Lilord of Tarreton, not a street-boy. We had no idea that his delusions had gone so far. It wasn't until a few days ago, when he turned up at Master Orien's memorial in an eye-patch and ragged trousers, that I put the pieces together. I sent Hulton and our driver out to search for him, and, well . . . you know the rest."

It was like looking at the past two weeks through a warped mirror. Or perhaps it was Isaveth's vision that had been distorted, and only now was she beginning to see Quiz clearly at last. Hadn't she wondered about his odd whims and reckless impulses, his mysterious past, his hostility toward the Lording from the first time she'd spoken Eryx's name?

Though he wasn't completely mad; he could still be clever, and funny, and kind. Delusional or not, there must have been moments when Quiz knew who he really was. Yet he'd allowed Isaveth to go on believing they were more alike than different, that he'd been cold and hungry as often as she had, and that he understood how frustrating it was to be a commoner in a city where nobles held all the power. Worse, he'd pretended he was helping Isaveth out of friendship, when he'd had his own secret motives all along. . . .

Eryx lowered himself into the chair behind the desk, bracing his elbows on the arms and steepling his fingertips together. "You're the young lady who was selling spell-tablets in the city a couple of weeks ago, aren't you?" He spoke in a soft, wondering tone, as though he'd only just made the connection. "Was that how you met my brother?"

Isaveth still had the handkerchief Eryx had given her, tucked away in the box that held her mother's lake-pearl necklace and the few other personal treasures she possessed. He'd been kind to her that day, and tonight had been no different: He'd given her a generous tea, apologized for the distress his men had caused, and now was talking to Isaveth so frankly she might have been his equal. Quiz had begged her not to confide in Eryx. But there seemed no reason to hold back now.

"Yes," she said, then added in a rush, "He thinks you killed Master Orien."

Eryx recoiled. "What? Why?"

"I don't know. Except Quiz—I mean, Esmond said whoever murdered the governor used Sagery as well as Common Magic, so we thought there must be a noble involved somewhere."

"And of all the nobles in the city, he suspected me." Eryx rubbed a hand across his eyes. "But Master Orien was my tutor as well as Esmond's, and I considered him . . . well, like a father. So when he told me he planned to support my Reps' Bill, I was overjoyed. I never dreamed anyone would . . ." He shook his head. "I still can't believe he's gone."

He sounded so bewildered, and so sad, that Isaveth's heart went out to him. If he'd played any part in the murder, it could only have been by accident. "Did you tell anyone what Master Orien was planning?" she asked. "Your father, maybe?"

Eryx's eyes flew open. "Great Sages, no! That would have been an unforgivable breach of trust. I did confide in two of our allies on the council, with Orien's permission— Lady Marcham and Lord Amaraq. But I assure you, they're both above reproach."

Isaveth bowed her head, despair welling inside her. She'd been so sure that finding Quiz would lead her to the murderer as well. But she'd pedaled across the city for nothing, and she was no closer to saving Papa than before.

"I didn't realize you felt so keenly about politics," said Eryx, leaning forward to peer into her face. "Unless . . . I hope you're not so terribly disappointed that I'm not a murderer?"

And that was so *Quiz* of him, despite the tailored suit and the two-reel-hero looks, that Isaveth couldn't bear it. She covered her face with her hands, and burst into hiccuping sobs. An awkward few seconds later Eryx offered her a handkerchief, which she took gratefully, but he didn't try to interrupt. Not until she had wept herself dry and slumped from sheer exhaustion did the Lording clear his throat and speak.

"Clearly there's something going on here that I don't understand," he said. "Would you do me the honor of taking me into your confidence? I might be able to help."

Isaveth was so tired she could barely think, and there was a cold lump of misery in her chest that had Quiz's fingerprints all over it. Except he wasn't Quiz at all, he was Esmond—and Esmond was insane. If the Lording didn't help her now, who would?

"It's my papa," she said. "I'm Urias Breck's daughter, and I've been trying to prove that he's innocent."

As Isaveth poured out her story, the Lording's expression alternated between astonishment and concern. When she finished, he let out a little laugh of admiration.

"I knew you must be brave and clever, to have tracked Esmond all the way here on your own," he said. "But

I'd no idea how extraordinary you are. You and my mad brother made a better job of investigating Master Orien's death than the Lawkeepers and the news-rags put together. Certainly you've learned more than I ever could."

"Then you believe me?" asked Isaveth, trembling with hope. "You can help Papa?"

Eryx's face sobered. "I wish I could," he said. "Master Buldage was never one of my favorite teachers at the college, and I wouldn't put it past him to murder someone. He undoubtedly had the skill to make an affinity-charm, and enough wits to manipulate this man—Remick? Sorry, Rennick—into helping him." He sighed. "But I'm afraid it's not so simple. I know the Healer-General personally, you see, and he gave me a copy of Master Orien's post-mortem. He found no evidence that anything but Common Magic was involved."

"But what about—"

"The silver Esmond found on his robe? The examiner noticed that too and put it to all the usual tests. It was nothing more than a melted waistcoat button."

Isaveth's stomach turned over. The stain on Orien's robe was the one clue she'd never doubted, or even thought to question. Yet she'd only believed it was charm-silver because Quiz had told her so. . . .

And now she knew with sickening certainty that she could never trust Quiz's word again.

"It does seem as though Mister Rennick was involved in the murder somehow," the Lording continued, rising from his chair. "I'll talk to the Lawkeepers tomorrow and urge them to bring him in for questioning. Still, given the evidence we have . . . I'm afraid it's hard to imagine how anyone but your father could have done it."

Isaveth's heart cried out in protest, but she had no strength left to give it a voice. She twisted Eryx's handkerchief between her hands and breathed slowly so she wouldn't cry again.

"You're welcome to look over the Healer-General's report, if you like," Eryx continued, opening a cabinet in the corner and taking out a large envelope. "It's a bit gruesome in parts, but quite comprehensive. Perhaps by the time you've finished, Esmond will have calmed down enough for you to say good-bye."

Esmond. Even the sound of that name was enough to make Isaveth's stomach clench. She knew she ought to pity Quiz, or at least be willing to forgive. But she'd believed in him, trusted him, and he'd failed her.

And now Eryx Lording, the shining hope of the city, the one who was supposed to bring justice to poor folk like herself, had failed her too.

"No, thank you," said Isaveth. Her voice sounded small, but if she spoke any louder, she'd end up screaming. "I don't want to talk to him. I just want to go home."

Once the Lording's driver had let Isaveth off at the top of Cabbage Street, she ran home as fast as her weary legs would carry her. She'd barely made it inside when Annagail flew out of the kitchen and seized her in a desperate hug.

"Thank the All-One," she gasped. "I was so worried, Vettie. Where have you *been*?"

There were at least five answers to that question, and Isaveth didn't want to talk about any of them. She pulled away from her sister and sat down on the stair. "I can't explain," she said wretchedly. "Not right now, Anna. Please."

"But . . ." Annagail hovered next to her, wringing her hands. "You're all right? You're not hurt?"

Oh, she was hurt. Every thought of Quiz brought a fresh stab of grief and anger, and for the first time since her father was arrested, a tiny part of Isaveth feared he might actually have done it. What if Rennick and Papa had plotted Master Orien's death together, as fellow stoneworkers and members of the Workers' Club? What if Rennick had panicked at the sight of Quiz because he'd

269

recognized him as Esmond Lilord and feared the Lording and a troop of Lawkeepers wouldn't be far behind?

But then Isaveth remembered the way Rennick had stared at her prayer scarf, the loathing in his voice when he spoke her father's name. He'd never work with a Moshite. And though it seemed impossible to prove otherwise, deep down Isaveth knew Papa would never take part in a murder plot, either.

"No, I'm not hurt at all," she said with as much conviction as she could muster. "I'm sorry I was late. It won't happen again."

Annagail dropped onto the step beside Isaveth and turned her face against the banister. She made no sound, but it took Isaveth only an instant to realize her sister was weeping. "Anna! What is it?"

"I had a message . . . from the Lawkeepers . . . this evening," gasped Annagail. "The Lord Justice asked Papa . . . if he was willing to be truth-bound . . . and he . . ."

She broke off, sobbing, while Isaveth waited in an agony of suspense. A moment ago she'd been exhausted, but now she'd never felt so wide awake.

"What?" she asked, clutching her sister's arm. "What did Papa say?"

"He . . . said no. And I . . ." Annagail sniffed and wiped her eyes. "I don't understand, Vettie."

Isaveth exhaled a grateful, silent prayer. "I do," she said, and went on to tell her sister everything she knew about truth-binding. When she had finished, Annagail looked as relieved as Isaveth felt.

"I had no idea it was so horrible," she said. "I thought if he agreed, they'd know he was innocent, and I couldn't imagine why he'd rather go to trial than speak the truth."

"Go to trial?" Isaveth sat up straighter. "They've fixed a date, then? When is it?"

Annagail brushed a knuckle across her cheekbone, wiping away the last of her tears. "It starts on Duesday. And oh, Vettie, I know it could be dangerous, but . . . I think I ought to go."

Three days from now. That left Isaveth only two days to find Master Orien's murderer—and one of them was Templeday, when the trams stopped running and every business in the city was closed. Unless the Lawkeepers found Rennick quickly and forced him to confess, there was no chance of stopping her father's trial before it started. And once it began, Isaveth couldn't testify, or even sit in the audience, because children weren't permitted in court.

Of course Anna had to be there for Papa. She was the only one who could.

Chapter Twenty-Four

ISAVETH WOKE THE NEXT MORNING feeling like she'd been drugged—or knocked out with a sleep-wand, which was probably more accurate. She sat up, knuckling the crumbs from her eyes. The little room was flooded with sunlight, and both the mattress next to her and the bed across from it lay bare. Somehow her sisters had got up and sneaked off to temple without waking her.

Which meant Anna had gone with them. And judging by the emptiness of the bedpost, she'd taken Mama's prayer scarf as well. Isaveth didn't know whether that was a good sign or not, but her brain was too foggy to think about it. She clambered out of bed and went downstairs to have breakfast.

Once she'd eaten the porridge Annagail had left for her and bathed last night's grime from her body, Isaveth felt better. But when she remembered her conversation with the Lording, the old hopelessness came flooding back. What could she do now? Without spare money for taxis to take her around the city, she was limited to the few places she could reach on foot. Besides, Eryx had forgotten to give back her satchel, so she didn't even have any spells left to protect herself.

She couldn't bear to leave Papa's fate in the hands of the Lawkeepers, especially after what she'd seen at Goodram's Wharf last night. But what choice did she have? Everything she'd learned about Master Orien's death had been cast into doubt, if not disproved altogether. And Quiz, with his bright mind and quicksilver tongue, his knowledge of Sagery and city politics, and his surprising talent (not so surprising now) for getting people to give him whatever he wanted, had vanished like a dream.

The thought of trying to prove Papa's innocence in just two days, with no one to help her and no evidence to support her claim, seemed so impossible that Isaveth was tempted to give up and admit defeat. But how could she? There had to be something she could do to help Papa, someone else she could talk to who might take an interest in his case. . . .

Su Amaraq! She'd told Isaveth to get in touch if she had any news to share. She'd also boasted that the *Trumpeter* had a reputation for telling the truth even when the other news-rags didn't. What if Isaveth offered Su a first-person account of the events at Goodram's Wharf in exchange for help investigating Papa's case?

Isaveth was halfway to the door before she realized her plan had two flaws. First, it was Templeday, so the *Trumpeter* office would be closed. Second, and far more fatal, were the names of the people Eryx Lording had told about Master Orien's plan to support the Reps' Bill: Lady Marcham . . . and Lord Amaraq.

Whether the latter was Su's father, grandfather, or uncle, Isaveth couldn't tell. But as long as there was a chance Lord Amaraq had played a part in Master Orien's murder, there was also a chance that Su was protecting him.

Yet whom else could she turn to? Whom, in all this great city, could she trust?

Isaveth was still brooding over the problem as she rinsed and scrubbed the dress she'd worn last night, then headed outside to hang it on the line. Preoccupied, she scarcely noticed the shadow on the far side of the fence, until a hoarse voice whispered, "Isaveth!"

Isaveth dropped the clothespin, and caught the dress just in time. "Morra! I thought you'd been arrested!"

The older girl gave a wan smile. "I can't talk long," she said. "Mam's that upset just now. But yes, the Keepers took me and Seward like all the rest. Only, the cells at the station were full, so they shoved us girls and a few of the younger lads into a little room and kept us under guard for half the night. Then they let us go with a warning."

No wonder Morra looked so exhausted. "What about your brother?" asked Isaveth. "Did they release him too?"

"Not yet, but we're hoping." Morra sighed. "Fear there's not much chance for Alban and the other leaders, though. They'll end up in Dern Valley, like as not."

"So that's the end of the Workers' Club," murmured Isaveth, but Morra shook her head with a vigor that took her by surprise.

"We're not giving up," she said. "It may look bad for us right now, but we've still got allies on the council, and the Reps' Bill isn't defeated yet."

"It isn't? When's the vote?"

"Tomorrow night. We may have lost Master Orien, Sages comfort him. But we've still got the Lording on our side."

Once, any mention of Eryx would have made Isaveth's stomach tingle with excitement. Now she felt nothing but a dull ache. "Of course," she said, trying to echo Morra's confidence. "Anyway, I'm glad you're home now. I'm only sorry I was off chasing Rennick and didn't get back to the wharf until it was too late."

"That's right! I'd forgotten all that, what with everything else going on." Morra clutched the top of the fence. "Did you catch him? What did he say?"

She sounded so eager, Isaveth felt a flicker of hope. Perhaps she wasn't alone after all. "We did," she began, "but—"

The Caverlys' back door crashed open, and Missus Caverly stalked onto the step. "You get inside this minute!" she snapped at Morra. "Haven't you brought enough grief on this family already?"

Morra turned crimson, and her mouth opened as though to snap back. But no words came out, and after a few seconds she deflated.

"Sorry, Mam," she mumbled. Then she turned away from Isaveth and slunk into the house.

On Mendday morning Annagail went to work at the college—bare necked as usual, but she hadn't returned the prayer scarf to Isaveth, either. She seemed calmer now, as though she'd let go of the doubts and worries that had been troubling her. Isaveth could only wish she felt half so confident.

"Is Quiz coming today?" Mimmi asked as the three younger sisters left the house. "I want another ride on his cycle."

Isaveth had been dreading this moment, but she knew it had to come sometime. She started to explain that Quiz had left the city, never to return. But then she spotted Loyal Kercher glowering at her from his front step, his sneer even more malicious than usual, and thought better of it.

"I'm sure he'll be back soon," she said, loud enough for Loyal to hear. The last thing she needed was for him to get cocky in Quiz's absence. "Now you two hurry off to Aunt Sal's. I've got some errands to run."

That much, at least, wasn't a lie. Annagail had given Isaveth a little money to buy groceries and other essentials—including the morning edition of the *Trumpeter*, which they hoped would tell them more about Papa's case. A brisk walk brought Isaveth to the local market, where she paid five cits for the paper, practically snatched it from the grocer's hand, and sat down at once to read it.

The leading story was indeed about Papa's trial, but to Isaveth's disappointment, it told her nothing that she didn't already know. She was about to turn the page when another headline caught her eye.

HEXTER BULDAGE APPOINTED GOVERNOR.

Her gaze drifted to the picture below, which showed the master standing at the entrance to Founders' Hall, holding his wand of office and looking modestly smug about his good fortune. It was much as Isaveth had expected, except for one detail.

Buldage had the wrong face.

Instead of the little bearded master who'd been so angry to find Isaveth looking at the wardrobe, this was his tall, gray-eyed companion, the one who seemed to have nothing to hide. In fact, he'd even opened the wardrobe door so she could look in. Isaveth stared at the new governor's picture, her heart sinking lower with every beat.

She'd jumped to the wrong conclusion. Again.

With a rush of anger Isaveth slapped the news-rag closed, but then a thought struck her. Shouldn't there be something about the incident at Goodram's Wharf? She opened the paper and scanned it until she spotted a small article in the local section.

DISSENTERS' RALLY ENDS IN ARRESTS.

It described how the Lawkeepers had broken up an illegal political meeting on Fastday night and taken its leaders into custody. But within a few lines it became obvious that the writer was reporting only one side of the story, because the arrested men and women were described as criminals with a history of violent and lawless behavior, and there was a vivid account of how the Lawkeepers had been "forced" to use shields and clouters against the "angry mob" who rushed to attack them.

Disgusted, Isaveth wadded up the *Trumpeter* and shoved it down the side of her basket. Anna could look at it later, but Isaveth never wanted to read that lying rag again.

When she returned to Cabbage Street, Loyal Kercher was lounging on his steps again, as though he hadn't moved since she left. But there was something odd about his expression: not surly as before, but gloating and even triumphant. Still, Isaveth had too much else on her mind to bother about it—until she got inside and found Mimmi huddled at the foot of the staircase, weeping.

"What happened?" Isaveth dropped to her knees and seized her little sister by the shoulders. "Where's Lilet?"

Mimmi hiccuped. "At Aunt Sal's. Only, Pem wanted to play dollies, so I ran home to fetch mine, and on the way . . ." Tears welled up again, streaking her dirty face. "Loyal to-o-ok my sho-o-oes."

"What?" Isaveth was appalled. Loyal might be a bully, but she'd never known him to attack someone as young as Mimmi. Much less steal something he had no use for. "Why?"

"He said . . . he said . . ." Mimmi sniffed hard. "I didn't . . . deserve them. Because Papa was . . . a murderer and you were . . . a dirty, tale-bearing . . ." She gulped. "I can't say it."

"You don't have to," Isaveth replied, hugging her. "Never mind, Mim. I'll make him give them back." Even if she wasn't sure how, and was more than a little afraid to try.

"You can't," Mimmi said miserably. "It's too late."

"What do you mean?"

"I begged him to give them back. I begged a lot." Mimmi wiped her eyes with the hem of her skirt. "I said I'd tell his mama. But he just laughed and told me to go ahead. Then he threw the shoes to his . . . his dog . . . and Bruiser . . . *ate* them. . . ." She hugged her knees to her chest, sobbing harder than ever.

Isaveth sat back slowly, staring at Mimmi. Then without a word she got up, walked straight out the door, and planted herself outside the Kerchers' cottage.

"Loyal!" she shouted.

He swaggered to meet her, his smirk more taunting than ever. "Bet you're sorry now," he said.

"Sorry for what?" demanded Isaveth, and he scoffed.

"Like you don't know. You thought you were clever, didn't you? Trying to get our relief cut off, all 'cause you were jealous we had a crystal set and you didn't. Guess you figured you could sit there and laugh while we were starving." His lips twitched into a snarl. "Well, it didn't work. And now we're onto you, Moshie girl. We'll teach you not to muck with us."

The anger drained out of Isaveth, leaving her chilled all over. "What are you talking about? I never—"

The cottage door banged, and Missus Kercher came flapping down the steps in her lounge-robe, like a great white bat. "You've some nerve, young miss," she rasped, jabbing a finger at Isaveth. "You'd think a girl in your place should know better than to spite her neighbors, but by all the Sages, you're going to regret it."

"I don't know what you mean!" Isaveth burst out. "I never told anyone about your crystal set!"

"Ha! Don't think you can play the innocent." Missus Kercher folded her arms, the curl of her lips even uglier than Loyal's. "I caught your boyfriend with the patch peeping in my window, sure as daylight. And my Loyal says you've been running wild all over the city with him, causing no end of trouble. You ought to be ashamed of yourself!"

Esmond again. And to think she'd believed he couldn't hurt her any worse than he had already. But he'd ruined every part of her life without even knowing it.

"You're wrong," Isaveth said hoarsely. "I would never." Then, as Loyal stepped menacingly toward her, she turned and ran.

Dinner in the Breck household that evening was even more subdued than usual. Annagail was so distraught she forgot to say the blessing, and no one had the heart to remind her; Lilet kept muttering darkly and glaring at her plate; and Mimmi was still sniffling over her lost shoes— which Loyal had tossed onto the front step only an hour ago, chewed to sodden ribbons that no amount of box-board or binding twine could repair. And since Annagail had thrown out the old pair, Mimmi now had nothing to wear on her feet at all.

"Stupid Kerchers," Lilet spat, and Mimmi burst into tears and dropped her bread on the floor. Isaveth picked it up and scraped it clean, then went to fetch more mus-tard for her.

"Hating people doesn't solve anything," said Annagail, but she sounded tired and less than convinced herself. "I'll go back to the Relief Shop tomorrow . . ."

She stopped, looking stricken, and Isaveth knew why: Papa's trial started tomorrow, so Anna wouldn't have time to go anywhere.

"I'll go," Isaveth said quickly. "First thing in the morning."

"But the Kerchers are stupid," insisted Lilet. "If they were worried about losing their relief, why didn't they spend the money Merit sent them a little bit at a time, instead of wasting it all on some fancy crystal set? You'd think they *wanted* to get caught."

"Merit, sending money?" Annagail frowned. "What are you talking about?"

Lilet looked at Isaveth, who admitted, "Well, I don't know for sure it was Merit. But where else could the money have come from? It's not like anyone else in the Kercher family has a job right now."

"Neither does Merit."

"What do you mean? Of course he does. He's working on the railway to Vesperia." Or at least that was what Loyal had told everyone when his brother left. And he'd sounded so smug about it, he surely couldn't have been pretending.

Annagail shook her head. "That's only what Merit told Loyal because he didn't want to hurt him. He was hoping to find work somewhere, eventually, but . . ."

"You mean he's a rail rider?" Isaveth exclaimed, and Annagail lowered her eyes.

"He didn't have a choice," she said softly. "There was nothing for him here."

Isaveth regarded her sister in amazement. She'd

thought Papa was only being silly when he teased Anna about Merit Kercher, but their father had been more perceptive than she'd ever guessed. "How do you know all this?" she asked. "Has he been writing you letters?"

"Only a couple," said Annagail, blushing. "I . . . I gave him a postage-mark and some paper when he left, you see. So I'd know he was all right."

Lilet scowled at her. "Traitor."

"Enough, Lilet," Isaveth warned, and turned back to Annagail. "But if Merit isn't sending money home to his family . . . where are they getting it from?"

There was a long silence while the girls looked at one another. Then:

"I told you," Lilet said defiantly. "The Kerchers are dirty spies."

Chapter Twenty-Five

REPS' BILL STRUCK DOWN IN COUNCIL.

It was the first headline Isaveth read when she opened her copy of the *Citizen* on Duesday. She'd gone to the Relief Shop as promised, and managed to find Mimmi a pair of ugly old slip-shoes that were broken down at the heel. Even those had cost most of her money, so the cheaper news-rag was all she could afford.

> **"Naturally, I'm disappointed," Eryx Lording told reporters after the vote. "But political change takes time. I still believe that one day my fellow lords and ladies will recognize the importance of equal representation for all of Tarreton's citizens, and until that day comes, I will continue to defend the rights of the common people as faithfully as I can."**

So that was that. The Workers' Club had lost, and Master Orien's murderer—whoever he was—had won. Despite Morra's optimism, despite all the letters and the speeches and the prayers, the ordinary folk of Tarreton were still at the mercy of their nobles. And though the Lording spoke confidently about a better future, there seemed no end to the city's troubles in sight.

The *Citizen* gave no news of Papa, either, except for a brief reminder that his trial would begin this morning. But Eryx had promised to have the Lawkeepers bring Tomias Rennick in for questioning—shouldn't there be something in the news-rags about that?

Isaveth scanned the local articles, looking for some hint that Rennick had been taken into custody, but she found nothing. Disheartened, she closed the paper and put it away.

When Annagail came home that night, she looked weary, but she had little to tell about the afternoon she'd spent in court.

"The adversary presented his case against Papa," she said shortly when Lilet and Mimmi pressed her for details. "And the Lord Justice asked him some questions. Papa won't get to defend himself until tomorrow, so nothing's been decided yet."

Only later, after the younger girls had gone to sleep, did Anna tell Isaveth the rest of the story. The court had heard testimony from several witnesses, including the cleaning maid who'd found Governor Orien's body (so she hadn't vanished after all, thought Isaveth) and the Healer-General, who'd examined him. The lawyer acting as adversary had also read statements from two unnamed informants who'd appeared before the Lord Justice in private, confirming that Papa had been a member of the Workers' Club and was known to hold a grudge against Orien.

"It shouldn't be allowed," said Annagail, gripping her teacup so tightly Isaveth feared it would crack. "People testifying without showing their faces, or even giving their names. How can Papa defend himself if he doesn't know who's accusing him?"

Isaveth felt the same way, but the Lord Justice had the right to accept private testimony if he chose, so there was nothing they could do. Still, it wasn't hard to guess who the anonymous witnesses must be.

"Rennick," she said bitterly. "And Mister Kercher, as likely as not. Oh, why are people so horrible?"

"Because we're Moshites." Anna spoke with quiet conviction. "But we can't give in to them, Vettie. We can't let them frighten us away." She took a deep breath. "I'm going to wear Mama's prayer scarf in court tomorrow. Not for me, but for Papa. You understand, don't you?"

Dread clutched at Isaveth, and she nearly begged her sister to reconsider. Papa had never paid much attention to the All-One or the teachings of Moshiel, so what difference would a prayer scarf make to him?

But then she realized that no matter how risky the gesture, Annagail was right. By putting on her prayer scarf where everyone could see it, Anna wouldn't only be affirming her own faith; she'd be reminding Papa of their mother's love, and the memories they cherished as a family. And she'd be showing that she was proud to be Urias Breck's daughter, too.

Until now Isaveth had believed, and she'd nearly convinced Anna as well, that their only hope of escaping poverty was to keep their Moshite heritage a secret. That might still be true, but maybe some things were worth suffering for. Isaveth set down her teacup and laid her hand over her sister's.

"Yes," she said. "I understand."

The next day was Papa's defense, and the wait for news was so agonizing that Isaveth could think of little else. She prayed that their father would be a good advocate for himself, that he'd have the wits and the courage to stand up to the adversary and convince the Lord Justice he was innocent. But when Isaveth met Annagail at the tram stop that night, one look at her sister's face told her those hopes had been vain.

Once Anna had stopped weeping long enough to describe what had happened, it was even worse than Isaveth had feared: Papa stammering out his argument before a pitiless adversary and a skeptical Lord Justice, with no witnesses and no evidence to support him. The best he could do was insist he'd had no motive to kill Orien, since the governor had offered him a job. But the Lord Justice dismissed the statement because Papa had no proof Orien had ever made such an offer.

At that point Papa begged the court to summon the messenger Orien had sent to find him, insisting the boy could confirm his story. But the Lawkeeper-General testified that his officers had visited every message service in the city, and none of them employed a boy with an eyepatch. . . .

"Quiz," Isaveth gasped, and clapped both hands to her mouth, afraid she might be sick. If she'd ever been tempted to pity Esmond Lilord, she could never forgive him now.

"I know." Annagail put an arm around her. "That's how I felt too. Where is he, Vettie? Why didn't he come?"

Isaveth knew the answer, but she couldn't say it. It would only destroy what little hope they had left. She leaned her head wearily against her sister's, and the two of them walked home.

By Trustday afternoon the tension in the Breck house was unbearable, with Lilet stomping up and down the stairs every few minutes, while Mimmi clung to Isaveth like a teary-eyed shadow. At last, in desperation, Isaveth dug out the copies of the *Trumpeter* and *Citizen* she'd bought earlier that week and gave her sisters each a section to read.

"We're going on a word hunt," she said. "The first one to find the word 'horse' wins. Go!"

Lilet muttered something about baby games, and at first Mimmi accepted her pages only with reluctance. But by the third round they'd risen to the challenge and started calling out new words for each other to find. Grateful for the distraction, Isaveth was playing along with them—the word this time was "healer"—when Mimmi jumped to her feet.

"I found it!" she exclaimed, thrusting her section at Isaveth. "Right here, see?"

She was pointing to a death notice in the *Citizen* that described the deceased woman as a former healer at

Sage Johram's Hospital. Isaveth was about to hand back the pages and declare Mimmi the winner of the round when her gaze fell to the entry below:

> **Tomias Arton RENNICK, twenty-eight years of age, found hanged in the grain elevator of Goodram's Distillery early Mendday morning. Death was evidently by his own hand, although he left no note. He is survived by a wife and one daughter. Memorial gifts and condolences may be left for the family at Fourways Unifying Temple.**

The paper tumbled from Isaveth's nerveless fingers, rustling to the floor. No note meant no confession, and no Rennick meant no hope of ever getting one. No way to tell what part the young stonemason had played in Master Orien's murder, no chance of finding out who'd paid him to do it. Isaveth stared past the bewildered Mimmi, too stunned even to cry.

She'd failed. They'd lost. It was over.

BRECK FOUND GUILTY IN GOVERNOR'S MURDER, blared the Fastday edition of the *Trumpeter*, while the smaller heading beneath read, BUILDER SENTENCED TO HANG. Yet the paper wasn't the only bad news Annagail brought when she returned from work that morning.

"Mister Jespers was in the court the other day," she said quietly to Isaveth as they sat together on the back step. Neither one of them had wept for Papa yet; the grief inside them went too deep for tears. "I didn't tell you because I thought he might not have noticed me, and I was praying he wouldn't say anything to Meggery. But . . ." She drew a shaky breath. "He did. I was cleaning the masters' lounge today when she came up to me and asked if I was Moshite."

There was no need to wonder how that conversation had gone, or how it had ended. "Did she say anything about Papa?"

"No. But I think she suspected. She was . . . I'd never seen Meggery so upset. She told me to leave the college straightaway." She twisted her prayer scarf between her hands. Then her eyes welled up and she whispered, "Oh, Vettie, what's going to become of us now?"

Isaveth had no answer. There were too many possibilities, each one bleaker than the last. And she still had to break the news to Lilet and Mimmi.

There was no supper that night, because no one could bear to eat. Mimmi shut herself in the bedroom and before long had sobbed herself to sleep. Lilet stormed out to the garden and threw herself into weeding, ripping up the scrub-grass and false mustard so savagely that Annagail had to rush to keep her from uprooting all their herbs and vegetables as well.

Isaveth sat down in the empty silence of Papa's room and tried to write, but there were no words for what she was feeling. She crumpled up the scrap of paper and flung it into the wastebasket, then flopped onto the side of the bed that had been her mother's and lay motionless, staring out at the darkening sky. Before long the exhaustion of her grief overcame her, and she closed her eyes.

She was halfway through a muddled dream in which Aunt Sal was scolding her for painting Mimmi's shoes purple when the chords of a familiar theme song tugged her awake. Isaveth sat up, dragging a hand across her eyes, as the voice of the narrator took over:

"Last time, our heroine was racing to warn Peacemaker Otsik of a plot against his life—only to be waylaid by a mob of clouter-wielding dissenters! Will she make it to the embassy in time? Find out on this episode of *Auradia Champion, Lady Justice of*—"

The sentence cut off abruptly as Isaveth slammed the window shut. She burrowed beneath the covers, dragged a pillow over her head, and huddled there until the sound of the Kerchers' crystal set died away.

* * *

Tap, tap.

Isaveth turned her head restlessly against the mattress, flinching as her cheek hit the damp patch where she'd cried herself to sleep. The room was completely dark, except for one dim stripe between the curtains.

"Anna?" she mumbled, but there was no answer. She climbed out of bed, padded to the door, and opened it.

No shadow on the landing, no footsteps on the stair. And when she looked in the bedroom she usually shared with her sisters, all three of them were crammed together in one bed, fast asleep.

Tap, tap, tap.

The sound was coming from the room she'd just left. Something—or someone—was at Papa's window. Isaveth pressed her back to the doorframe, swallowing fear. Was it a hungry redcoon? A burglar? Or perhaps Loyal, climbing up under cover of night to torment her?

Tap, tap went the noise again, and then a frantic hiss, "Isaveth!"

Relief washed over her. She ran to Papa's window, flung the curtains wide—and there he was, crouched like a pale spider on the outer sill.

Quiz had come back.

Chapter Twenty-Six

BUT NO, THE BOY outside the window wasn't Quiz; he couldn't be. Because Quiz had a patch over his right eye and a thin, slanting scar beneath it. While this boy wore nothing on his face but a round lens in a wire half frame, and the blue eye behind it showed no trace of injury at all.

"Isaveth, please." His voice came low, muffled by the glass between them. "Let me in. Give me a chance to explain."

He wasn't dressed like Quiz, either. His bare head shone white gold in the moonlight, and though he'd rolled up his shirtsleeves like a workman, his waistcoat and trousers looked new. Wild speculations raced through Isaveth's mind—what if Quiz and Esmond were identical twins separated at birth, and one of them had gone to live in the Sagelord's house while the other had been raised by commoners? Perhaps they'd met by accident a few months ago, and they'd been switching identities ever since. . . .

No, that was ridiculous, like the plot of a bad talkie-play. But if there was any chance that she'd been mistaken about Quiz—or Esmond—Isaveth needed to know. She heaved the window open, then backed up quickly as he folded himself through.

"Phew!" he gasped. "That was no fun at all." He pried something off the bottom of one shoe heel and dropped it into his pocket, then straightened and gave Isaveth an apologetic smile.

"I'm sorry I couldn't come before," he said. "I tried, but Eryx caught me."

Isaveth knew who he was then, and that there had never been more than one of him. The sheepish expression was so Quiz it hurt her, but the cultured cadences of his voice could only belong to Esmond, Lilord of Tarreton.

"You shouldn't have come," Isaveth told him, edging around the far side of the bed. She reached for Papa's lamp, but it was empty.

"Allow me," said Esmond politely, drawing an engraved charm-case from his waistcoat. He opened it, tweezed out a thin square of silver, and murmured three words she couldn't hear before snapping the charm in half and tossing the pieces onto the mattress between them.

At once the room lit up—not with the sunny brightness of one of Isaveth's tablets, but with a subtler, blue-tinged radiance that gave them just enough light to see each other. Esmond tugged the curtains shut and turned back to Isaveth.

"I'm sorry I didn't tell you who I was," he said, "and I'm even more sorry about your father. I would have testified at his trial if I could, but Eryx burned my patch and street clothes, and this is the first chance I've had to get away."

He didn't sound insane. He didn't even look ill. Isaveth gripped the bedpost to steady herself, no longer knowing what to believe. "You were Master Orien's message boy," she said, unable to keep the accusation from her voice. "You never told me that, either."

Esmond lowered his eyes. "I know I should have. I would have, if I'd thought it would matter. But I couldn't . . . I didn't know how to talk about him at first, and then it was easier to go on pretending he was a stranger than explain. He was the reason I became Quiz in the first place, you see."

A little of Isaveth's anger ebbed away. "He was? Why?"

"He wanted to know what was happening in the city.

He didn't trust the *Trumpeter* and the other news-rags to give him the real story. So I offered to disguise myself and sleuth around a bit, and . . . well, it became a regular thing."

"But if he asked you to find Papa for him, you must have seen him on the day of the murder," said Isaveth. "So why wasn't your name in the secretary's book?"

"Oh, I never came to the college as Quiz. There were too many people there who would recognize me, and he didn't want anyone to know we were working together. So we mostly talked by charm-band."

Isaveth knew little about Sagery, but she understood the concept of charm-bands well enough. They came in pairs and could only be used to communicate with whoever had the matching half of the set—like Auradia sending one of her secret messages to Wil Avenham, or the guard calling in from the Dern Valley gatehouse. They were rumored to be expensive and extremely difficult to make, but that would surely have been no obstacle to a skilled Sage like Master Orien.

"You must have been close to him, then," she said. "If he trusted you that much."

Esmond breathed in and said, not quite steadily, "Very."

A few heartbeats passed in silence while they gazed at each other. Then Isaveth walked around the bed to stand in front of him, an arm's length away. "You didn't think I would trust you, though. Not if I knew who you were."

"Well," Esmond said, "would you?"

It was a fair question. Oh, Isaveth would surely have been grateful for his help at first, the same way she'd been grateful when the Lording slipped that money-note into her handkerchief. But she'd always have felt awkward around Esmond, conscious of her inferior position and her inability to repay him in kind. She certainly wouldn't have dared to boss him about, or tease him—in fact, just thinking about some of the things she'd said to Quiz brought a surge of blood to her cheeks.

"See?" said Esmond. "I knew it would never work. And I couldn't tell you the truth about my eye, either, because you were all swoony over Eryx—"

"I was not!" Isaveth protested, and then it struck her. "What about Eryx?"

In answer Esmond reached up and unhooked the half glass. Wearing it, he'd looked like a healthy young noble with somewhat old-fashioned taste in eyewear. Without it . . .

"Oh, Quiz," whispered Isaveth. He did have a scar after all—and a blind, milky cloud where his pupil should be.

"The glass is illusion-charmed," said Esmond, putting the lens back in place and blinking both eyes at her to show how perfectly they matched. "Father had Master Orien make it for me, so no one would know what Eryx did."

Isaveth sat down on the corner of the bed, stunned. "He did that to you? When? And *why*?"

"Last harvest, a couple of weeks before the parade." He sat next to her, his hands on his knees. "He'd asked me to join him for fencing practice, but really he wanted to coax me into one of his schemes. I said no, and he . . . well, I suppose he wanted to teach me a lesson."

He touched his scar—it was strange to watch the tip of his finger vanish behind the glass. "Father was livid, of course, and Mother had hysterics. But Eryx swore on his life it was an accident. In the end even Civilla believed him, and she usually knows better. So they decided to cover it up, and I had to play along."

No wonder he'd looked so miserable during the parade, trapped in the carriage next to Eryx. Yet it seemed impossible that the Lording could be so wicked; it was almost easier to go on believing Esmond was mad. Isaveth stared at the rug, her insides churning with bitterness, reluctant sympathy, and a small, gnawing worm of doubt.

But doubt of whom? Of Eryx, of Esmond, or only of herself?

"I don't blame you for being angry," Esmond said

quietly when the silence became uncomfortable. "I would be too. But I never meant to hurt you, Isaveth."

Isaveth said nothing. What difference did it make what he'd wanted, when he'd ended up hurting her anyway?

"At first I felt guilty for crashing into you when I was running away from Eryx, and it seemed only right to try and make it up to you somehow. And since we both wanted to find out who'd really killed Master Orien, helping you made all the sense in the world. Except once I got to know you better, and we became friends . . ." His expression turned wistful. "I knew I couldn't go on being Quiz forever. But I wanted to make it last as long as I could."

Was this some twisted attempt at flattery? Isaveth felt a sudden, savage impulse to hurt him. "Eryx was right," she said. "You *are* mad."

"Is that what he told you?"

She'd expected Esmond to be furious, but he only sounded resigned. "Of course he did. I should have known. Well, perhaps I am a bit odd, compared with him. Though I do at least know that murdering people is wrong. Let alone sending an innocent man to the gallows for it."

Fresh grief stabbed into Isaveth, and she gave a shuddering gasp. How could she have forgotten that this wasn't about her own sense of betrayal, but about Papa's very life? And how dare this boy be the one to remind her, when he had everything and she had nothing?

For one blind moment she wanted to hurl herself at Esmond and pummel him with her fists, shout her rage and misery into his face, even shove him out the window and not care how or where he fell. Yet all the while his words kept echoing in her mind: *Innocent man. Innocent man. Innocent man.*

"Why?" she asked at last, choked with the effort of holding back tears. "Why did Eryx kill Master Orien?"

Esmond looked up at her, transfigured. Then he leaped off the bed, dropped to one knee on the dusty floor, and seized Isaveth's hand in his. "Thank you. *Thank you.* You won't regret asking that question, I swear." He let her go and jumped up again, practically vibrating with energy. "It's a long story, though, and there's not much time. Will you come with me? I can explain on the way."

Isaveth blinked, flabbergasted by his sudden change of manner. "The way to what?"

"Did I forget to mention that part? I'm sorry, I'm an idiot." His teeth flashed in a feral grin. "We're going to ruin Eryx. And save your father."

"The thing about Eryx," said Esmond as he and Isaveth hurried up the coal-lane toward Grand Street, "is that he's a complete fraud, and it astonishes me that more people haven't figured that out yet. I suppose it's because he's been politicking for only a year or two, and everyone's so relieved he doesn't act like Father. Still, when you think about it, what has he actually *done* to help the city? He scatters promises like a great puff-weed, but none of them land anywhere."

He was talking so rapidly and striding so fast, Isaveth could barely keep up with him. Her mind was a fog of confusion, her heart raw with grief and newfound hope; it was hard to know what to think, let alone believe. Yet Esmond must be exaggerating. How could Eryx be so popular, especially with people like Morra and the Workers' Club, without having done *something* right?

"What about the Reps' Bill?" Isaveth asked.

"Exactly," said Esmond. "What about it? Everyone thought Eryx was terrifically brave for standing up to Father and the other nobles and proposing such a radical change in the council. Except he knew from the start—or at least he *thought* he knew—there was no chance the bill would pass. It was all a scheme to boost morale in the city, make himself look like a hero, and keep the workers from burning down Council House and marching on Rollingdale."

Isaveth stumbled to a halt, appalled. If Esmond was right, then Eryx hadn't merely disappointed her—he'd deceived her at every turn. He'd lied about Esmond's madness, he'd lied about the Healer-General's findings, and most cruelly of all, he'd lied about not knowing Tomias Rennick.

How could she have been so naive, so gullible? Eryx had led her to believe that he cared about justice as much as she did, and that she could trust him to talk to the Lawkeepers on her behalf. Yet it was all promise and no substance, like giving a soother to a starving baby. He'd never had any intention of letting anyone find Rennick, much less question him, at all.

By the time she caught up to Esmond, he'd reached the top of the lane. Isaveth half expected him to drag Quiz's pedalcycle out of hiding, but instead he walked to the curb, pulled a cab-hailer from his pocket, and snapped the slim wand in half.

A bright blue spark shot high over Grand Street, and presently a spell-taxi pulled up beside them. Self-conscious, Isaveth tugged at her wrinkled dress and climbed in.

"Rollingdale Court," said Esmond, passing a money-note to the driver. "Quick as you can." He slid the privacy window shut, then settled back as the cab took off toward the city center.

"You're certain your brother's gone out?" asked Isaveth, rubbing her bare arms. Fairweather was drawing to an end, and the nights had grown cooler; she wished she'd thought to wear a cardigan, but it was too late now. "He won't be back anytime soon?"

"Not if we're lucky," said Esmond. "The trick's going to be getting into his study, but if the door's no good, we can always try the window. I've got a couple of float-charms left."

So that was how he'd got up to Papa's room. "And you think he has Rennick's suicide note?"

"That would mean Rennick actually committed suicide, and I don't think he did. But I'm sure Eryx made him write a confession before sending him to kill Orien—in fact, knowing Eryx, he wouldn't have paid Rennick a cit if he hadn't. He always likes to have insurance, you see, in case anyone's tempted to betray him."

Which meant that even if they did find the confession, it would read as though Rennick were solely responsible for the crime. It wasn't exactly the Auradia-style justice Isaveth had been hoping for, but right now she'd settle for anything that saved Papa from that noose at the Dern Valley Jail.

"Good," she said. "So now all we have to do is find it."

Esmond gave her a quizzical look. "I must say you're taking the idea of Eryx being wicked awfully well. What convinced you?"

Late though her change of heart had been, it took Isaveth only a second to know the answer. "He talked as though Papa were guilty," she said. "You never did."

Esmond went still, as though she'd surprised him. Then he reached over and took Isaveth's hand, his long fingers curling warm about her own. They sat in silence, not looking at each other, as the cab sped toward Rollingdale.

Chapter Twenty-Seven

IT WAS STRANGE getting out of the cab with Esmond—who looked very much the young noble, despite his grime-streaked clothes—and walking back to the Sagelord's mansion. All Isaveth's instincts urged her to stay low and creep through the shadows as before, but Esmond strode purposefully up the drive as though he had nothing to hide. Which it turned out he didn't, since the house was empty of all but a few servants.

"Some sort of fund-raising event for the hospital," he explained as he led her up the steps. "I pretended to have one of my beastly headaches so they had no choice but to leave me behind. I knew Eryx had told the servants to watch me, so I locked myself in, dug up a spare charm-case he didn't know I had, and floated out the window. I doubt anyone even knows I'm gone."

Esmond slipped the signet ring from his finger and

pressed it to the door, which promptly clicked open. With a wary glance back at the driveway, Isaveth followed him in.

The entry hall was cool and quiet, the chandelier dimmed to twilight gray. Isaveth slipped off her shoes, seeing that Esmond was already carrying his, and the two of them padded up the staircase to the upper level.

When they reached the landing, Esmond caught Isaveth and drew her back. A maid in house uniform stood at the far end of the hallway, peering into the gilt-framed mirror. She smoothed her apron, tucked a strand of her brown hair back beneath her cap, then took up a stance against the wall, watching at the final door.

"I knew it!" whispered Esmond, so close his lips tickled Isaveth's ear. "Wait here a minute. I'll deal with this." He pulled his charm-case from his pocket, tweezed out a strip of coppery metal, and set off boldly down the corridor.

"Good evening," he sang, and the maid jumped to attention. Isaveth ducked back around the corner as Esmond continued in the same blithe, even silly tone:

"Did Eryx ask you to keep an eye on me? That was thoughtful of him. But then, my brother's always looking out for other people. Your name's Ellice, isn't it?"

"Y-yes, milord."

"I thought so. Lovely name, Ellice. Do you like it here? It's a bit nicer than the college, isn't it?"

"I— I—"

"You used to clean Master Orien's office, am I right? It must have been a nasty shock for you, finding his body and then having to tell the Lawkeepers about it. I'd think that would make anyone want to disappear. Especially once Eryx was kind enough to pay you a visit and invite you to work for us instead."

With every word his voice grew fainter. Isaveth didn't dare look, but she could picture him approaching the maid step by step, smiling innocently all the while. "You'd do anything for my brother, wouldn't you? Or at least you'd do anything not to lose your job here. Trouble is, I fear Eryx won't be too pleased when he finds out you let me escape. Unless we give him a reason to believe it wasn't your fault."

"I c-can't think what you m-mean, milord."

"That's all right, I'm going to explain. See this bit of the floor outside my bedroom, where it's nice hard marble? I'm going to drop this sleeping-charm onto it, right where it would be if I'd slipped it under the door. Now imagine what you might do if you heard me making escaping sorts of noises inside and you had no idea the charm was there. It's an easy trick to fall for; might happen to anyone. Eryx can hardly blame you, and I won't say a word. Does that sound fair?"

The maid let out a whimper. Then came an agonizing twenty seconds of silence, followed by the muffled thump of a body hitting the carpet.

"All clear," called Esmond, and Isaveth hurried to help him drag the unconscious maid out of sight.

"When did you work all that out?" she whispered as the two of them searched her pockets.

"I should have guessed a lot earlier, if I hadn't been so busy running around with you." Esmond walked back to Eryx's study and crouched, squinting at the door. "I didn't even know we had a new maid until a few days ago. But once I found out she'd been hired two days after Orien's murder, it wasn't hard to guess why."

"You mean she saw something that could prove Eryx did it?" Like walking in on him poking about the masters' wardrobe, perhaps—although in that case, he'd have had to bribe the porter and anyone else who might have seen him in the college too. . . .

"I doubt that," said Esmond, peering into the keyhole, "or she wouldn't have been so quick to accept his offer. But Eryx doesn't like to take chances, and keeping Ellice close would keep her from talking to anyone who might cause trouble. Su Amaraq, for instance."

"Su? But I thought—"

"Oh, she's as dazzled by Eryx as anyone else, at least for now. But she's clever and she's curious, and she's not afraid to ask pointed questions. I don't think it'll be much longer before she realizes something's not quite right with our hero the Lording and decides to look into it. Now, let's see. . . ."

Frowning in concentration, Esmond eased his charm-tweezers into the keyhole, held them still a moment, and drew his hand back again. "Done," he said, turning the tweezers to show her the tiny crystal they held.

"What's that?"

"It's supposed to warn Eryx if his lock's being tampered with, but I'm pretty sure I managed not to set it off. Do you have any of that neevil paper about you?"

"I'm afraid not," Isaveth said. "Eryx's guard took my satchel, and he never gave it back."

"I'll bet I know where it is, then. But it'll have to wait." Esmond took a dab of wax from his charm-case, laid the crystal in its center, and rolled it up. "That should do it. Where's that key ring we took from Ellice?"

As he eased the key into the lock, Isaveth braced herself, but the door opened without so much as a creak of protest. They stepped through, into the darkened study.

"That was a little too easy for my liking," said Esmond, closing the door carefully behind them. "But we're here now, so we'd better get to work." He turned, frowning at the bookcase. Then he wrapped a handkerchief around his fingers, stepped up to the mirrored panel in its center, and pressed it.

The mirror swung outward to reveal a hidden alcove, tall and deep as the bookshelf but stocked with liquor and glasses. Esmond stepped inside, tapped on all three walls, then backed out and shut the panel again. "Nothing in there but the obvious. I doubt Eryx would be unimaginative enough to hide a safe behind any of the paintings . . ."

"Apparently not," said Isaveth, after a moment's search. "What about the books?"

"Even less imaginative," said Esmond, "but I suppose there's no help for it." He pulled a volume from the shelf, flipped it open, and put it back again. Isaveth moved to the far end and did likewise. By the time they met in the middle, it was clear that all the books were genuine.

"No space for a cupboard behind the shelves, either," mused Esmond, "unless it's invisible and hangs over the lobby. The desk, then."

Isaveth opened all the drawers, which had been left tauntingly unlocked and contained nothing out of the ordinary, while Esmond crawled beneath to knock for hidden compartments—but of course there were none. Isaveth was peering into the potted plants, and Esmond had started rolling back the carpet, when the glass doorknob rattled and began to turn.

Esmond swore under his breath. Before Isaveth could protest, he opened the secret cupboard and bundled her into it, shutting the panel just as the lights came on and Eryx Lording strolled in.

"Hello, little brother," he said mildly. "I see your headache's better. Have you found what you were looking for?"

Trapped in the narrow space, surrounded by bottles and glassware that might rattle at any moment, Isaveth stood motionless, afraid even to breathe. With the study fully lit she could see a little—very little—through the crack in the door. But that only meant Esmond hadn't shut it properly, and if Eryx turned . . .

Esmond must have realized his mistake as well, because he walked to the other side of the room, drawing Eryx's attention with him. "No, of course I didn't find anything to prove you killed Master Orien," he said, tugging at his rolled-up shirtsleeve as though itching to pull it down. "Though you can't blame me for trying."

"Can't I?" said Eryx. "For accusing me, your own brother, of a capital offense? For prying into matters that are none of your business and putting the future of this city in jeopardy?" He shook his head. "I think I *can* blame you, Esmond. If you're too young to understand politics, you shouldn't meddle."

"Oh, I understand *your* politics well enough. Peace and prosperity for everyone, eventually—so long as they keep trusting you to fix their problems, instead of doing anything to help themselves." Esmond leaned on the back of the armchair, his half glass glittering coldly in the light. "That's why you came up with the Reps' Bill, isn't it? You knew the commoners hated Father for not listening to them, so you seized the chance to trick them into believing you were on their side."

"I *am* on their side," Eryx retorted. "I want what's best for the people of Tarreton, and the last thing we all need is a revolution. Father's dragged this city into the gutter; it's my responsibility to lift it out again. And you poking about in my study, looking for proof that I'm a monster, is *not helpful*, Esmond."

Isaveth gave an involuntary shudder. Even in anger Eryx's tone remained pleasant, but now she could hear the teeth behind it.

"But you are a monster, aren't you?" said Esmond. "What else do you call someone who would turn a desperate man into a killer, send him to murder an old family

314

friend, and let a widower with four daughters hang for it?"

Eryx pinched the bridge of his nose. "I may regret this," he said, "but it seems only fair to ask. Why would I do any of those things?"

"Because you want to become the greatest Sagelord in Tarreton's history," said Esmond. "You're arrogant enough to think you can fix everything that's wrong with this city, but to do it, you need power. So of course you couldn't let Orien support the Reps' Bill, because if it passed, then you and Father would lose control over the council, and you'd have to get the commoners' approval to build this glorious future you keep talking about." He paused, then added in a bitter undertone, "Besides, Orien was one of the few people who knew what a brute you can be."

"So that's what this is about," said Eryx, and now he sounded both weary and sad. "I told you it was an accident. I said I was sorry—truly, deeply sorry—and that I'd give my own eye to replace yours if I could. Everyone else believes me. Why can't you?"

"Oh, I don't know," said Esmond with an ironic tilt of his head. "Maybe because I'm the one who lost the eye? And because it happened right after I refused to help you poison our father so you could become Sagelord in his place?"

Horror rippled through Isaveth, and she pressed her

lips tight to keep from crying out. She hugged herself and breathed shallowly, more frightened for Esmond and herself than ever. If Eryx had been willing to plot murder against his own father, what might he do to them?

"That was merely a bit of black humor." Eryx made a dismissive gesture. "It had been a long day, and you know how exasperating Father can be. I spoke without thinking."

"You never do anything without thinking. If Father's still alive, it's only because you've figured out how to get around him." Esmond gripped the chair, flushed with rising anger. "What did you tell him? That it was too late to save his reputation, but not too late to keep his power? That it was all right for people to despise him, as long as they still loved you?"

"Without a Sagelord, Tarreton would fall into chaos," Eryx told him patiently. "You know as well as I do that the common folk aren't ready to govern themselves." He turned toward the bookshelf, and Isaveth shrank back in alarm. If he opened the panel . . .

Esmond stepped in front of him. "You won't be governing anyone soon if you keep drinking whenever things get tense. Or do you think Father started out *wanting* to ruin the city?"

Eryx stopped and stared at his brother, his brow

creased with pain. Then he walked to the armchair and sat down. "So first I was a murderer, and now I'm a drunkard? I knew you hated me, but I didn't realize you despised me as well."

"Oh, please," said Esmond scornfully. "You're not a victim—you never have been. Unlike that poor fool Tomias Rennick, whom you paid to kill Orien. And then had him murdered too, so there'd be no one to tell the Lawkeepers how you'd done it. Well, except maybe the Healer-General, but I'm guessing you bribed him to hide the evidence."

He crossed the carpet and sat in the chair opposite Eryx, careful not to glance at the panel where Isaveth was hiding. "I suppose Orien being so busy with the new charmery was what gave you the idea to make it look like one of the workers had done it? And using an affinity-charm to set off the exploding-tablet would give it that touch of irony, not to mention keep you and your accomplice away from the scene of the crime. I imagine it was you who gave Rennick the charm and told him how to use it? Or did Hulton give him your orders instead?"

"This is ridiculous," said Eryx. "You're overwrought—"

Esmond waved this aside. "It's all right, I was only curious. In any case, you promised Rennick you'd have Father recommend him for the charmery project, so he wouldn't be tempted to doubt that he had a future. But you knew Master Orien wouldn't cooperate, since he was still hoping to rehire the man he'd picked for the job the first time: a Moshite named Urias Breck."

Isaveth pressed her hands to her mouth, aghast. Was Esmond right? Had framing Papa really been Eryx's plan from the start?

"Your spies had told you that Breck was a member of the Workers' Club, and that he blamed Orien for the loss of his fortunes. And since Rennick despised Breck already, that made him all the more willing to carry out your plan." Esmond leaned back in his chair. "Have I forgotten anything?"

It was agony to watch him act casual when his emotions must be running as high as Isaveth's own. But it was even more difficult to look at Eryx, who was regarding Esmond with a mixture of sorrow and an almost tender pity.

"I almost wish I could say no," he said. "I can see this fantasy means a great deal to you. However, you've overlooked a rather important point. You keep insisting an affinity-charm was used to kill Master Orien. But it couldn't have been this Rennick fellow who put the charm in his robe, since the records show Rennick's first and only visit to the governor's office was on the day of the murder. And it couldn't have been me, because I was nowhere near the college that week—in fact, I was quite publicly elsewhere the entire time. So if neither Rennick nor myself had any opportunity to plant the charm on Master Orien before he died . . ." He spread his hands. "How could either one of us have killed him?"

Esmond made no answer. His face turned pale, then red, then white again, until Eryx said gently, "I've done my best to be patient with you. But I'm afraid all this has only confirmed my fears. Your mind is unbalanced, Esmond. You need help."

He sounded so apologetic, so genuinely concerned. If Isaveth hadn't known that he'd lied to her, she might have been tempted to believe him. How could they make him give up Rennick's confession if he wouldn't admit he'd had any part in the crime?

"I had your room guarded only because I couldn't be here to look out for you," Eryx continued in the same compassionate tone. "I was afraid you might do something rash if you were left alone, and I was right. Don't you think it's time you stopped pretending, Esmond? Master Orien is dead because Urias Breck killed him. No matter how you feel about Breck's daughter, that's the truth of it."

Esmond said nothing. His head was down, his eyes on the carpet; he looked utterly defeated. Isaveth shifted her weight from one aching leg to the other, her brain working at furious speed. If neither Eryx nor Rennick had had the opportunity to plant the tablets on Orien, then who . . . ?

The answer came to her then, so quick and sure it left her breathless. She'd nearly lost faith, but her instincts had been right all along.

She didn't realize she'd gasped aloud until Eryx started to his feet. His gaze swept over the bookcase . . . and locked, unblinking, on the crack in its mirrored door.

Isaveth's skin broke out in turkey-flesh. She had no idea what Eryx would do to her, but the set of his jaw warned her there could be no more hiding now. She sent up a silent prayer to the All-One, and stepped out of the alcove.

"I know how you killed Master Orien," she said, forcing herself to look straight into Eryx Lording's face. "You didn't just use Tomias Rennick. Master Buldage was working for you as well."

Chapter Twenty-Eight

IT WAS A BOLD ACCUSATION, and Isaveth could only hope she'd guessed right. But the spasm of anger that crossed Eryx Lording's face reassured her. Quickly she stepped around him and moved to join Esmond as she went on.

"Ellice caught Buldage slipping the tablets into Orien's robe, didn't she, the night before the murder? She may not have realized what he was doing, or known enough to tell the Lawkeepers. Still, you couldn't afford to let anyone else question her, so you coaxed her to come and work for you instead."

Eryx's dark brows lifted. "Good evening, Miss Breck. I wondered if you might be joining us."

Even now he refused to give up the role he'd been playing: the honest young politician with a dream of equality and prosperity for all, plagued by two foolish children inexplicably bent on ruining his good name. The hypocrisy was maddening, but it was also reassuring. If Eryx did anything to harm her, he'd be admitting that Esmond was right about him.

What if Isaveth played along, then, instead of arguing? Eryx was so good at flattering others, perhaps he wasn't entirely immune to flattery himself.

"I think you do care about the people of Tarreton," said Isaveth, clasping her hands behind her back so they wouldn't tremble. "Even if you think they can't rule themselves as well as you can rule them. And I'm sure you couldn't bring yourself to murder anyone, especially a man who'd taught you since you were a child, unless you believed it was the only way to save the city."

Eryx didn't reply. He studied Isaveth with a faint crease between his brows, as though everything about her puzzled him.

"I don't know if Rennick killed himself or not," Isaveth went on resolutely, "but he's dead now, so he can't betray you. And Buldage can't turn against you without ruining himself. I know the truth, but nobody's going to believe me. All I want is to save my papa, and you're the only one who can do that now."

She looked up at the Lording, tears shining in her eyes. "Please, milord. I promise I won't tell Papa what you did. I won't tell anyone. Just save him, and I'll be grateful to you forever."

Eryx cleared his throat. "This is rather awkward," he said. "I'm not quite sure how to reply. Even if I agreed that your conclusions are accurate—which I couldn't possibly do, of course—I'm not sure I can trust my brother to take the same, shall we say, generous view of the matter. . . ."

"Oh, shut up, Eryx," said Esmond bitterly. "Do you really think I'd tear our whole family apart and let Isaveth's father hang just to spite you?" He stood up, pulled a scrap of black cloth from his pocket, and flung it onto the table between them. "There's the cloth I cut from Orien's robe, with the charm-silver on it. Now turn Rennick's confession over to the Lawkeepers, and let Isaveth's father go."

Isaveth held her breath, afraid to interrupt, as Eryx's gaze flicked to Esmond. "That's quite a sacrifice, little brother. After all, with me disgraced you'd be a step closer to becoming Sagelord."

"Only if I assassinated Civilla first," retorted Esmond. "And unlike some of us, I have no interest in killing people. Or ruling the city, either."

"Perhaps," said Eryx. "But as you're so convinced that I killed Master Orien, having a dead workman charged with his murder is bound to be painful for you. It might even seem that you'd failed to avenge him."

Esmond's throat bobbed as he swallowed. "It doesn't matter," he said huskily.

"No?" Eryx glanced at Isaveth. "Or maybe you've found something that matters even more to you. Enough that you'd do anything to make her happy."

If she thought she'd seen Esmond red before, it was nothing compared with now. "Eryx—"

"Don't worry, brother, I'm sure she's conscious of the honor you do her." His tone was kindly, even sympathetic. "Still, even if Miss Breck shares your feelings, I'm sure she's sensible enough to realize that nothing can ever come of it."

A tingling flush spread through Isaveth, starting from her fingers and toes and burning up through her stomach. She'd begged Eryx to do the right thing by her father, and she still hoped that he would. But he was enjoying this—enjoying the power she'd given him, and using it to torment Esmond.

"Don't," she blurted out. "You've already won, can't you see?"

"Have I?" Eryx's gaze remained on his brother. "I believe there's one thing we still have to negotiate. Roll down your sleeve, Esmond."

Esmond flinched as though his brother had jabbed him. Then he unrolled his shirtsleeve and took off the charm-band he'd been hiding. "Fine," he said sullenly. "Take it. Probably nobody at the station was listening anyway."

"Do you really think it would make a difference if they were?" asked Eryx. "The walls of this study are shield-charmed, so no signal can travel in or out. You can't listen to a crystal set in here, let alone send a message. Still, I admire your ingenuity." He took the bracelet from Esmond's hand and tucked it inside his jacket.

"Now that's settled," he continued briskly, "it's time we finished this. Miss Breck, it's possible Mister Rennick left some kind of confession. It could be that his wife kept it hidden from the Lawkeepers, to spare their daughter the shame of knowing her father was a murderer. But if she knew it could save an innocent man . . . well, perhaps that might persuade her to turn it over."

Isaveth felt as though a millstone had been lifted from her shoulders. "Thank you," she whispered, but Esmond held up a hand.

"Eryx," he said coldly, "you can do better than that. How does she know this isn't just another of your pretty promises? I think it would be best if you got into that *very fast* spell-carriage of yours and drove over to see Missus Rennick right now. I'm sure it won't take you more than a few minutes."

Eryx's eyes narrowed, and Isaveth feared he would refuse. But at last he said, "Very well. As long as both of you sit down in those armchairs and stay here until I return."

"Our solemn word on it," said Esmond. He walked to the farthest chair and plopped down, leaving Isaveth to take the other. "See? Nice, obedient children. Now you can lock us in and go."

"I can't believe you were wearing a charm-band that entire time," said Isaveth when the Lording had gone. "Did you know he was going to walk in on us? Was that your plan to catch him all along?"

"For all the good it did," said Esmond gloomily, but there was a wicked glint in his eye. He dragged his chair close to Isaveth's, wriggled to the edge of the seat, and leaned forward, beckoning her to do the same.

"We're not beaten yet," he said so quietly she had to read his lips. "We might still be able to catch Eryx, if my plan worked."

"What plan?" Isaveth whispered, and Esmond flashed a grin.

"That charm-band he took from me wasn't transmitting," he said, "it was recording. Once I steal it back from him, we'll have proof of everything he said tonight. But that can wait. I won't do anything to put your father in danger."

Relief warmed Isaveth all over. She'd hated to let Eryx get away with murder, even for Papa's sake—but if Esmond was right, she wouldn't have to. Of course, the Lording hadn't actually confessed to arranging Master Orien's murder, but the record of tonight's conversation ought to make his guilt plain enough.

"I don't know how to thank you," she began, but Esmond shook his head.

"Don't. I'm still kicking myself for not figuring out it was Eryx from the start." He gazed past her, his expression pensive. "I knew he was obsessed with becoming Sagelord and remaking Tarreton in his image. But even after what he did to my eye, I didn't think he'd really go so far. I kept thinking—hoping—it was somebody else."

And with that the last speck of resentment Isaveth had felt against him faded away. She reached out and put her hand over his. "I'm sorry I didn't believe you earlier," she said.

Esmond turned his palm over, fingers grasping hers. "Isaveth," he said, "I know I'm not Quiz, not really. But even so . . ." He looked up into her face. "Do you think we could go on being friends? Because I would like that very much."

"I . . . I don't know," said Isaveth. "How can we, really? You're the Lilord, and I'm just a girl from Cabbage Street."

And a Moshite girl, at that. Even if Esmond didn't care where Isaveth went to temple, his family and friends surely did.

"You're not *just* anything," Esmond protested. "You're ten times more clever and interesting than the girls I go to school with—and the boys, too, for that matter. Besides, we make a good team. . . ." He stopped, his head snapping up. "Wait. I think that's Eryx coming back."

"Already?" asked Isaveth. She'd thought the Lording would at least carry out the pretense of driving across the city, but it seemed he'd dropped even that.

Esmond got up, drawing Isaveth with him. "One last thing," he said in a strangled tone. "Could I—would you mind if I kissed you?"

Isaveth's mouth dropped open. She stared at him, too astonished even to blush.

"Sorry." He let go of her, ducking his head ruefully. "That was a stupid thing to say."

"Not *stupid*," said Isaveth, finding her voice with an effort. She felt as though the ceiling had fallen on her head. "It's just that I . . ."

She had no idea how to finish the sentence, but mercifully, she didn't have to. The door opened, and Eryx Lording stepped into the room.

"I trust this is what you were looking for," he said, handing an envelope to Esmond, who opened it and scanned the contents before nodding agreement.

"Though if you don't mind," he said coolly, tucking the envelope under his arm, "I'll deliver it to the Lawkeepers myself."

"As you like," said Eryx. "In any case, it's getting late, and the others will be back soon. I think it's time I took Miss Breck home, don't you? We wouldn't want to distress Mother."

"No, of course not." Esmond turned to Isaveth. "Don't worry, I'm sure my brother will see you safely back to Cabbage Street. Because it would distress Mother even more if I had to kill him."

That startled a laugh out of Isaveth, but Eryx didn't smile—and neither did Esmond. He made a little bow over Isaveth's hand and walked out.

The Lording's open-topped sportster was the most elegant vehicle Isaveth had ever seen, let alone ridden in. Under any other circumstances, the buttery softness of the leather seat and the breeze tossing her hair would have delighted her. Yet she was all too conscious of Eryx's brooding presence at her side, the way his fingers clenched the steering yoke as they coasted through the twinkling lamp-lights of Rollingdale toward the darker streets beyond.

She wasn't afraid that he would hurt her, not exactly: Even if he had plotted Master Orien's murder, strangling a twelve-year-old girl with his own hands didn't seem like something Eryx would do. Still, the journey back to Cabbage Street felt twice as long as any tram ride, and Isaveth almost wished she'd refused the Lording's offer and walked home instead. When at last he stopped the carriage, she scrambled out so fast she nearly fell.

"Miss Breck," said the Lording, and Isaveth froze. She wanted to slam the door and run, but she didn't dare risk offending a man so powerful—or so dangerous. She turned back and gave Eryx a watery smile.

"I'm ever so sorry," she said. "I didn't mean to be rude. I was thinking about my sisters—they must be terribly worried about me. But I'm grateful for all you've done tonight, I really am—"

"No need for that," Eryx interrupted her. "There's just something I'd like to say to you before you go."

He patted the seat beside him, and Isaveth's heart sank. She forced herself to open the door and sit down again as the Lording leaned back, gazing thoughtfully at her half-lit street.

"I couldn't say this to Esmond," he said, "because he'd

never believe it. But I think . . . I think perhaps you might." He switched off the carriage and turned to her. "It wasn't my idea to have Master Orien killed. It was my father's."

Isaveth clutched the door handle, feeling as though the earth had shifted beneath her. "I—I beg your pardon?"

"I blame myself," said Eryx distractedly, "because I told Father that Orien meant to support the Reps' Bill— or at least that I'd heard a credible rumor to that effect. I should have known he would take it as a personal betrayal." He sighed. "I tried to appease him, but he was too angry. For a moment I feared he meant to charge off to the college and murder Orien himself."

"So you offered to do it for him?" The words came slowly, rough with disbelief.

"What else could I do? If I hadn't taken over the assassination, my father would have bungled it and taken our whole family down with him. At least I could handle the matter discreetly, so there would still be something left for the rest of us to inherit when Father died."

Eryx laid his gloved hands on the steering yoke, flexing them as though they ached. "I knew Buldage would do anything to become governor, and since Rennick was already selling secrets to the Lawkeepers, I knew he would do anything to save his wife. I knew

331

Orien had been frustrated at having his plans for a new charmery canceled, so I encouraged Father to reverse his decision and tell Orien to start hiring workers right away."

Which had not only provided Eryx and his fellow conspirators with a number of plausible suspects for framing, but kept Orien too busy to notice what they were up to. He'd gone to his death full of happy plans for improving the college, and the end had come so suddenly he probably didn't feel a thing. It was the sort of scheme only Eryx Lording could come up with—ruthless and oddly generous at the same time.

"Why are you telling me this?" asked Isaveth. "Are you asking me to forgive you?"

If so, he'd be disappointed. She had no right to absolve him from what he'd done. Besides, until Eryx confessed his guilt to the people he'd wronged, and showed true remorse and repentance, it would be wrong to pardon him anyway. She might not be as devout a Moshite as Annagail, but she did know that much.

"Of course not," said Eryx. "But since you worked so hard to uncover the truth, it seemed only fair to give it to you. And since we're speaking frankly . . . I'd like to make you an offer as well."

There was no threat in his tone, but Isaveth felt suddenly wary. She edged closer to the door. "What kind of offer?"

"Simply this. I know my brother too well to believe he would take my advice, especially now. But you strike me as a wise young lady." He reached into his jacket, drew out a billfold, and opened it. "If you were to decide it was undesirable for your friendship with Esmond to continue, I believe he'd respect your wishes."

He flicked out a money-note between his fingers, holding it just high enough for her to see. "I'm sure your family could use a little financial help. Perhaps you might think of their feelings, even if you find it hard to reconcile your own?"

He was offering her a regal—half a month's wages. Isaveth was so flabbergasted, all she could do was stare.

Eryx must have misinterpreted her hesitation, because he pulled out a second note and held it next to the first. "You drive a hard bargain, Miss Breck," he added with a sliver of a smile. "Though you must realize that Esmond will soon lose interest in you anyway. I'm only trying to make it a little less disappointing when he does."

His expression was arch, his dark brows slightly raised: It was clear that he expected Isaveth to take the money. How could a girl in her position do otherwise? Yet though she was still flustered by Esmond asking to kiss her, and not at all sure how they could go on being friends without great difficulty, Isaveth felt no impulse to accept the Lording's offer. All she could find in herself was revulsion, and a touch of pity.

No wonder Eryx had been willing to arrange his old tutor's murder, if he believed things like friendship could be bought and sold so easily. Everything was negotiable to him, even his principles. But what was the point of being wealthy and successful if you had to betray all the people who loved you to get there? Was it really worth having everything if it cost you your soul?

Isaveth opened the carriage door and climbed out. "Thank you for your offer," she said as she shut it again. "But I think we'll manage."

"I beg your pardon, Miss Breck," said Eryx, "but do you not realize what I'm offering you?"

He sounded not only shocked, but faintly alarmed—which made Isaveth even more sure of her decision. Not because she liked Esmond, but also because he'd been right: They did make a good team. Together, they'd solved Master Orien's murder and cleared her papa's name . . . and now Eryx Lording, the second most powerful man in the city, was afraid of them.

"I do realize," Isaveth said politely, stepping back from the carriage. "I'm just not interested. Good night, milord."

Epilogue

ON THE DAY ISAVETH TURNED THIRTEEN, the sky was clear and sunny, though the crispness in the air hinted at harvest and school to come. Since Papa was still recovering from his time in prison, and Annagail had yet to find another job, Isaveth didn't expect much in the way of presents beyond the traditional lie-in while her sisters made her breakfast. But when Mimmi proudly carried up the tray with its plate of potato frycakes and bowl of creamed wheat, there was a little cloth-wrapped bundle sitting on it.

"It's from Lilet and me," she said, bouncing as Isaveth untied the ribbon. "We made it collecting bottles. So you can buy something you really like."

Inside were fifty cits, lovingly polished until the copper shone bright as mage-gold. It must have taken her sisters at least three weeks to earn. Isaveth was about to protest, but Lilet gave her a look so fierce that she shut her mouth at once. It was clear that if she tried to argue, her sisters would never forgive her. So she ate her breakfast meekly, allowed Annagail to fuss with her hair, then hugged her family farewell and went off to buy her birthday present.

She hadn't been downtown since she and Esmond parted, and even the most crowded streets seemed strangely empty without him. It was hard to believe she'd never see Quiz sauntering up the sidewalk with his hands in his pockets or zooming through the traffic on his pedalcycle again. In no mood to linger, Isaveth made straight for the stationer's and spent every cit that Lilet and Mimmi had given her. Then she tucked her parcel of ink and paper under her arm and headed home.

No sooner had she started down the coal-lane, however, than she spotted Loyal swaggering up from the other end. Until now Isaveth had done her best to stay clear of the Kerchers, not knowing what trouble they might make for her next. But the Loyal's cruel smile on his face, and the knowledge that if he got hold of her precious writing paper, he'd tear it up just for spite, filled her with new determination. She marched to meet him and spoke up in her boldest voice.

"Don't even try it, Loyal. From now on you're going to leave me and my sisters alone."

He sniggered. "Who's going to make me, your patch-faced boyfriend? I haven't seen him in weeks."

"No," said Isaveth, "and you won't see him again. But I don't need his help to make you listen. Because if you bully me or anyone else in my family again, I'll tell everyone in the neighborhood that the Kerchers have been spying on them and selling their secrets to the Lawkeepers."

Loyal turned crimson. "That's a lie," he spat, but his eyes darted in all directions, and Isaveth knew her threat had struck home.

"Tell that to the Caverlys," she said. "Ever since Morra and Seward got arrested, they've been wondering how the Lawkeepers knew where to find the Workers' Club that night. Once I explain how your family managed to afford a crystal set, though, I'm sure it'll all make sense."

Loyal shifted from one foot to the other, his tongue working around his stained teeth. He didn't reply.

"Well?" Isaveth prompted. "Do you want to tell your parents we have a bargain? Or would you rather be shamed out of the neighborhood than deal with a Moshite?"

"Fine." He aimed a savage kick at the dirt. "I'll tell them."

"Good," Isaveth said, and walked past him without looking back.

* * *

"Vettie! Guess what came while you were out!" Mimmi grabbed Isaveth by the hand, and practically yanked her inside. "Papa, is it ready? Can I show her?"

"Almost, almost, my Mirrim." Urias Breck's voice boomed from the front parlor, where Lilet stood blocking the door to keep Isaveth from seeing in. "Just a minute . . . yes, that's done it. Come here, Vettie."

Mystified, Isaveth put down her package from the stationer's and walked to meet him. Papa opened his arms, and she snuggled into them. It felt good to lean against his solid warmth, knowing it meant he was home, he was safe, and most of all, he was alive. All because of her—and Esmond.

"You have a wealthy admirer, my Vettie," he said, turning her gently to face the sofa. "And whoever it is seems to know you pretty well. How do you like your birthday present?"

There it sat upon the end table, the most perfect crystal set Isaveth could have wished for. Nothing fancy, or even new: It was an older model with a slightly worn cabinet and tarnished dials. But when Papa switched it on, the music that flowed out was the sweetest she'd ever heard.

"There was a note in the box," said Lilet. "Only it had your name on it, so Papa wouldn't let us read it." She thrust the letter at Isaveth. "Here."

Birch-white paper, smooth against her hands. The

envelope had been sealed with crimson wax; Isaveth broke the stamp eagerly and drew the letter out.

> *Dear Isaveth:*
> *I hope this news won't upset you (and if it does, I hope the gift will make up for it). But I found your satchel the other day, so I took the liberty of showing your neevil paper to Mistress Anandri, and she was quite impressed with it.*

"Who's Mistress Whatsit?" asked Mimmi, peering beneath her elbow.

"She works at the college," said Isaveth distractedly. "Go away, Mim. I'm reading."

Mimmi gave a gusty sigh. She would have flopped onto the sofa to wait, but Lilet dragged her out the door. With exaggerated care Papa tiptoed after them, and Isaveth went back to her letter.

> *She introduced me to a former student of hers who owns a spell-factory, and we showed him how the paper works. He became extremely excited and begged us to sell him the rights. I told him they weren't mine to sell, but that if he wanted to make you an offer, I'd be happy to pass it on. So this letter is to notify you that*

J. J. Wregget, president of the Glow-Mor Light and
Fire Company, is offering five imperials for the full
and exclusive rights....

Five imperials! Isaveth clutched the page so hard it crumpled. That would buy new clothing and shoes for everyone in the family, and food for weeks to come. Annagail could stop job-hunting and go back to school. Papa would still need work eventually, but now he could look for it without fretting over the coal bill or the rent. For the next few months at least, their money troubles were over.

If that seems reasonable to you, I'd be honored to
handle the arrangements on your behalf. All you need
do is sign the bottom of this letter and send it back to
me, and I'll get started right away.

Respectfully yours,
Esmond, Lilord of Tarreton

P.S. I still haven't got that bracelet back from Eryx
yet. But I'm working on it.

A smile broke over Isaveth's face. She pressed the letter to her heart, and ran to tell her family.

Acknowledgments

I could not have written this book without the help of many friends and colleagues, who deserve all the thanks I can give them: Chandra Rooney and Sarah Rees-Brennan, who made Encouraging Noises when I told them my concept for the book; Josh Adams, my savvy and supportive agent; Reka Simonsen, my wonderful North American editor, who loved Isaveth and Quiz from the start; Peter Anderson and Deva Fagan, who shared my journey through the wilderness of the first draft; Brittany Harrison, whose insightful critique showed me how to take Isaveth's story to the next level; Stephanie Burgis and Simon Bohner, who read my revisions chapter by chapter and reassured me I was on the right track; Liz Barr, Emily Bytheway, and Deva Fagan (again) who read and commented thoughtfully on the second draft; Sarah Prineas and

Ishta Mercurio-Wentworth, who helped me solve some last-minute editing problems; E. K. Johnston and Erin Bow, for tea and sympathy; and my family, for giving me all the time, space, and support I needed until the book was finished. I am deeply grateful to you all.

TURN THE PAGE
FOR A SNEAK PEEK AT

A Little Taste of Poison

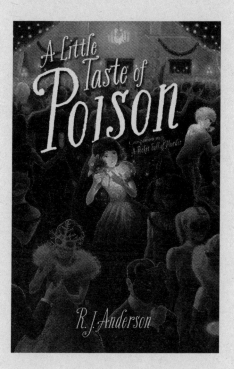

Isaveth sat stiffly in the leather chair, hands clenched on the brim of her hat and heart pounding in her throat. The reception room was hot and smelled of baccy; a clump of snow melted off her boot and plopped onto the diamond-patterned carpet. She longed to take off her coat, but the wool was too damp to lay it on her lap, and she could see nowhere else to put it.

On the opposite wall, a brass plate trumpeted the name of the man Isaveth had come to see: J. J. WREGGET, PRESIDENT. Meanwhile his personal secretary, lean and elegant in a brown suit that nearly matched his skin, shuffled papers while speaking to the call box on his desk: "I'm sorry, Mister Wregget is in a meeting. . . . Pardon? . . . No, he's booked until next Mendday."

Isaveth shifted uncomfortably. This sumptuous ultramodern office, the inner sanctum of the Glow-Mor Light and Fire Company, was no place for a stonemason's daughter from Cabbage Street. Especially one barely thirteen years old. What could the president of the biggest spell-factory in Tarreton want with her?

True, she'd invented a magic-resistant paper that was perfect for wrapping spell-tablets, and once Mister Wregget had seen it he'd been eager to buy the recipe. But that was months ago, and Isaveth had nothing more to offer him. Even the five imperials he'd paid her—half a year's wages for poor folk like herself—was spent now, gone to pay off old debts and buy her family warm clothes, boots without holes in them, and other long-overdue necessities. In fact, if Papa couldn't find better work than the odd jobs he'd been doing, they'd soon have to apply for relief again.

Dread clutched at Isaveth's chest. What if the president wasn't pleased with her invention? What if he'd called her here to demand his money back?

Perhaps she'd been reckless, coming all the way to the Glow-Mor office by herself. But Papa hadn't been home when the message boy delivered Mister Wregget's summons, and Isaveth hadn't felt comfortable showing it to her older sister, Annagail—let alone the younger girls, Lilet and Mimmi. After all the troubles they'd been through since their mother died, she hated to tell them anything until she was certain it was good news.

Right now, though, she'd settle for it not being too crushingly bad. Sweat prickled beneath her collar and she fumbled open the top button of her coat, but it didn't help. She felt ready to faint by the time the outer door swung open at last, and a balding, ruddy-faced man in a striped waistcoat strode in.

"Miss Breck!" he enthused, engulfing her hand in his big pink one. "What a pleasure. Tambor, take the young lady's coat."

Isaveth struggled out of her winter things and piled them on the secretary, then hurried to catch up as Mister Wregget marched into his office. He sat down, gesturing her to the chair in front of his desk.

"I'm a straightforward man, Miss Breck," he said as the privacy door swung shut, "so I won't bore you with a lot of preamble. How would you like to go to Tarreton College?"

Isaveth goggled at him. Tarreton College was the most exclusive upper-grade school in the city, where the children of the nobility and wealthy merchant families received the finest education—general and magical—that money could provide. He might as well have asked Isaveth how she'd like to fly. "I—I've never dreamed of such a thing, sir."

"Then you need to dream bigger, young lady! Because I'd like to offer you this year's Glow-Mor scholarship." He leaned back, smiling beatifically. "I know it's a mite unusual to start partway through the year, but you're a bright girl, and I'm sure you'll soon catch up. And if you make it through fallowtime and planting terms with good marks, we'll renew the offer next harvest: full tuition, with all books and materials included. What do you say?"

He couldn't be serious. Or if he was, he must be losing his mind. The magic taught at Tarreton College was Sagery, an ancient craft very different from the spell-baking Isaveth had learned from her mother. Instead of recipes using magewort, binding powder, and other cheap ingredients, Sagery relied on precise formulations of precious metals and gemstones to create the kinds of charms only wealthy folk could afford. Its secrets had been jealously guarded for centuries, and some even considered it sacred; it was no craft for a commoner, as the proud masters and mistresses of the college would surely agree.

"Sir," said Isaveth faintly, "I'd be honored, but they'll never—"

"I know what you're thinking," interrupted the president, wagging a finger at her. "Don't worry, Miss Breck; I wouldn't be making this offer if the college wasn't willing to accept you. I know you come from humble stock and your family's had more than its share of troubles, but to my mind that just proves what a resourceful young lady you are. That's the sort of brain I want working for my company, the kind of boldness and sharp thinking that will give Glow-Mor the edge!"

His confidence was buoyant, and Isaveth's hopes rose-with it. Maybe this wasn't a mistake after all. Maybe this was what she'd been praying for ever since Mama died and Papa lost his business, a chance to make something of herself and lift her family out of poverty. . . .

Except for one hard fact, dragging her back to earth like an iron anchor. If she'd merely been poor, then Mister Wregget's offer might be seen as an act of charity, a way to enhance his company's good name. But as far as most people in Tarreton were concerned, Isaveth was much worse off than that.

"It's kind of you to say so," she said, forcing the words past the lump in her throat. "Only you don't seem to realize . . . I'm Moshite."

Even as she spoke, she braced herself for his reaction: the hiss of breath, the lowering brows, the frown. But to her surprise, Wregget threw back his head and laughed.

"Honest to a fault, Miss Breck! I see I haven't mis-judged you." He folded his hands across his belly, still smiling. "True enough, your . . . er . . . religious background did raise a few eyebrows among the masters. But as Spellmistress Anandri pointed out, there's nothing in the college charter to prevent Moshites from attending. As long as you work hard, obey school rules, and pass your exams, they've got no right to turn you away."

Isaveth had only met Spellmistress Anandri once, and only because her friend Quiz—otherwise known as Esmond Lilord, youngest son of the Sagelord himself—introduced them. Still, the woman had seemed impressed with Isaveth's skill at Common Magic, and even helped bring her magic-resistant paper to Wregget's attention. With such a respected member of the college on her side, perhaps Isaveth's acceptance wasn't as unlikely as she'd thought.

Still, just because the school had no grounds to refuse her didn't mean Isaveth belonged there. She might not even be safe, if anyone recognized her from her last visit, when she'd posed as a cleaning maid to investigate the old governor's murder. . . .

Especially since the current governor of the school, Hexter Buldage, had been part of the conspiracy to kill him.

"I can see you have doubts," said Wregget, "and I can't say I blame you. I'm sure it all sounds a bit too good to be true. But I'll tell you a secret." He leaned closer, voice dropping to a confidential rumble. "Buying that recipe of yours was the best decision I've ever made. Thanks to Resisto-Paper, we've become the leading spell-tablet manufacturer in the city, and orders are pouring in from all over Colonia. You've *earned* that scholarship, is what I say, and anyone who thinks otherwise will have to deal with me!" His hand smacked the desk, making Isaveth jump. "So what's your answer, young lady?"

Isaveth twisted her hands together. Yes, going to Tarreton College would be risky. There were plenty of people, including Esmond's villainous older brother, Eryx Lording, who wouldn't want her to succeed. If Isaveth failed, she'd not only bring disgrace on her family, she'd be confirming what most Arcan and Uniting folk already believed—that Moshites were worthless troublemakers, and everything bad that happened to them was their own fault.

Yet she wouldn't be alone at the college: Esmond would be there too. Isaveth still wasn't sure how to feel about the charming rogue of a street-boy she'd befriended four months ago turning out to be a noble in disguise, especially since they couldn't spend time together any-more without causing a scandal. But at least she'd be able to see him now and then, instead of only writing letters.

Besides, she wanted this. Inside her, beneath the worries and doubts, lay a simmering excitement ready to bubble over at any moment. To face the odds and defy them, to bravely march into danger instead of shying away—wasn't that what her favorite talkie-play heroine, Auradia Champion, would do? There was no guarantee Isaveth would succeed at the college, but if she didn't at least try, she'd regret it for the rest of her life.

Isaveth took a deep breath and smiled at Wregget. "Thank you, sir. I'd love to accept."

Dear Isaveth, I'm afraid I've got bad news. . . .

Esmond rubbed his forehead, staring at the freshly penned words. How was he going to tell her? He was still struggling to get over the shock and disappointment himself. All those weeks spent hunting for the evidence that would prove Eryx guilty of murder, and now . . .

A throat cleared behind him, and Esmond jumped. He flipped the paper over, though he had a sick feeling Eryx had already seen it, and twisted in his chair. "What do you want?" he snapped.

"Mother sent me to call you to supper." As always, his older brother's voice was rich, mellow, and maddeningly calm. "The bell rang five minutes ago, but it seems you were . . . distracted."

He'd come up on Esmond's blind side, and not by mistake: the illusion-charmed lens Esmond usually wore lay unheeded beside the ink blotter, and the scar that ran from brow to cheekbone was plain to see. Not that Eryx would be likely to forget which eye had been injured, seeing as he was the one who'd done it.

Inwardly Esmond seethed, but he kept his expression neutral as he studied the young man who'd made himself the most trusted politician in the city, even as he secretly bribed, blackmailed, and—if necessary—murdered anyone who dared to get in his way. Eryx Lording, Sagelord Arvis's favorite son . . . and for all that they both pretended otherwise, Esmond's most bitter enemy.

"I'm not hungry," he said.

Eryx's brows arched. "Considering your usual rampaging appetite, I find that difficult to believe. To whom were you writing, may I ask? Surely not that Breck girl. I thought we had an agreement."

He hadn't read the letter, then. Or maybe he had, and he was just toying with Esmond. With Eryx, you could never tell.

"Well, you know," said Esmond, "I've been thinking about that. You already burned my street clothes, and Father made me charm-swear not to dress up like a commoner or sneak out of the house again. Then you warned me that if I tried to see Isaveth, you'd have your thugs pay her family a visit—"

"Thugs?" Eryx gave him a pitying look. "Really, Esmond, you sound like that ridiculous *Auradia* show you love so much. I merely remarked that after all Urias Breck had been through since he was arrested, and how hard young Isaveth had worked to clear his name, it would be a shame if they had to endure any further misfortunes."

"Yes, quite," said Esmond. "I'm sure you've lost whole seconds of sleep worrying over it. But it's occurred to me that you could have kept me in line more easily by telling Father about Isaveth, instead of making vague remarks about me 'keeping low company' and 'disgracing the family name.'"

He cocked his head to one side, studying Eryx through his good eye. "Only you don't want to tell him, do you? Because that would mean admitting you botched up, and Urias Breck's daughter caught you framing her papa for a murder *you* helped commit."

Eryx sighed. "We've talked about these delusions of yours before, Esmond. Is there a point to this?"

"Maybe not," said Esmond. "But it's an interesting thought. After all, if I'm not allowed to talk to Isaveth anyway, what's to keep *me* from telling Father the whole story?"

Eryx regarded him steadily for a moment. Then he snatched up Esmond's sheet of writing paper, crumpled it, and tossed it into the fire. "I think you'd find that less satisfying than you imagine," he said coolly. "Remember what happened the last time you accused me in front of Father?"

A dull heat spread beneath Esmond's collarbones. He wouldn't soon forget the agony of Eryx's fencing sword lashing his eye, or the keener torment when Esmond realized that no one—not his mother, not the Sagelord, not even his sister Civilla—was prepared to believe it had been anything more than an accident.

That was the curse of having a silver-tongued demon for a brother. If it came to his word against Esmond's, Eryx would always win.

"In any case," Eryx went on, "if you want to sulk over missing your girlfriend, that's your business. But you know how Mother feels about family dinners. You wouldn't want to upset Mother, would you?"

Esmond was tempted to treat that question with the scorn it deserved. Lady Nessa's fragile nerves were notorious: She'd always be anxious about something, whether her youngest son came to dinner or not. But Lord Arvis was also waiting, and defying him was another matter.

Grudgingly Esmond picked up his half glass, hooked it into place, and rose. He was taller than his brother when they stood side by side, but Eryx didn't allow him that satisfaction; he turned and strode out, leaving Esmond to trail after him like a servant—or a dog.

> *Dear Isaveth:*
> *I'm afraid I'm a stinking failure as a detective, which means the men who killed Governor Orien and nearly got your papa hanged for it are never going to pay. Also, Eryx caught me writing to you, and if he tells Father I've been "fraternizing with commoners" again I won't have to worry about his dodgy liver— he'll die of apoplexy instead.*

But that was black humor, and self-pitying besides, and Isaveth wouldn't think much of either. She'd watched her mother die of a wasting illness and her father get dragged off to jail, and it had only made her more determined to stand up for justice and protect the people she loved. Esmond's family might not need him—or even care about him—the way that Isaveth's did, but he could do better than that.

> *Dear Isaveth:*
> *I'm afraid we've had a bit of a setback, and by "a bit" I mean "I just found the only evidence we had*

against Eryx burned and smashed to bits," which is the opposite of what I'd hoped to tell you. But I haven't forgotten what my brother did to your family, and I promise that somehow, I'll make him pay for it. Don't lose heart.

P.S. Have you decided if I can kiss you yet?

That was better. More like Quiz, the jaunty street-boy he'd pretended to be when he first met Isaveth, the bold and funny part of him that she liked best. Even if the last thing he'd said to her had been so embarrassing that he could only recover by turning it into a joke, they were still friends and he hoped to keep it that way.

For now, though, writing Isaveth was out of the question. It could be weeks before Esmond's brother stopped watching him, and if one of Eryx's spies found their secret letter drop it would be disastrous. He could only hope she'd be patient, and not worry too much that he hadn't replied.

"What do you mean, boy, keeping us all waiting on you?" demanded Lord Arvis as Esmond came into the dining room. His father sat at the head of the long table, a big man whose muscles had long ago turned to fat, eyes deep-set in a sallow and blotchy face. Esmond's mother had once remarked wistfully that in his youth the Sagelord had been handsome, even dashing. But that was hard to imagine now.

"I apologize, sir," Esmond answered, chin up and voice strong. The Sagelord hated slouching, mumbling, and all other hints of cowardice. He also despised excuses, so Esmond added, "I should have been paying attention."

"I'll say you should," growled his father. "Sit down and let's get on with it."

He snapped his fingers and the footmen leaped to attend him, filling his wineglass and whisking a cloth napkin into the scant space between his belly and the table. A platter of bread, pickled vegetables, and cheese was set before him—Lord Arvis would have nothing to do with soup, though his wife ate little else—and the evening meal began.

"My darling," Lady Nessa murmured as her husband raised the glass to his lips. "Your liver . . . ?"

Lord Arvis slammed down his wineglass, sloshing red onto the damask tablecloth. "Take this away," he barked at the servant. "Are you trying to poison me?"

Stammering apologies, the footman rushed to obey. Esmond pitied the man; if he hadn't poured the wine, the Sagelord would have lambasted him for forgetting it. Lord Arvis's healers had warned him not to drink alcohol, but whether he chose to heed them depended on his mood, who else was drinking, and how well he happened to be feeling that day.

The healers had also recommended a strict diet, but as Lord Arvis slathered his bread with butter and helped himself to two kinds of cheese and a pickled egg, it was plain that he had no use for their opinion. "And I don't need you fussing over me either," he told his wife, who shrank back and said no more.

"So," the Sagelord went on when the silence around the table had grown unbearable. "What did *you* do with yourself today? Something useful for a change, I hope."